On the Edge of Broken Pieces

Elizabeth Arroyo

On the Edge of Broken Pieces
Copyright © 2023 Elizabeth Arroyo
All rights reserved.

ISBN: (ebook) 978-1-958136-66-9
(print) 978-1-958136-78-2

Inkspell Publishing
207 Moonglow Circle #101
Murrells Inlet, SC 29576

Edited By Yezanira Venecia
Cover Art By Bookish Gals

DEDICATION

For Julisa

ELIZABETH ARROYO

DEDICATION

For Julisa

ELIZABETH ARROYO

PROLOGUE

The sharp wind cuts through the night. Despite wearing my thick winter coat, I'm freezing as I stand outside the van's open door. No one is in the driver's seat yet.

Beatrice, my older sister by a year, is holding on to her fraying Raggedy Ann doll so tight that her knuckles are white. My mother is holding on to my little sister, Katie, on her lap. There's panic and desperation in my mom's brown eyes. A plea for help.

I feel the silent scream inside the van.

The hairs at the back of my neck stand on end.

Dad's hand lands on my shoulder, pushing me toward the passenger side. "Get in." He's holding the door open for me.

Get in.

Run.

Do something.

I get in. The van's sliding door slams closed behind me, locking all of us inside of what feels like a coffin. The headlights slice through the night. Shimmers of snow hang in the air.

Dad jumps into the driver's side and turns the key. A prayer that the old conversion van has met its demise echoes

1

in my thoughts. I pray for it not to start. For Mom's God to save us.

The thing spits on.

The vibration rattles my teeth. Or it could be the cold. Or the fear. I smell the rancid stench of beer on my dad's breath. I hate beer. I hate that smell. His eyes are bloodshot, and he wears that expression that always scares me. He glances in the rearview mirror and snarls at my mother.

He hates her.

I feel it in my soul.

He hates us because we are a part of her.

I'd gotten so used to their arguments and fistfights that I slept through this one. I didn't even care what started it this time—my dad's nightmares or the fact that he drank too much. No food in the fridge or that small sports car he'd bought. Their fights have never scared me like it does now. I want it to stop.

"Where are we going?" I hear the fear in my own voice.

"North," he says. "You liked Canada, remember?"

Canada in winter?

"But it's cold," I try to reason. "The road's icy."

He told me to get bigger *cojones*. My dad never liked me acting less than a man. Said he'd have to buy me a dress if I started acting like a girl.

I try to act like a man and be brave, my heart pounding so hard against my chest.

The van rumbles angrily underneath my seat as he presses the accelerator deeper. The treacherous, icy roads make us slip.

The world around me turns into a dark funnel. I see the lights on the dashboard. I hear my mom and sisters' soft sobs behind me, and I smell my dad's bad breath.

I look over. The speedometer reads seventy.

Thick white snow falls from the sky—one my mother's God created. A sky that has already dropped four inches of snow with an expectation of eight before all this is over. The snow sticks to the road. It isn't a lot of snow, but it's enough to force the van to slide. We all feel it. I instinctively clutch onto the armrest and the door. I hate snow.

"Papi, please." Tears close now. My throat tight.

That sets him off, and he drives faster.

"Armando, *por favor*," my mother pleads from the back.

I want to tell her it's too late. I want to tell her she should've protected us from the monster in our house. I'm angry at her because I'm afraid of him.

"Cállate la boca," he snaps at her, hatred spilling into his voice.

He transformed into a demon—charred, sunburned skin, sharp features, and a scowl forever etched into his face. But his red eyes draw all his other features together.

I hear Beatrice start to cry. "Papi, please," she says in her tinny voice. "We don't need to get there so fast."

"It's okay, Mama," he responds without looking at her, gripping the steering wheel tighter. "Do you trust your papi?"

My heart tears a little bit knowing that he's making her feel bad. He always makes Beatrice feel bad for taking sides. Beatrice is hypersensitive and is always afraid when Dad drinks. She even hides the knives when our parents fight.

"Yes, Papi."

"Don't be scared. Everything's going to be okay."

He doesn't let up, and I know we aren't going to be okay.

Okay stayed in my bed with whatever God Mami was praying to right now. *Okay* decided to take a vacation and leave the Morales family to die.

Bright lights explode out of nowhere. The world turns inside out. I hear screams. I'm not sure if it's mine. I'm flying out into the night's frigid air. The screams silence and the cold wraps me in pain for a floating second. Then I feel nothing.

CHAPTER 1

I sat outside the principal's office, bobbing my knee up and down to a tune in my own head, leaning back with my eyes closed. The nightmare last night was still curling somewhere in my mind, fading like all nightmares eventually do. I struggled to remain focused on my current surroundings, which happened to be awaiting trial at Locke Academy. I'd transferred into Locke midsemester after my old school banned me for something that wasn't even my fault! My aunt Carmen got me into this private hellhole after talking to some rich guy with perks. After a month of playing nice, I got called into the principal's office for threatening to pull the spine out of a fellow twelfth grader's throat. A bit over the top, but I'd been pissed. And he'd been the idiot to believe me. Well, come to think of it. Who was sitting in the principal's office awaiting judgment? Not him. I was clearly the idiot. At least I hadn't hit the guy. My words had been enough for him to scamper away.

"Mr. Morales?" Mrs. Collins called out twice before I acknowledged her. I didn't want to seem overly antsy. "Dr. Newman's ready to see you."

I wiped my sweaty palms on my gray slacks, then fixed my blazer. The tie felt like a noose around my neck. The whole uniform made me itchy as hell. I walked inside the principal's office. I've been in quite a few of these over the years. They always looked the same: certificates hanging on the walls, family pictures on a large desk where the warden sat waiting, a smaller round table for more intimate conversations in a corner, and a shitload of self-help books on shelves that screamed, *I am the authority figure! You are mine to control!*

Yeah, not working.

The only difference in this office was the guy already sitting in front of Dr. Newman's desk. I caught myself checking him out. Platinum blond hair cut short and neat, light blue eyes that seemed to glow when they caught the light, and smooth features I'd expect a rich, spoiled brat could afford. Too perfect. And his clothes were all pressed and shiny. Not a secondhand purchase for sure. Then he smiled, revealing pearly whites. I rolled my eyes almost to the back of my head. Couldn't help it. I decided to keep my attention on Dr. Newman. At least I knew she was human and not a humanoid altered to perfection. "Uh, should I come back?" I asked, my voice sounding huskier than usual due to my throat still being scratchy from my screams last night.

"No," Dr. Newman said and pointed at an empty chair next to the guy. "Xander Gael Morales?" she asked. As if she hadn't sent for me.

"Yes, ma'am," I said and plopped down on the chair beside Mr. Perfecto. Doing so, I caught a whiff of fabric softener puffing out of my clothes. My aunt Carmen liked the clothes to smell clean. It tickled my nose.

I caught Mr. Perfecto shift in his seat, his nose flared. I struggled not to roll my eyes again.

"Thank you for joining us," she started, as if I had a choice. I didn't mention that part. She apparently liked to live in la-la land. "I'd like to officially welcome you to Locke Academy. This is Wade Wilson." She motioned to the guy beside me. Not a question yet. I kept my mouth shut. She went on. "Mr. Wilson has graciously agreed to show you around, be your sponsor, available if you need assistance. That sort of thing."

Okay, so color me nasty, but I just threatened George Purdy, or whatever his name was, with bodily harm, and Dr. Newman was now making a rich avatar my shadow? This had to be some psychology bullshit she just learned in school. I turned to look at Wade, then back at her. "You mean like some sort of service dog?" I asked. Couldn't help it.

Wade chuckled and hid it with a cough as Newman glared at me. *That* expression I recognized and was oddly comfortable with. "Mr. Morales," she said stiffly, lacing her fingers on top of her desk, spearing me with blue eyes. Not much diversity in this school. I must've stuck out like beans on white rice. "Mr. Wilson has graciously volunteered to help you acclimate to our beautiful, *safe* school."

"You're kidding, right?"

She looked on the verge of tossing me out into the street. *That* look I understood too. Then she led my eyes to Wade. Something about his perfect face and smile bothered me. Rich, conniving, brat wanting something.

"I assure you, my involvement with you will only be to help you acclimate until Dr. Newman believes you've settled in," Wade piped up just like a perfectly trained avatar.

Yeah, throw that in my face. I turned back to Newman. "This is my punishment?"

"We don't punish students here, Mr. Morales. We assist in developing moral character in ways that will benefit the student population, or would you prefer expulsion?"

I shifted in my seat. "For one threat? I didn't even hit the guy. That's kind of excessive, don't you think?"

"Ah, but this is not your first threat to a student, is it, Mr. Morales?"

No, it wasn't. She had my file sitting on her desk. Fighting had been my thing. A way to calm my nerves. "It is for *this* school," I answered.

I didn't like this principal. She was smart and cold.

I turned back to Wade and gave him my once-over that was usually filled with all kinds of "don't mess with me" vibes. Except that the guy gave me a totally different vibe. I couldn't quite place it, but it made me uncomfortable. "Fine," I said, turning back to Dr. Newman. "Not like I have a choice."

"You always have a choice, Mr. Morales. This"—she gestured to Wade, who shifted in his seat, the first visual cue that suggested he wasn't a bot but may actually be a real live boy—"or expulsion. There won't be a problem here, correct?"

If I messed this up, I'd never get the rest of my blood money. I had to graduate high school to get out of Aunt Carmen's house before I tested the ripping spine out of the throat visual in my head. "Correct." I grumbled. "No problem."

"Are you okay with this arrangement, Mr. Wilson?"

There was a long silence, and I didn't look his way. Not sure what he was getting out of this, but it had to be worth it. "Yeah, I'm good," he finally said.

She got to her feet. "Great. Just come see me if you encounter any problems. I'm sure Mr. Morales will benefit from all you have to offer."

Wade gave me a *yeah right* look but nodded in agreement.

"Mr. Morales, I will be keeping my eyes on you. I believe in you."

Oh, yeah, this woman was *good*. I almost snorted. Thankfully, I caught myself.

I rushed out of there, and Wade caught up to me at my locker. I wished he'd just go away. "Why the hell did you agree to this?" I asked instead, not paying attention to what the hell I was pulling from my locker. Paper. Book. A week-old sandwich. Nope. I put that green shit back.

He leaned against the locker beside me and crossed his arms across his chest. "I have my reasons," he said with a smug expression.

"Fuck you, Wilson," I responded. It would've sounded more severe if my voice hadn't cracked.

He chuckled at my expense. I already hated the guy. "Okay, listen," he said. "This will be painless. Just stay out of trouble. Reach out to me if you find yourself considering hitting someone, killing someone, or bad-mouthing someone, and I'll talk you down from it." With his hand extended like some homeless person begging for a couple of bucks, he lifted two perfectly trimmed brows, waiting for my answer that I didn't give. He had to have plucked or some shit and he still looked manly. Didn't look pretty at all. No femininity about him. Reluctantly, I unlocked my cell phone and dropped it on his palm. He typed his contact information in it, then handed it back to me. "Just text me with your name and I'll save your info." I reached for it, but he held it firmly, inciting a sort of tug-of-war. "I need verbal confirmation that you understood."

"I got it, dickwad," I said, sharply pulling back my phone.

He narrowed his light blue eyes at me. "That's considered bad-mouthing. Do I need to give you a reprimand?"

I slammed my locker shut with more angst than I should've had this early in the day. I tried to flank him, but he blocked my path. Apparently, he didn't like being ignored, and I didn't give a shit. The guy wasn't as tall as me, but he still had this strong presence and stubborn way that made hitting him too damn tempting. Hitting him would be bad. I didn't want to make the five o'clock news.

Students heading to class gave us a look. I usually didn't care about being eyeballed, but being eyeballed with him suddenly made me uncomfortable.

"How about every time you swear, you have to do something for me?"

I snorted. Couldn't help it. "Hell no."

He grinned at me like a shark. Not that sharks grinned or anything. Come to think about it, I'd never even seen a shark up close and personal. WTF? My brain had spazzed out for a moment staring at his lips, and I lifted my eyes from that shark-like grin to his eyes. It did not make me feel better.

"Well, I'll have to record all your failings to Dr. Newman. Is that what you want? She won't be pleased."

"Wow, really? You're going to go there?" I felt my stomach clench. "Fine. I'll work on my bad-mouthing."

He nodded. Victory was his. This round. "Good. I'll see you at lunch."

"Uh, no."

"You need to expand your friendship pool." His eyes lifted to a group of guys walking toward him. All his likeness. I couldn't tell them apart. Blond hair, blue-eyed jocks. His clique. He smiled and I had to look away from him to avoid feeling ... I didn't know what the hell I was feeling. The need to punch his perfect face or draw it.

I did neither.

Thankfully, the wave of guys pulled him in, and he started walking away from me. "Lunch," he said, laughing at something one of them said. "I'll see you at lunch," he called out, and every student looked my way, curious as to who Wade Wilson had embraced into his pool of friends.

I hated him.

I let out a breath as soon as he was gone and headed to class.

CHAPTER 2

Trini Chan stood waiting for me just outside class as I headed toward lunch. I tugged at my tie again, loosening it, but she stopped me. At five-feet-nothing, she had to tiptoe, and I had to lean down for her to slip the knot back up to hide the open button. "You'll get demerits for not wearing it correctly, trust me."

I did trust Trini. Probably the only person I did trust in all of California. I couldn't look away from her warm expression. Her eyes were dark brown, her features petite. She could almost fit in my pocket.

"There," she said and tapped my tie. "Better." Her smile warmed all my insides. Something must've shown in my expression because she said, "What? Do I have something in my nose?" She wiped her small nose.

"No," I said. "Well, maybe a hoagie."

"Eww," she squealed, making me laugh. Then she slapped my arm, taking that moment to slide her hand down until she linked our hands.

Trini and I had a mutually beneficial relationship. After I kicked her boyfriend's ass for slapping her in a very public and video-surveillanced parking lot (I had the video in case the douchebag started something again), we started dating.

Except, it was in name only. She wanted to have a reason to avoid the loser, and I wanted everyone, including my aunt, to think I'd finally kicked the habit of getting into trouble. Funny how people believe a girlfriend could pacify a guy. We didn't kiss or have sex, though, and we'd agreed this would only be temporary. Six weeks at most. We had three left to go.

But I really liked Trini as a friend. And I would protect her from anyone who would seek to hurt her. "How'd it go with Dr. Newman?" she asked as we stood in line to get our tray of food. At least the food here did not suck. Yay for a sixty-thousand-dollar-a-year tuition.

"It went," I said.

"So, no suspension, expulsion?"

"Nope. I got it covered." I picked up a tray and juice and followed her to our regular table near the weebs and brainiacs, away from the jocks and Barbies. I totally forgot about Wade until he came up on Trini with that freakishly genuine smile of his. I almost tossed my tray on the floor and pulled her away from him.

They hugged.

She knew him.

And I suspected the worst-case scenario imaginable.

When Trini turned back to look at me with a hint of blush on her face, that sealed the deal. I'd been used. "Don't be mad," she said in that voice that made me melt. "Please. I did it for you."

I wasn't sure what she did for me, exactly. I knew it had something to do with Wilson showing up in Dr. Newman's office to act as mediator and savior, though. And I didn't like it. I still followed her to the JB table, where she apparently decided to lead me. Yeah, I could've bolted for the weeb table where we had been discussing the latest episode of *Attack on Titan*. (Okay, so anime was my reprieve from the dark cruel reality of my world. I'd prefer the dark cruel reality of someone else's world.) But Trini was my girlfriend. If I simply abandoned her, I wasn't sure how that would look. I didn't know anything about girls or girlfriend etiquette, even if it was fake, so I followed like a puppy.

The group at the table were all speed-talking over themselves about some boarding competition. Maybe they had friends in boarding school. Who cared? Wade gave me a quick chin-up acknowledgment, then cleared his throat, as if he were Xerxes ready to send his troops to conquer. Damn, that guy got on my nerves. They all settled like minions as he introduced me to Piper, Nick, Taylor, and Theo.

I nodded at each in turn and sat down beside Trini, who smiled at all of them too. The silence lasted two seconds before they went back to their discussion.

Trini leaned into my ear and gave me the rundown of who they were. Piper Harrington was heiress to a large fashion conglomerate, which was why she hated this school. Uniforms sucked. Nick's father owned a chain of restaurants in the Bay area, Taylor's mother was a famous actress I'd never heard of, and Theo's dad owned a slew of resorts along with Wade's father. Compared to them, Trini's thirty-million-dollar net worth was peanuts.

Yeah, I wanted to drive a screwdriver in my eye just being here.

I kinda zoned out until Trini elbowed me and I realized everyone was looking at me because Wade had said something. "What?"

"Skiing? We go every weekend. You want in?" Wade said as if he'd just announced I'd won the lottery.

I gave him my brightest fake smile. "Uh, no. Thank you. Though it would be nice to see you belly flop."

That wasn't that funny, but everyone roared with laughter. "You have no idea who he is, do you," Theo asked.

"Wade Wilson. Teacher's pet." I shrugged. "Rich. Jock. Am I close?"

Wade gave me a smirk with hard cold eyes that spoke volumes to how pissed he was, even though he was trying to hold it back. "Why don't you show me your skills, then you can talk shit," he said.

Everyone went *oooo*, as if we were going to start boxing. Instigators on his side. I felt Trini squeeze my knee under the table, a warning to keep my mouth shut, but keeping my mouth shut wasn't in my skillsets. "I ain't got nothing to prove to you."

"Really? Because you're such a badass. All bark."

I hadn't actually ripped Purdy's spine out. "Fine," I finally blurted, getting to my feet so I could at least be taller than him. He had to look up to meet my eyes, and I liked that. I liked intimidating Wade fucking Wilson. He didn't back down like the others. He looked as if he were having fun. Too much fun, actually.

"Next weekend. The first run. Ours," he said.

"Fine."

"Fine," he repeated.

And that had been the start to one messed-up series of events that knocked down the brick wall I'd erected over my soul. The tower, the curtain wall, the keep, all of it shot to shit because I hadn't known anything about Wade Wilson.

CHAPTER 3

"You gotta be kidding me." My blood ran cold.

Trini watched me from her perch on the bleachers during gym the next day. "You don't have to do it. He was being an ass because, well, you were being an ass."

We lived in California. There was nothing but water surrounding us, so when Wade had mentioned skiing, I had quickly assumed water skiing, like, on water. But nooo, the guy was an Olympic Gold Medalist in snowboarding. Snow!

Fucking snow.

I glared at her. Hard *not* to think this was her fault for setting me up. "What did you trade for my exoneration from Newman?"

She slipped her puffy bottom lip into her mouth. I've never kissed her, although I knew she'd let me if I tried. I didn't. Which was a weird feeling. Not wanting to kiss your fake girlfriend who saved your ass from expulsion. "He wants to meet my brother." Brother? I never knew she had a brother. Outside of school, I knew nothing about Trini. "He's back from college."

"Why would he want to meet your brother?"

She arched a brow as she grabbed my phone out of my hand. Wade's info was still on the screen. Yeah, I'd just looked him up. She searched through my phone until she came to something to show me, then she handed me the phone back. A picture of Wade, definitely Wade at a club in the arms of a guy who looked older. *Olympic Gold Medalist Wade Wilson was spotted in the arms of Caleb Knight, the heir to a multibillion-dollar fortune. Caleb, eighteen, has denied any involvement with the seventeen-year-old teen.*

The article went on to note that Caleb was soon seen in the arms of some female model. I instantly didn't like the creep and hoped the article got it all wrong. I felt a tinge of pity for Wade, but then I remembered it *was* Wade. Arrogant, conniving, got-his-way Wade. And gay. I did not see that one coming.

"He's gay?"

Trini gave me a *duh* look. One I was getting used to where Wade Wilson was concerned. "Uh, yeah, very," Trini responded.

I didn't care that the guy was gay.

I cared that Wade *used* me.

"You didn't have to do that," I finally said to Trini.

She shrugged. "It's what friends do for each other. You did more for me, remember?"

I wanted to forget.

"So, about this skiing thing," she started. Oh God, I wanted the ground to swallow me. "Maybe we can put laxatives in his milk. Give him the runs." She cupped her mouth and giggled. It made me feel better. I took a seat next to her. Our shoulders brushed, and I couldn't help but to always notice her small frame. Her delicate features. The need to protect her from harm ingrained inside me. Trini deserved better than me or the prick who'd slapped her.

"Maybe I can break his leg," I said as a joke.

She stopped laughing and gave me a soul-searching look that suddenly made me uncomfortable. I bumped her shoulder with mine. "Kidding. Ha. Ha," I said dryly, hurting a little bit inside that she could think I'd do such a thing.

She curled her arm around mine and drew me closer.

Then she pulled me into her and kissed me on the cheek.

"What was that for?"

"I know you're not as evil as you think."

She was wrong. I let my family die. I let an innocent man take the blame for our accident. And I got blood money for it. I swallowed back the lump in my throat. "You don't know me very well, Trini."

She gave me her cute, cocked-head look that compelled me to give her anything she wanted. My heart, my soul, all my darkest secrets. Thankfully, I was saved by the bell.

She hopped to her feet, and we started heading back to the lockers. "Do you need a ride after school?"

Getting a ride was one of the perks of having a fake girlfriend with a license and car to match, but I had group therapy after school. My stomach rolled just thinking about it. "Nah, I'm good. But thanks. I'll see you tomorrow." I planted a kiss on top of her head, and we separated to head into our respective locker rooms.

I didn't feel comfortable ditching my clothes in front of these morons who didn't give a shit about sporting their junk around as if they were gods. Living in a group home, I'd learned to be wary of locker rooms. I had learned to strategically dress without having to expose myself too much. To be quick about it before pricks started their shit. Like prison, group homes were a cesspool for perverts and bullies.

I gave my immediate corner a quick glance, saw it empty, and quickly lifted off my gym tee, dropped it on the bench, and plucked up my white T-shirt. Just as I had it over my head, Wade turned the corner, and I suddenly forgot how the hell to dress. My head missed the hole, my arms didn't fare much better, and it took me a few seconds longer than necessary to finally cover myself. I sneered at him. "What?" I snapped.

Wade blinked a couple of times, as if trying to get the vision of me out of his eyeballs. He didn't have time to say anything when his entourage appeared behind him. They shoved him on their way to their lockers without paying any attention to me. I waited until he disappeared with them, and the coast was clear to drop my shorts and pull up my pants. Unfortunately, despite gym being the last class of the day, I still had to wear my uniform. I had made the mistake of changing into my street clothes the first day and got a warning. After shrugging into my white button-down shirt, anchoring my tie around my neck like a noose, and shrugging into my blazer, I shoved my gym clothes into the locker and slammed it shut. As if on cue, Wade—his hair wet, his lower body wrapped in a towel—made an appearance again because he just had to rile me up. I felt my own heart start to race.

"Hey," he said easily. Almost friendly. "We're heading to Dogs to get a bite to eat. You wanna come?"

Hell no. "Is this you trying to expand my friendship pool?" I asked with a sharp edge to my voice. I didn't like being his charity case, or his reason for getting hooked up with another guy. For a moment, I could've sworn he looked vulnerable. Nervous even. I wanted to tell him I knew who he was, and he could drop the damn act. I didn't.

He finally shrugged. "Your call."

"Thanks, but no thanks. I'll pass." I flanked him, brushing his shoulder as I moved away from him and the rest of the laughter that exploded behind him.

"Damn, Wade Wilson got turned down." I heard a voice say behind me. "Record this shit."

"Fuck you," Wade said back. He said something else, but I was already at the exit and didn't stop.

Breathe, Xander. Prison is a choice. Punching Wade Wilson would lead to prison. A choice. You don't want to go there. I heard Beatrice's voice.

It took me another moment to remember my sister was dead.

CHAPTER 4

Dr. Reyes had his office south of Malibu inside a loft on the fourteenth floor. I stopped at Mrs. Flores's desk, and she nodded at me before she buzzed the door so I could go inside. Apparently, nutjobs were sometimes volatile and Dr. Reyes had added an extra layer of security. Not sure where that left Mrs. Flores, since she was out in the open. Maybe she had a better life insurance plan.

The group room was spacious, with dark blue walls and bright orange and green furniture. The walls were plastered with positive quotes that made me grind my molars. At least the images did not have snow.

The tall ceilings and bright recessed lights made me feel as if I were incubating inside an eggshell waiting to be hatched. Seemed appropriate. In one way or another, we were trying to break free from the shell imprisoning us by society, by family, by the president, who fucking knew? Every time I ended up in this place I felt as if I needed to chisel my way out. It jarred something inside my mind, drew me back to a place I did not want to be.

Yeah, we were all chicks trying to hatch out of our very own hell.

A board covered the east wall, our names on top of the

separate sections. Each section looked like a pinball machine. A small silver ball rested on a spindle on top. Once released, it would navigate down the intricate bumpers and angles until it settled on a theme we'd be forced to talk about if we had nothing to offer the group.

Four options lay under my name. Art. School. Bullies. Friends.

It meant that Carmen must've called Dr. Reyes to let him know about my threat to Purdy.

Sage and David were already seated when I arrived, and Jack came in behind me. His eyes quickly roamed around the room, counting the number of furniture pieces. Dr. Reyes had once made the mistake of having an odd number of pieces and Jack had walked out of the room, deciding to stay in the lobby where there were six chairs and not seven.

It meant that we always had an empty chair.

Counting the even number, he sighed and headed toward Sage. Sage wore white chinos and a pink button-down rolled at the sleeves. His blond hair styled in a perfect quiff with a fade. It made him look retro with all the bright colors he wore. He had soft features, a strong chin, and was handsome, like all the other rich assholes that had a lineage stemming from royalty. He sneered in much the same way, too, and scooted further away from Jack as he took a seat next to him.

David's dark eyes just watched them both as if he were plucking some sort of code from their actions. David Grayson was some rocker's son. At seventeen, he'd already been tatted up his sleeves, and I could see artwork trailing under his tee. The guy was every parent's nightmare. He had metal practically everywhere—ears, nose, tongue, brow. He wore leather and a faux hawk and had a better leave-me-the-hell-alone look than I did.

Out of all of us, Jack looked the most normal. If I could even use that word to describe us. In simple jeans and a UCLA T-shirt, he didn't scream get the fuck away from me.

And then there was my stupid ass wearing my school

uniform, minus the tie and blazer, which I had shoved into my backpack. They all lifted their eyes to me. I needed to complete this shit to get my *Get Out of Jail Free* card and leave for college. This therapy shit hanging over me tethered me here. I probably should've ditched it, but after the stupid threat and the principal on my ass, I'd need all the brownie points I could get when my court date came around. I'd been charged with assault for hitting a dude with a two-by-four and sent to Boys Home for Delinquents. Actually, it was just named Boys Home. I was released with the understanding that I would continue to see a therapist and complete the anger management group with these morons.

Dr. Reyes was a handsome man who carried himself professionally. Always wore a suit and tie and shiny shoes. His dark hair combed to the side. His brown eyes behind wire-rimmed glasses were kind. He smiled at all of us in turn, giving us his attention for the few seconds it took to glaze over us, then he sat in one of the available chairs. At least they were comfortable. I realized I was still standing, so I sat down too.

"As we begin," he started. "I wanted to remind you that this is a safe space. What is said in this group will remain in this circle of trust."

Sage shifted. "Or y'all get sued. I'm assuming the NDAs have been updated."

Dr. Reyes didn't react to Sage, which was a skill in and of itself. We all had to sign NDAs, which made forming this little group harder than for regular folks who didn't have billion-dollar trust funds or whatever. "Yes, Sage, everything is up to date." Dr. Reyes paused slightly, giving Sage a moment to process the safety of NDAs. "Now that we got that cleared up, who wants to go first today?"

No one moved for a few seconds until Dr. Reyes lifted his eyes to the board.

"Oh, for fuck's sake, I'll go," Sage said and pulled out his notebook from his purple satchel. This was nothing new. Sage usually started discussions. I pegged him to have a short fuse and preferred to get shit over with than haggle over trifles like who should go first. Realizing he really didn't need his journal to talk, he elegantly crossed his legs and placed the journal on top of his knee. "I got angry at my brother this week."

That was nothing new either. From what I could tell, Sage's older brother was a homophobic prick like his family.

"On a scale of one to ten?" Dr. Reyes asked.

Sage scratched his chin. The guy had no hair on his face, and I wondered about the rest of his body. More than once. Then I fought not to get a visual of Sage naked, hairless. There was something wrong with me. Duh, I was in therapy.

"A six," he answered.

"And how did being angry make you feel?"

Sage lifted his blue eyes to the chart on the wall that listed emotions. It went from frustrated to homicidal. No one tested the homicidal bit, sure that Dr. Reyes would have to report us despite the signed NDAs. "I felt annoyed."

"Do you care to share the lead-in to this emotion?"

The questions were always the same. Who precipitated the emotion? Define the emotion and rate it on a scale of one through ten. What drove the emotion? What was the outcome? And how could we have reacted better? Then the consequences and what we learned from it.

Always the same bullshit.

I ran my palms against my pants.

Sage's eyes misted and he turned away from the group, staring at the wall in front of him. I didn't think the optimistic memes did anything to make him feel good.

"He was with his college friends at home. They were being homophobic pricks like always. He didn't stop them. Said I should try a blow job from a girl. He said a mouth is a mouth and it shouldn't matter. I told him he should get a blow job from a guy and tell me what the difference is. His friends started laughing, and he called me a defective gene splice that should never have been born."

The room was so silent, even Jack stopped counting. That act gave me hope that maybe, one day, I could change too.

"Then what did you do?" Dr. Reyes prompted.

"I unzipped my pants and took a piss on his shoes."

It took a moment for me to register what he'd said, and then I started to laugh. The response was so random. I never thought Sage would've had it in him. I kinda felt happy for the guy. My response made everyone else laugh and Sage smirk. Granted, we probably weren't supposed to encourage such behavior, but I didn't care. Outside of this circle, we knew shit about one another. Hell, we'd probably ignore each other if we ever bumped into each other in the real world. But inside the circle, we were all the same: little chicks under the heating lamp.

"Okay, okay," Dr. Reyes started to settle us down. "Let's regroup."

We regrouped to talk about other weird shit the guys did when they'd been pissed. Jack had cut his mother's embroidered napkins into twelve even strips when she made him feel inadequate. That was his emotion all the time. Inadequate. David had glued one of his father's dresser drawers shut, and they had no clue what the hell had happened. Neither father suspected it had been David. Thought it was a defect in the dresser. I had mentioned my threat to Purdy. That had everyone laughing too. Then Dr. Reyes had us evaluate what we could've done instead. Like breathing and visually thinking of positive things. Sage mumbled that him pissing on his brother's shoes was a positive image. That set everyone off into laughter again.

Surprisingly, the hour-long session went by quickly, though something about the session made my gears spin more than usual. My fingers itched to draw, and when I got home, I drew Sage pissing a beam of flame into his brother's friends. The whole place caught fire as a result. It wasn't one of my best works, but at least it was something I could relieve from my already dark soul. I drew Jack with his napkin. Only in my drawing he had made a long rope he used to shimmy down the tower of inadequacy he'd been locked inside. And I drew David with the glue, locking up all the demons in a chest. They were all warped versions of superheroes, taking back control of their lives. It made more sense through art than verbal expressions. Although, I didn't draw myself ripping Purdy's spine. Apart from senseless threats, I'd done nothing to make myself feel better. Nothing to stop the nightmares.

In the end, they always just came at me like jagged-edged swords. I could do nothing but scream.

That night, I woke up to a night terror. Light seared my eyes. I dropped on all fours and crawled to the wall, sitting against it and drawing my knees tight into my chest. Carmen in front of me, mouth moving, trying to touch me. I couldn't hear her. I didn't want her to touch me.

"Don't touch me! Get out! Get out!" I covered my ears. Something instinctual. I was never getting put back together again. Ever.

I rocked myself as the tears broke free like wraiths pulling out the dark inside my soul. I needed to cry. I needed to scream. I needed to be angry. I needed to be empty inside.

CHAPTER 5

Carmen gave me *the* look as I entered the kitchen in the morning. I had woken up on the floor. The night terror a bad one. Moe sat at the table dressed in his work uniform, sipping his coffee. He eyeballed me as if I were a serpent ready to strike and he needed to keep line of sight. After four years of this shit, you'd think I'd be used to it.

"Bad night?" she asked.

I rubbed the back of my neck and popped it. "I don't remember," I lied. I wasn't about to get into details with her. Details I'd never told a living soul. She offered me her cheek and I kissed it.

Carmen was mom's youngest sister and the only one without kids, so I'd ended up at her doorstep. Never mind that I came with a thirty-million-dollar lottery ticket. A million for my caretaker, which allowed Carmen to buy a decent car to get to work, and Moe bought a truck he used for his work in construction. They'd also managed to put a decent-size down payment on a two-bedroom house in Santa Monica. Not cheap, so all good.

The rest I'd get after I graduated high school. After I got kicked out of the neighboring public school system, Carmen put me in Locke Academy filled with rich kids. She thought it would be good for me to hang around other types of people—expand my friendship pool—in hopes that I'd leave my violent tendencies behind. Little did she know it made me more of a target. At least in the public school system I could blend in. At Locke, I stuck out like a stain on white linen. Something needing to be scrubbed away and forgotten.

"Are you taking your meds?" Moe asked.

"No," I said with a bit more defiance than intended. "Makes me feel like shit."

"Language," Carmen scolded.

I caught the look they gave each other. I didn't care. I wasn't going back on meds. Ever. I sat down and silently ate my breakfast, one arm slung around the plate as if needing to protect it. Some things were too ingrained to change. My experience with people taking away my food was one of them. Seeing possible threats *everywhere*, another. The reason I was hard to love. I knew that the first time I ran away, and Carmen had cried for me. Instead of feeling bad for causing the tears, I felt angry.

Moe sighed and got to his feet, abandoning his coffee. He kissed Carmen and ruffled my hair, something he always did. "Have a good day at school," he said and walked out.

I smoothened out my hair. Not that it would do any good. It was long and did what it wanted. Carmen sat next to me. Our drive usually took thirty minutes, and we still had thirty to spare.

"I'm going to get dressed. Finish up and clean up, yeah?"

"Yeah."

I finished my breakfast and cleaned the plates on the table. We never talked about my night terrors or the accident. Carmen gave me space I didn't know what to do with, because sometimes I *wanted* to talk to her. Being a nurse, maybe she could tell me what was wrong with me. Fix me so I felt less broken inside.

That was a dangerous feeling to have, and I shoved it away as soon as I thought about it.

The thirty-minute ride to school was usually our talk time. This time she talked about my visit to the principal's office. The threat I gave the kid, which she laughed off. Wiped a few stray tears. "You have a wild imagination if you think you could pull someone's spine from their throat."

I guess I did. A morbid imagination.

"How was group yesterday?" she asked.

I shrugged. "It was okay. I can't talk about it or I'll get sued."

She rolled her eyes. "I feel sorry for some of these kids sometimes. Parents can be so icky."

Icky. I liked that. For the most part, Carmen wasn't like an icky parent. And I owed her my life too. "Your appointment with Dr. Reyes is Saturday morning. I have to work. Will you be able to go on your own?"

"Yeah, I'm good." I hated individual therapy. It rattled things already loose in my head.

"Good," she said.

"Oh, before I forget, I was invited to go skiing next weekend. Is it okay?" Although I wanted her to say no, I knew she wouldn't. The whole "giving me my independence so I wouldn't run away" mentality was a double-edged sword sometimes.

"Of course. That's great."

I didn't think it was great. I was actually terrified. I'd never talked about my fear of snow to Carmen. No need. We lived in California. No snow unless you went looking for it. I told her about Wade and she laughed that I didn't know about the gold medal thing. She knew Trini and I were a thing, although she'd never met Trini. She believed me. I told her they were friends and Trini asked him to mentor me since he was all perfect and shit. Too damn perfect. I didn't mention that part or the part about wanting to punch his lights out.

When we reached the school, I grabbed my bag from the back as she said her goodbye.

I hated goodbyes.

Wade was leaning against my locker, eyes cast down looking at his phone while the world passed by around him. Everyone glanced his way as if wanting to watch the spectacle that was him. I had to admit, that was a sight to see. I still couldn't decide if it was a good thing or a bad thing. I didn't want it to be a thing at all. After I'd done my homework—too late as always—I learned that he had very powerful sponsors. Everyone wanted the gay athletic poster boy on their team. He'd done underwear ads, showing off skin. Nice skin. Too weird to think about. He'd also done ads for shoes, colognes, and of course ski equipment. And let's not forget his rich daddy's resorts. I also found more information about his rumored fling with Caleb Knight. Wade hadn't interviewed since then, and his performance on the snow had been steadily declining. Of course, rumors attributed that to a broken heart. I scoffed at the thought. I didn't think Wade had a heart to break in the first place. Yet here he was, leaning against my damn locker, acting as if he didn't give a shit about the world around him.

Lucky him.

It sent me in a bad mood. I didn't want to even think about why. "Move," I ordered.

Slowly, he lifted his light blue eyes to mine, and I had to remember to breathe. Then that slow smile transformed his face, making him look younger somehow. "Someone is very prickly," he said. "Got up on the wrong side of the bed?"

"On the floor, actually," I blurted and regretted it the moment that smile fell. "Move," I rushed in, reasserting myself as being in control. He pushed off my locker, giving me enough space to get my things.

"What are you so pissed about? It's too early to have kicked someone's ass or make a wager you're going to lose."

"I didn't make a wager, and you cheated," I snapped back. "You failed to mention your professional status."

He chuckled. It was nice to hear. Made me smirk. I pulled it back quickly before he could see it. "You totally had no clue who I was? I have to up my PR game."

"I'm not into your scene. Don't be too surprised."

He leaned one arm against the locker beside me to look at me. "You will next weekend. I might be able to fit in some lessons for you if you ask nicely."

The guy loved himself way too much. I realized there wouldn't be a competition at all, if I decided to even go. Maybe I should bail. That would've been the smart thing to do, but for some damn reason I couldn't grasp, I wanted to go, to see what put that gleam in his eye, to see him in live action on the snow. Maybe it'd help with my own fear of the white powder. Wade cocked a brow at the silence.

"Fine, yeah, unless you want to bail." Brave of me to put it in his court. Not.

"Nope. I'll make time for you." Those words made heat creep up my neck and, thankfully, he changed the subject. "Speaking of teaching. I made you a schedule since I'm a good mentor and want to see you thrive." He shoved a sheet of paper into my hand. A list of subjects and days and times for tutoring. "It won't hurt."

I shoved it into my bag and slammed my locker shut. "Why? It's not like you care."

He cupped his chest, above his heart. "You break my heart."

I rolled my eyes. "Stop the play. Trini told me why you did it. Don't use me to make her a pimp for your fetish, *asshole.*" I sounded less angry than I felt, which surprised me. I shouldn't be this angry. Who cared who Wade dated and how he got dates? Not me.

His eyes slitted and he bit his bottom lip. Yeah, I looked before I snapped my eyes back to his face. "It's none of your business," he said, his voice taking a sharp edge to it that I found enlightening.

I could push some more of Wade Wilson's buttons and see what made him tick. "It is when you use me. What? You can't find your own boyfriend?" I couldn't believe I was having this conversation with him. In school!

The space between his brow folded and his eyes

darkened. Even his lips tightened, and I had to struggle not to stare. Why did I have to struggle not to stare at those lips? Why did my stomach twist into tight knots? I needed about a year of sleep to settle my nerves.

Wade's mouth slowly lifted into a nefarious grin, as if he knew something I still had yet to grasp. Then he licked his lips. "Jealous?"

I felt my blood drain away from my body and my lips part in shock. I bit them closed, slammed the locker, and walked away. Jealous? Why the hell would I be jealous? For one, I hated Wade Wilson. And two, I wasn't gay.

"No seas maricón."

My father's voice felt like nails being drilled into my brain. *One foot in front of the other. One foot in front of the other.* Anger and darkness coiled around me. I clenched my fist, digging my fingernails into my palms until I felt a touch of pain. I needed to hit something. Feel the corresponding flutter of pain from my knuckles zing up my arm to my elbow. If I hit something hard enough, I'd feel it in my neck. Better than this … this thing writhing inside of me.

I'm not gay. I would prove my father wrong.

I didn't settle until third period, when I finally sank into art.

Words could never clearly articulate how I felt. But art held no boundaries. It was something I'd always been good at. I'd doodled since I could hold a pencil. I doodled when Mom and Dad had argued and fought. I drew vivid scenes of destruction. I drew abstract swirls through colors. I didn't need words. Words had to make sense. They had to be in order, whereas art drew on chaos. An organized chaos I didn't want to make sense of. I just fell into it.

Mrs. Rashard walked around the class and just nodded her approval of my piece. When I finally looked up at it, I'd drawn a dark blotch speared with a lighter shade of shadow. An omnipresence under a dull streetlamp, watching, waiting. I couldn't tell if that was me or my father. Maybe both.

The bell rang and I hid my canvas behind others against the wall as Mrs. Rashard spewed our assignment. Before I could escape, she called me over. She was a petite woman with a pixie cut that framed her face. She wore loud colors and hooped earrings that pulled on her lobes. She also smelled of berries. I liked her. Maybe because like me, she seemed to always have smudges of paint on her fingertips or in her nail beds. A true artist.

"Mr. Morales," she said. "I didn't get to welcome you. A transfer student."

"Yes, ma'am," I said. I could be polite too.

"I'm taking a few of the students to the art institute next week." She handed me a field trip permission slip. "I'd like for you to join us."

I felt my cheeks grow warm. "Okay."

"Will you be applying to any art schools?"

I swallowed the lump in my throat. I hadn't thought that far into the future. I always felt like a drifter. Always on the edge of life and not truly living. I just wanted to survive high school. "I haven't thought about it."

"You should," she said with a smile that pulled at the tan lines on her face. "Maybe the trip will inspire you."

I nodded and walked out, shoving the paper into my bag too.

CHAPTER 6

Ayúdate, que Dios te ayudará.

Help yourself and God will help you.

That had been my mother's favorite saying. Along with *Tú no te gobiernas.*

She owned us.

Sitting in Dr. Reyes's office, this was me, helping myself. I wasn't asking God for help though. I still had a hate-hate relationship with him. I stopped praying in that van right before we hit the truck and my family died.

Dr. Reyes had been paid for by the Brody Foundation—the media went hard on the billion-dollar med tech corporation after one of their drivers slammed into a family van, killing himself and the family, leaving one sole survivor. Me. I'd been almost dead as the news filled with my sob story. I'd woken up to my family dead and a deep pocket. As if money could soothe the soul. I hadn't complained. It certainly made my extended family picking me up easier despite my four years of rebellious hell.

The office door opened and out strolled Adam Brody. I'd met Adam at a function I'd been invited to by the Brodys for the hearing impaired. Adam had lost his hearing in a car accident. I didn't know much else about him. I pulled back against the seat, hoping to disappear, when he spotted me and smiled.

Instinct had me smiling back. I got to my feet and took his outstretched hand for a handshake. "Xander," he said. All glimmering eyes and rainbows.

"Adam," I said back.

He released my hand and took a seat beside me. The most awkward moments are recognizing someone when you're about to have your emotions jacked, your mind sledgehammered, and quite possibly your sanity skewed. Adam didn't seem to get it.

"How's it going?" *Duh, I'm here.* He seemed to notice. "Apart from all this. How's your new school?"

I almost grimaced. "You helped Aunt Carmen get me into Locke?"

He shrugged; a hint of a blush scattered on his cheeks. "She called me after your altercation and asked. It's the least I could do."

I looked down at my hands, feeling my guilt rise to the surface, afraid he'd see right through me. "School's good."

"How about you call me." He pulled out a pen and wrote his number on a torn piece of magazine paper and handed it to me. "Anytime. Call."

Like Wade, he waited for my verbal confirmation. "Yeah, sure."

Thankfully, the receptionist called my name. I would never call Adam. Ever. I shoved that piece of paper into my bag.

Dr. Reyes's office smelled of mint. Cooler than the waiting area. I felt goosebumps rise along my skin. I sat down on the sofa while he spoke on the phone. I'd been seeing Dr. Reyes since Carmen fetched me from Chicago. I'd suffered a broken left humorous that had to be put together with plates and pins. I'd had a concussion and would never be able to play contact sports without risking death. Mom had been right in calling me hard-headed all those years. The reason I survived the impact.

The night terrors came soon after. And they still haunted me.

Dr. Reyes finally hung up and rolled his eyes. "Sorry about that." He sat down.

I shifted nervously. A twitch I couldn't quite settle or get used to.

"Would you like something to drink?"

Always the same question. "Nope. I'm good."

He smiled, smoothing out his wrinkles, which made him look young. I liked the guy. He seemed genuine, not that I had anyone to compare him to. My dad had been a bad drunk. My uncles were an echo of that lifestyle. A male figure to look up to hadn't been in the cards for me. And I had to remember that Reyes got paid to see me. Hell, he probably cursed me as soon as I walked out the door.

"How's everything going?"

"Good," I answered. Short and sweet until he started drilling and spreading the core of the questioning. Something he was good at, too, since I found myself telling him about the threat I made to Purdy at school. About Wade. Dr. Reyes knew about the gold medal thing, which made me feel like a fool for not. Dr. Reyes laughed at that. I didn't mention how Wade made me feel all knotted inside. I didn't tell Dr. Reyes I wanted to hit things, or of the darkness writhing inside of me. Or of hearing my dead sister's voice in my head. I had to deal with that shit on my own.

Then we sidled into the dream world. My night terrors. My brain felt like soup afterward, and I was no closer to doing anything to stop them. He brought up survivor's guilt. It was a real thing, I knew this. He brought up PTSD, Intermittent Explosive Disorder. Labels to put me inside. I got it. I really did. But it still didn't answer my writhing question that had me in knots. What the hell could I do to make it stop? I wanted to get off this fucking merry-go-round. I wanted to stop fumbling in the dark on the cusp of my nightmares. I wanted this guilt thing, something I could almost touch, out from inside of me. I got no answers, no solutions that didn't include me drugged on psychotropic meds. I wasn't doing it. I swore never to put any type of drugs into my body. I wasn't going to turn out like my dad, and I was old enough to make that decision.

Dr. Reyes believed I should try this art school and gave me my own homework. He wanted to see my dream journals. Although I said yes, I wouldn't show him any of it. They were too dark, too personal, and would rat me out as the liar I was. But I smiled and left without another word of it. I felt as if I'd left a piece of my sanity in his office. Not sure that's how therapy was supposed to work.

That evening, my mental health came into question again as I looked at myself in the mirror wearing black slacks, a white button-down, and my school shoes—they were the only dress shoes I owned. I flattened my untamed curls, but they just sprung back to life in defiance.

"You look very handsome," Carmen said from the doorway. "Does this mean I finally get to meet her?" Nervously, I smoothed out my blazer. Or actually Moe's blazer. I didn't have one without the school's embroidered patch on the chest.

"I'm meeting her at the place."

Carmen gave me a look but didn't press the issue. Thankfully. I hated lying to her about actually being Trini's boyfriend. Though tonight's date was real. A double date with Wade and her brother, Lincoln. I should've said no, but Trini's pouts killed me every time. The whole thing had sounded better in my head. I'd go to dinner with my girlfriend so that Trini could complete her end of the bargain that had me out of expulsion. Despite Dr. Newman's claim that Locke did not punish their students, expulsion and detention were still very much part of the school disciplinary system. They just called it some other bullshit like Character Development Classes, or Group Building Exercises. In the end, expulsion meant staying your ass at home and detention meant scrubbing toilets.

The thought that Trini made a bargain at all with Wade for me still made me bristle. Carmen took that as nerves. "Don't be so nervous," she said and helped me with the tie around my neck.

"I'm not nervous."

I could hear Beatrice inside my head giggle at my lie.

The Uber driver left me in front of a very fancy restaurant that featured linen tablecloths, comfortable chairs, and low intimate lighting. The hostess gave me a once-over, his nostrils flared, and I tried not to touch my hair, as if it had put that look there. "Uh, Chan, reservation for four?"

His eyes lit up. "Ah, yes, follow me."

Trini beamed at me as I reached their table. "You made it."

I didn't think I was that late. I sat next to her, and she leaned in and gave me a kiss on the cheek, just close enough to my lips that I could taste the strawberry lip gloss she wore. Then she turned to her brother. The guy looked like smooth sandstone: dark hair, light eyes, sharp features, and older. According to Trini, Lincoln had just graduated college with a Culinary Arts degree. Wade thought I could be jealous of the guy. I almost snorted to myself. I was not jealous of Lincoln Chan. I had nothing to be jealous about. "Lincoln, this is my boyfriend, Xander."

Boyfriend. The sound of it unsettled me a little bit.

He gave me a curt nod. "I was starting to think you didn't exist."

"Whatever," Trini said. I could hear the eye roll.

My eyes found Wade, who looked really good in his natural element. Although I'm pretty sure he gave thought to his outfit, it looked as if he just threw things on. A salmon-colored button-down—opened at the throat—no tie, with a blue blazer. If I could see his feet, I'm pretty sure he wasn't wearing socks. He looked so Californian.

"Xander," he said. His voice husky, as if threatening me.

"Wade," I said back with that same tone.

One thing being on the run taught me was to acclimate quickly in strange environments, and this was a very strange environment. Wade and Lincoln talked about the menu in detail while Trini gave me a comforting squeeze under the table.

"You look nice," she said.

Instinct had me looking down at my tie. "Not the first time you've seen me in a tie, Trini."

"Yeah, but you still look nice."

I tried not to roll my eyes. Instead, I told her the same thing. She did look nice too. I almost died when I picked up the menu. I didn't know what any of it was. "You're going to have to order for me," I whispered to Trini.

Trini did order for me and what came was something that I should've returned to the ocean. It wasn't that bad, though I couldn't really enjoy it with the glares Wade was throwing my way, as if I were going to steal the china.

After dinner, Trini and Lincoln excused themselves to go to the bathroom, leaving Wade and me alone.

"So—" he started.

"I'm not going to steal anything," I cut him off. The confusion on his face made me feel like an idiot. "You keep looking at me as if I'm going to bolt with the crystal."

"That's glass."

"Whatever. Stop looking at me like that."

Wade smirked, sending a shitload of tension into my gut. "Am I making you uncomfortable?"

I leaned forward to whisper harshly. "You are such a suck-up."

He quickly lowered his eyes, skimming the drink menu in his hands, although I knew he wasn't going to order anything. He couldn't. He was still underage. "Wow, you have a way with words. I'm a suck-up and a whore."

Heat lifted to my cheeks. "I never called you a whore."

"You said Trini was my pimp. That makes me a whore."

He pinned me with his eyes. Those baby blues that shouldn't be on someone so damn handsome already.

Handsome? What?

I tore my eyes away from him, looking at my own drink menu. "I didn't mean it like that."

"How *did* you mean it?"

"Not like that." I felt guilty. "I'm sorry," I mumbled.

He didn't say anything, and I looked up at him. "I must've missed something. What did you say?"

Asshole. Of course he'd milk it. "I didn't mean to say that. I was just angry."

"Are you ever *not* angry?"

"Not around you, apparently."

He chuckled, twisting my insides.

He ignored me when Lincoln and Trini returned. He ignored me at school the next day too. I participated in Mrs. Rashard's art trip, and it only solidified my intent *not* to study art. Artists were batshit crazy. I was done with crazy town. Been there. Done that.

ELIZABETH ARROYO

CHAPTER 7

Although to Californians a low temperature of fifty was cold, it didn't compare to the arctic temps I'd experienced in Chicago. People here actually looked for snow and cold weather by driving up the crazy mountains. Yeah, that's what awaited me this weekend because of my stupid pride.

I called Trini. We'd spoken yesterday about the skiing disaster awaiting me. If I didn't show up, I would never hear the end of it. And if I did show up, I'd probably end up back on the train to hell. And the messed-up thing of it was, I hadn't spoken to Wade since our double date. He hadn't been near my locker, hadn't made any attempt to talk to me during lunch. Although that's what I had wanted, it left me feeling raw inside. I shouldn't have cared nor felt the need to ask him why he was avoiding me.

I'd been dismissed.

Just. Like. That.

It made me wish I had a snow mound in my backyard to practice skiing just so I could give him a decent run for his money. Not happening. I'd seen footage of him at the Olympics. The guy was extraordinary. Weightless in the sky as he spun and twisted his body to land solidly on snow.

Snow.

Fucking snow.

"Hello?"

I hadn't realized I dialed Trini. "Hey," I said. "Am I free?"

She chuckled. It warmed my insides. Solidified me to this plane of existence. How one person could do that to me scared me. I had protected her, and she had protected me. Like …

Papi, please. We don't have to get there so fast.

Family.

I pressed my fingers to my eyes, pushing that shit back. Way back. I couldn't let it out. Not here. Not now.

"Not likely," she answered, tearing me from the dark road trying to swallow me.

I released my eyes and caught my surroundings. Might as well put my big boy pants on. I hadn't seen snow since the accident. "Just so you know. I've never skied before. I don't own a winter coat, goggles, hat … hell, I don't even have gloves."

She giggled. "We can get that there. I'll pick you up on the way. Just text me your address."

"Are you sure?"

"I'm sure. Link is driving."

Great. I sent her my address, and a few hours later, a dark SUV coasted into the driveway. I hopped inside, did the whole chin-up, what's-up gesture to the guy. He didn't particularly seem to care for a conversation with me. I was okay with that.

We drove out of the city, toward white-capped mountains. They talked about college life. Where Trini would be going. Brother-sister shit, while I white-knuckled the door handle throughout the last thirty miles of winding icy roads.

Trini Chan was the only person I'd go to hell and back for. And Trini Chan *had* sent me to hell. A cold, wet, icy hell.

Trini snatched glances my way and gave me a preoccupied look.

PTSD. PTSD. I have PTSD. Post-traumatic stress and snow and ice on roads are my trigger. I shouldn't be here. I shouldn't be here.

Don't be a pussy, Xander. Swallow it. My sister had a way with words.

Yeah, I was at war with myself.

We made it to the biggest house I'd ever seen propped against the snowy mountain. Another two SUVs were parked outside the three-car garage bay. The sliding door was open despite the nippy wind and cold. We had stopped to buy my winter gear and rent my ski equipment, which I didn't intend on wearing or using. Ever.

"I'm not promising anything, Trini," Link said.

They both got out of the truck and headed for the house. I stayed behind, swallowing back the fear and panic that had edged its way to the surface of my psyche. Painfully, I opened my palm and released the door handle, allowing myself to step outside. Snow crunched under my Chucks. Not fresh powder, more like ice. I kept one hand on the truck for balance as memories tugged at my wiring, firing networks I wanted to douse in water and short circuit.

"*No seas maricón,*" my father's voice boomed in time with my pounding heart.

"*Armando, por favor,*" my mother begged.

My sisters softly crying.

Then the sunrise crept into the sky, sending a burst of orange light just at its apex. Until the sound of crushing metal exploded.

I couldn't breathe.

I slipped on the snow and vomited the undigested coffee and bread I had this morning until there was nothing left.

Emptied out.

If only I could spew my soul with it.

"That's gross, dude," Theo said from the door.

I looked at the sliding door to see an audience. Wade among them, though he didn't wear gross on his face like the others. His expression was softer, kinder. I looked away from him, feeling my cheeks dampen, and I wiped my eyes.

Then Trini was there, lending me her shoulder and walking me inside the house.

The big ass house. They didn't care that we tracked mud inside. Mixed with the other muddied footprints. She left me in the bathroom.

"Is he okay?" I heard Wade at the door.

"I think so. I think the drive made him dizzy, that's all," Trini said.

I was grateful for her explanation, unsure what I would've said instead. I washed my mouth out with water, splashed water on my face, then walked out.

One of the SUVs already left and everyone but Wade and Link—who were talking in the kitchen—and Trini, who was on the sofa, stayed behind, waiting for me.

Wade looked at me but said nothing.

"You okay?" Lincoln asked.

"Yeah. Just the drive."

"You'll get used to it."

Why? I almost asked. I was never coming back to this place. Ever.

Wade gave me a once-over I didn't appreciate, then lifted his chin. "You good to go up. You don't have to."

I knew I didn't have to. But I still had to. "Yeah, I'm good."

He nodded, taking in my bullshit, and led us out. I got more views of snow and tall mountains and more snow. Wade smirked in my direction, and after giving up on teaching me anything, he disappeared up the mountain with Lincoln. Trini found it in her heart to remain with me and guide me through this hell.

"Ready?" she asked.

Ready? On snow? Me? Yeah, nope. The moment Trini found it entertaining that I couldn't figure out the mechanism on the skis to free myself, I knew I was so damn doomed. I couldn't even remember why the hell I decided to even do this.

Right. Pride, asshole. Pride got people killed.

Luckily for me, Trini had no desire to leave my ass. She guided me safely to the spot where the others had claimed land. I was part of Wade Wilson's entourage. And he made it a point to shine like a bad penny. Fake ass surprised that a couple of photographers were there taking pictures of his awesomeness. I had to admit, he was in his element. I couldn't see his face with the hat and goggles, but I imagined what he must've looked like free flying off the snow mounds, which seemed made especially for him. While others looked tense on the thing, Wade looked like magic. Then the real magic happened when we moved to the halfpipe.

A sudden jealousy spiked through me that someone could be so perfect at something. That someone like Wade, who probably grew up with a silver spoon in his mouth, had this love rushing through his veins while I was stuck as an angry asshole. The dangerous question of why bounced around my mind, and I couldn't pull the shit out of my head. Why had my family died and not his? Why was he so blessed and not me? Why did he have everything, and I had shit, not even a soul anymore? Why was I such a fucking downer?

I didn't remember myself before the accident. I was numbed to the world. Hiding in my game system, my thoughts, my fear. I'd lived in shadow for so long I didn't even know how to step into the light. I didn't know how to be heard. I realized I didn't have anything to say that deserved the light.

Wade slid to a perfect stop to my left on the bottom of the incline and pulled out his headgear. That damn smile sprayed on his face made him look radiant. I didn't want to punch him this time. I wanted to be the focus of it. To be in its trajectory. I wanted that smile to be just for me.

Before I could decipher any of that shit, I pushed away from the crowd that wanted a part of that too and made my way down the mountain. Alone.

A few hours later, as I began to wonder if my ass had gotten frostbite from sitting on a bench all afternoon watching the families and kids slide and fall and laugh, I caught sight of a group heading down. Couldn't miss Trini's bright purple puffer jacket. My moment of insane jealousy had dissolved, and I was just happy seeing her happy. Twenty yards away she caught sight of me and waved. And that's when some fucker on skis forced her to stop. His back to me, I only caught a glimpse of sandy blond hair as he pulled off his headgear.

Chad fucking Jones.

I jumped to my feet and ran.

CHAPTER 8

The instant the idiot pulled off his headgear I knew the guy was going down. Hard. Adrenaline fueled my veins. The rush of it made me feel alive. With a loud *oomph*, I tackled him onto the snow. Both of us wearing thick ass jackets made everything sluggish. On slo-mo. Trini fell on her ass, still on her skis as we rolled around in what I'd imagined a couple of penguins would look like if they decided to duke it out among each other. The puffer jackets were too thick to inflict any kind of real pain.

Just as I decided to go for his exposed face, I felt someone grab the back of my jacket and toss me to the side like a sack of shit. I slipped on my hands and knees on the snow before getting to my feet. Theo, the big ass mofo, stood with a hand flattened against my chest while Wade stood near Chad and Trini, who looked at me as if it were my fault.

Nick and Taylor waved their hands, ensuring the crowd around us that we were okay. Just a game of suicidal tackle.

Trini looked beside herself. "Xander, don't," she said.

Those two words cut through me like an ice pick through the ribs. Despite our thing being fake, it had been to protect her from this prick who hit her. "Don't what?" I spat out, wiping my chin. I'd been on edge since I got here. Trini defending Chad made it all worse. I shouldn't have come. I didn't belong here. I didn't make friends or have girlfriends. I shouldn't care about people. Eventually, they hurt you.

"I just want to talk to him."

I took a step toward Chad, intending on beating the hell out of him, but Wade stood between us. Although I was taller than Wade, I couldn't hurt him. I didn't want to hurt anyone that didn't deserve it. "Let it go, man," Wade said. "It's her choice."

Bullshit. Trini couldn't make that decision. I looked around for Lincoln, but he wasn't around.

Wade cocked his head at me, already knowing who I was searching for. "Lincoln had a call to take," he said so only I could hear.

I turned to Trini. She reminded me of Bea, or the person Bea could've become had she survived, deepening my need to protect her. "Trini." My voice broke. "Don't do this."

"It's just a talk. I'll be fine." The light tone in her voice sounded forced. She wasn't fine. Probably would never be fine, but it was still her choice, and I had to respect that. Like it or not. And I wasn't a fool. Talks with exes would lead to reconciliation. It always did.

Without a word, I turned around and started away from them. She wanted to talk, fine. But I wasn't leaving her alone with that prick. I plucked my skis from the ground and turned, almost slamming into Wade. Even with only the guy's light blue eyes visible, he made me itchy. I looked past his shoulder at Trini and Chad moving away from the group.

"Where are they going?"

He shrugged. "Looks like to the lift."

"Okay, then, let's go." I started walking forward until he grabbed my arm and stopped me.

"She wants to talk to him." He reminded me as if I hadn't heard.

"Yeah, I heard. I'm not going to interrupt the talk, but I'm not leaving her with him unprotected. He hurts her, and I'll kill him."

I could've sworn I caught a smirk under Wade's cowl, as if he approved. "Okay. But let's give them some space." He told the others we'd meet up with them later and started walking away from me and toward the lift. I had to half run to catch up with him while trying to clumsily not impale him with my skis. He seemed to notice my inadequacy and stayed at a safe distance from me. At least until we caught the line to the lift. "What's your deal anyway?" he asked. "With her."

The glower remained on my face. I felt it pull the muscles cramping from the cold. My lips were already cracking, and I noticed him lower his eyes to them. My stomach rolled inside of me thinking about Trini with Chad, not because of Wade. Not because of Wade. "She deserves better," I finally admitted. "Better than him and better than me."

He looked at me as if he wanted to call my bullshit, but it wasn't bullshit. Trini did deserve better.

Trini and Chad climbed on the lift, and we waited a few carts before getting on ourselves. Wade had to steer me into the lift and instructed me how to hold the skis so I wouldn't impale him. We finally sat shoulder to shoulder inside the tight seat, and my heart rate kicked up a few notches as the ground fell below us. I held on tight and shut my eyes. I hadn't realized I was also afraid of heights.

"So," Wade said beside me, breaking me from thoughts of doom. "If she deserves better than you, what do *you* deserve?"

A fair question. One that startled me. I turned to look at him and the light hit his eyes, making them look like clear pools of water. With his hair fitted into the beanie, his eyes became the prominent feature on his face, and it was hard to look away from them. He tilted his head and lifted his eyebrows, waiting for my answer. My reaction to him pissed me off. I should know better than to feel—whatever this was. Anger was better, safer. "What kind of question is that?"

His full lips tilted on one side in a half smile, as if he figured something out I was still clueless about. "You're not that bad, Morales."

"I like hitting people," I reminded him.

"Okay, maybe you are bad. But you hit people who deserve it."

I clenched my teeth, my jaw muscles complaining as I looked away from Wade.

He leaned in closer, his breath touching my cheeks. "And you're afraid of heights, apparently, and snow," he said. "So why did you come out this weekend at all?"

Good damn question. For some reason, admitting I was an idiot wouldn't cut it. "Pride," I answered, knuckle-gripping the bar keeping me from falling to my death. "I'm not afraid," I said dryly. "I just like my feet planted."

"Afraid," he mocked, smiling.

I flinched when we made an unexpected stop and the thing swayed.

"And cute when you're nervous."

"Don't call me cute. Ever," I said through gritted teeth, although I felt my cheeks heat up. "I'm not cute. Cute and me do not mix. Cute is for teddy bears and unicorns, I am neither."

Wade laughed. A sound that sounded so sweet and made me smile. "Great," he said. "Now I have this visual—"

"I am going to push you off this thing if you finish that statement," I cut him off, imagining what visual he had of me and wanting to shove it out of my own brain.

He laughed, and I liked the sound of it. I liked the look of him, too, and that was the problem. I'd never been so shallow as to be interested in glamour. Rich ass wipes who thought the world owed them had not been my thing. I'd been surrounded by boys my whole life, even Jace, whom I found to be the most beautiful person on the planet, and I'd never felt this … this … discombobulated. Thankfully, we arrived at the top of the mountain before I could continue thinking about what that all meant. We were basically pushed off as the lift lowered, and I stumbled forward almost stabbing a guy's eye out with my skis.

"Sorry," I mumbled.

Once free from the crowd I took a moment to look around and gasped. Surrounded by a million ways to die— jagged edges, sharp peaks, and a quick death over the side of the cliff. And snow.

The white powder mocked me.

I'd survived snow in Chicago to die of it in California. How the hell did that make sense? My chest tightened and I suddenly couldn't draw breath.

"Are you okay?" Wade asked beside me.

No. I wasn't okay. I was so screwed. "I'm so screwed," I said.

Wade didn't get it. He didn't get the level of fear that clenched me like a vice grip. He didn't get that I'd been dead in the snow for hours before help came, that I'd seen my mother's face turn green, then blue in the cold as death and ice consumed her. That my imagination ran wild as I thought of my sisters somewhere in the snow and whatever lurked in the silent dark around us.

He didn't know.

"Xander," he snapped. He stood directly in front of me, cupping my face. I hadn't even realized he had moved. His cold gloves on my face made my body shudder, but his face so damn close to me made me forget my fears and want things I shouldn't want. "You're going to be okay. Look at me."

I met his light blue eyes competing with the bright blue skies behind him. "I shouldn't be here," I mumbled. *With you.*

"You're here for Trini, remember?"

Right. Trini. "I have to make sure Chad doesn't hurt her," I mumbled like an idiot.

"Right. That's why we're here. Now, relax. You're fine with me. I'm not going to let anything happen to you."

Those words drove a wedge into my heart. I'd never heard them before. No one bothered to protect me from anything, from anyone. Hearing it from Wade, the sincerity in his voice, made all my insides heat up. I still couldn't get words out.

"Now, let's get you into your skis. Yeah?"

I nodded. My cheeks still cupped in his hands. Then he released his hold over me and instructed me how to shove my booted feet into the skis. It took a few tries, but I finally managed to secure them to the boot. He, on the other hand, held his snowboard under his arm and walked beside me.

"We could walk down the mountain. No need to test gravity," he said, reassuringly. Although I knew he could fly off the mountain if he wanted to. He wouldn't leave me. Not in this place anyway.

Okay. "I can walk. Sure." I slowly used my skis in a walk-like fashion while he chuckled beside me.

"That's good," he said, as if I were a two-year-old. "And if you have to stop, you can always drop to the side. Okay?"

I nodded. Sure. I could fall. Falling was easy. "Why don't they have rails to avoid falling off the mountain? That would've been nice."

He snorted this time. "What would be the fun in that? The point is to jump off things."

"I thought the point was to survive down the mountain."

"Yeah, that would be a plus."

The guy was nuts. Like creepers, we followed behind Chad and Trini, who carried themselves differently now. Trini leaning a bit more into Chad's space. Yeah, they were getting together. Which meant she was dumping me sooner than expected. Surprisingly, I didn't feel hurt about that. I knew we'd always just end up as friends. But I still had a gut feeling that Chad was still a violent asshole and Trini deserved better.

"Are you okay?" Wade asked beside me.

Trini took that moment to laugh at something Chad said. They still hadn't noticed us following them. "They're getting back together," I admitted.

"Yeah," Wade said with a sigh. "It looks that way. You're not going into a murderous rage. What's up with that?"

We moved slowly, which was hard with the slip and slide of the skis. "We weren't really dating," I admitted. Something no one knew. I wasn't sure why I told Wade. A weight lifted off my chest.

"Really dating?" Wade asked. "What does that even mean?"

I lowered my cowl and noticed him quickly looking at my lips then back at my eyes. I restrained the urge to shudder. Too damn cold. "She wanted to avoid Chad, and I wanted to appear, I don't know, normal I guess, so we agreed to act like a couple." I glared at him. "Tell anyone and I'll toss you off this mountain."

Wade laughed again. "You do like your threats."

I shrugged and turned back to Trini and Chad. They had settled into a rhythm and looked like a couple.

"So you weren't together. No kisses or anything?" Wade sounded almost hopeful. As if reveling in my pathetic-ness.

"No. Just friends," I said without sounding upset or deflated. Just the truth.

"Great, that's—"

I narrowed my eyes at him.

"—uh, great."

"What's so great about that?"

"Well, for one." He gestured toward Trini and Chad. Duh, I wasn't really getting dumped, having never been really dating. "And friends are always better. You need more of those that you wouldn't punch." Suddenly, Wade looked nervous again. As if he itched to get as far away from me as he possibly could get. His eyes roved over the mountain and something like hunger flashed into his expression. This was his joy, his happy place, and he had stopped to guide me.

I felt like a fool. "You win. I totally bombed this skiing thing."

He chuckled and slapped me on the back. "I was messing with you. I knew you didn't have a chance. I'm Wade Wilson."

"Well," I said, feeling my stomach clench, "at least you got what you wanted out of this, right?" I didn't realize I was angry about that until I heard my own edgy voice, and I felt the need to leave Wade and Trini to their own mistakes. I had my own to deal with; I didn't need their shit too. "Have fun with Link," I said, just as I took off down the mountain.

I'd meant to slowly navigate down like I'd done from the halfpipe. Except, I'd gone the wrong way. I knew that the moment I started picking up speed.

I was so screwed.

CHAPTER 9

I wasn't used to asking for help, getting help, or anyone saving my ass. I needed to get away from Trini and that asshole Chad. And I needed to get further away from Wade fucking Wilson. The guy was relentless. I hated the way he kept looking at my lips. The way he called me cute. The way my stomach took a nosedive to my knees whenever he smiled. And thinking about him with Lincoln Chan. The shit was too damn raw.

Fess up, bro. You are gay. You knew it the moment Papi told you not to be.

I swallowed the lump in my throat, hearing Beatrice's voice in my head. The distraction made me miss the last optimal dropping point before my descent into hell, and I didn't know how to stop.

"You lose control, just drop to the side," Wade had suggested. Except the side was filled with jagged rocks and trees. I'd hit something and die. Trying to stop only made me go faster. Thankfully, there weren't that many people on this slope to see my ultimate last-second fail. My life flashed before me. I had two options as the path veered right: take my chances and drop to the side, or pray to a God I no longer believed had my best interest to save me from

cracking my head against stone or tree, or jump off the fast-approaching ridge. I didn't know what lay beyond the precipice. Maybe another snow mound. Maybe the edge of the mountain and a thousand-foot drop. Maybe a fucking rainbow.

A familiar feeling of having no control over my fate swept through me. My dad testing fate and losing. My mom never standing up for us. Bea hiding the knives. Katie too young to know what any of it meant. Maybe this was the way I'd go. Death missed me last time in a different snowbank. Maybe, this time the snow would end me.

I dropped my ski poles and inhaled, ready to launch forward and at least try to land on my two feet. Then out of nowhere I got the wind knocked out of me. I fell head over teakettle until my body stopped moving. Lying spread-eagled on the snow, I half-expected fate to laugh and have someone impale me with their skis. A few moments passed until I opened my eyes to blue skies and took stock of my injuries. My ribs hurt and I'd lost my skis but not my limbs. I sat up and turned to the edge of the trees, and my heart stumbled. My chest tightened, and I bit down to hold back a cry.

Wade lay on his back near the tree line. I couldn't see his face with those damn goggles he wore, and I couldn't tell if he was breathing through the puffer coat. I crawled toward him, sliding a few feet on the decline, and shoved up his goggles. His eyes were open, his breathing suddenly started, as if he'd been holding his breath, and he turned on his side and coughed.

"Are you okay?" I asked. All I needed was the damn guilt trip for having killed a gold medalist trying to save my ass from being an idiot on skis.

He sat up. "I hate you," he said with little venom in his voice. "I really do." He got to his feet with a grunt and plucked his board, securing it under his arm, then he collected my gear and only tossed me the poles. The skis he kept under his arm too. "Fuck you and skiing. I catch you on my mountain and I'll kill you myself."

With that, he stomped off.

I didn't feel the pain on my side until I got up on my feet and followed his brisk walk down the mountain.

And that apparently ended my skiing career.

Wade didn't even look back to see if I was following. Pissed didn't begin to define his current status. I thought he was actually going to throw me off the cliff at one point. I couldn't be sure if his current state was because I forced him to save me or because I had almost killed him for saving me. Probably both.

Breathing hurt. I knew my ribs had taken the full impact of that tackle, so I kept my left arm against my body. I was used to pain. This pain. Getting jumped at Boys Home had been a regular thing for loudmouths. What could I say? I was a loudmouth. I owned it and the consequences that came from it.

I didn't follow Wade to the parking lot where I suspected he took off without me. Instead, I waited for Trini. Despite the bogus shit she'd just pulled, I needed to make sure she was okay. I wouldn't survive another guilt trip. I caught sight of her where I had planted myself earlier before Chad's beatdown. I couldn't even think of his name without growling. She'd been waiting for me, apparently. My chest felt too damn full at this point.

"I can't believe you're doing this," I said.

"It's not like we were ever a real couple," she said back, without a hint of malice in her voice. True.

"And if we were? If I wanted us to be?" I didn't, but if it would keep her away from him, I would.

She slipped her bottom lip into her mouth. "He never hit me before then."

"It always starts somewhere."

"He promised he wouldn't do it again."

"They all say that." I should know.

"I have to try."

"Why?"

"Because I love him."

And there it was. The reason I would never love anyone. "Are you sure this is what you want? Him?"

"Yeah, I'm sorry."

"Me too, Trini." I walked away from her. I had no lifeline here. No way out of this fucked-up shell I called my mind and body. I didn't belong here. I didn't belong anywhere. California had never been my home. The boy who did nothing when his father beat his mother. That did nothing when his family was killed. I turned into an angry seventeen-year-old waiting for the darkness inside to tear through every fiber of my being. It would, eventually.

I had run away so many times only to be hauled back by the cops. Moe and Carmen had fought about what to do with me until the night I'd been arrested for assault. The judge decided to give me a chance and instead of juvie, or prison, I'd been sent to Boys Home. I spent ten months trying to remain sane there. It was also where I met Jace. I wondered how he was doing. If he ever thought about me.

Shaking my head, I wiped the memory clear of my mind. I couldn't go there. I had to let all that shit go. I walked into the small town with my heavy boots crunching the snow-covered ground under me. I hadn't paid attention on the drive to this place and had no idea where Wade's house was.

Fucking hell.

Then, as if I needed to be shitted on further, thick snowflakes started to lazily fall from the sky. I pulled off my right glove with my teeth and caught a few flakes on my palm, making sure it wasn't some trick of the eye. Nope. Snow.

I hated snow.

I slipped into a coffee shop and removed my headgear to place my order. I sat at a small table wedged in the corner. Instantly, I started to sweat. My Henley clung to my back, and I couldn't peel my coat off due to the reminder every time I moved that I bruised a rib. I pulled out my phone, which miraculously survived my fall, and placed it on the table. There were always options. Not that any would be good ones. I found myself with two: call Wade for directions or try to hike it back home. An Uber from here would cost the same as a damn plane ticket. And I didn't think anyone would pick up a six-two, hundred-and-eighty-pound Latino mammoth in this neck of the woods. This was God punishing me, because while I didn't believe enough to get anything good out of life, I attributed all the bad shit to Him.

Better to face the squadron. I texted Wade.

Me: I've been dumped by my GF. Homeless in snow. Lost. Should I take my chances and head home?

Yeah, I sounded as pathetic as I felt. I wanted him to feel guilty, should he ignore my call for help and I die because of it. My phone pinged ten minutes later, and I knew he'd let me stew on purpose so that I would realize he was in control of my very fucked-up predicament. I may have played the same card if the situations were reversed.

I sipped my now cold coffee. The barista shot me a few glares, as if expecting me to rob the place. Okay, so I didn't blend in. It didn't mean I was a criminal. Though, technically, I was a criminal. My records were confidential because I was a minor. I'd get a clean slate in a few months when I turned eighteen. I looked at Wade's text. Not in any hurry to respond to him.

Let him stew.

Him: Where are you?

He even took his time to properly spell all the words and not use just R and U. I ignored the text and scrolled through my phone for other possible ways out of this town. I could rent a car for forty bucks if I had a license and a parent to sign. I didn't even know how to drive. My options were limited. I had to call it. After twenty minutes, I texted him back.

Me: It's snowing.

His text came through instantly, which made me smile and, okay, feel a little bit special.

Him: Yes. It is. Are you going to tell me where you are?

I could imagine his pissed-off expression and found myself smiling. Which was totally insane on my part.

Me: I hate snow. I texted back, ignoring the second half of his inquiry. I glanced at the window and the sticking snow.

Him: Snow is good for skiing.

Me: I don't ski.

Him: No, and you never will. Ever.

I smiled at that. I hadn't remembered anyone actually caring for me before. It was kind of nice and irritating at the same time.

Me: Do you care about me? I texted back. Couldn't help it.

Him: Where. Are. You.

I didn't think he wanted to flirt. Was that what I was doing? Flirting with him? Having never done it—and why should I with Wade fucking Wilson—I wasn't sure. I returned to being pissed instead.

Me: Taby's Cafe.

Him: Not far. On my way.

Me: Don't drive.

The thought of him driving in the snow made me panic.

Him: Walking.

I let out a relieved breath.

When Wade walked in, everyone, and I mean *everyone*, farted rainbows and confetti. Strangers approached him for selfies, handshakes, pointers on things like a McTwist, which had me thinking of McDonald's shakes, and 1440 halfpipes, which had me thinking of a bomb Jace had once shown me how to make. Not the inhaling kind, but the smoking, explosion kind. I had no clue what the hell they were talking about, but by the time Wade actually got to my table, I had learned it had to do with snowboarding. Thank you, Google. When he finally sat across from me, the barista, who had been sporting a weathered scowl at me, had suddenly turned twenty years younger and projected her own rainbow at Wade.

Fucking hell.

She even put his drink in front of him while everyone else had to order at the counter. "The regular?"

"Yeah, thanks," he said with that genuine bright smile he wore so well.

He shrugged out of this coat and remained in a black Henley. His cheeks were flushed, his hair tousled with sprinkles of snow already melting on the crown of his head, and I was struck by how handsome he looked, which forced me to feel suddenly uneasy and look away from him.

"I'm still pissed at you," he said. "Just so you know."

I lifted my eyes to the crowd and noticed some still taking photos. The last thing I needed was any type of attention. To be on some trending photos of us. Or of him and me in the background. I pulled on my hood low over my eyes and stood up as he scowled up at me. I dropped a twenty on the table. "I'll wait for you outside." Ignoring his confused expression, I walked out.

A thick layer of fresh snow clung to the ground and was still falling. I was itching to go home. He made me wait as more people started to show up to become his bestie. By the time he came out, my fingers were frozen.

"You are a very rude person," he snapped.

No one had ever called me rude before. I've heard violent, loudmouth, disrespectful, criminal, and asshole. Rude was a new one for me. I followed him because I had no choice, and shit got even more toxic when we made it inside the house, as if he'd been waiting to combust in the privacy of his own home behind a locked door. He dropped his snowboard just outside the door and I did the same just before stepping inside the house. He turned to me with a vicious look on his face. The left side of his nostril raised with his lip curled up in his version of a sneer. "You are the most insufferable, stubborn asshole on the planet!"

I didn't expect that. He tore out of his winter gear. I

couldn't do the same, although I was sweating again. My body hurt too much to move. "Me?"

"Yes, you."

"Why, because I don't kiss your ass like the world does?"

He was suddenly in my space and my body became aware of his nearness, as if I'd been zapped by an electrical charge that burned my skin and my insides. "Because you are a careless ass who thinks of no one but yourself."

Not what I expected him to say. I was a bitter, angry ass that preferred to punch someone than talk to them. Not careless and not selfish. "You don't know shit about me."

"I know you almost got hurt today. You could've been killed! Didn't even try to avoid the fall!" His voice cracked and concern dampened his eyes.

I knew he was right. I've seen the news of ski accidents killing people, but I pulled all that back. I didn't need, want, or deserve his concern. "I didn't ask you to risk yourself for me."

"No, you didn't."

We were standing so close that I was pretty sure he would've been able to feel how fast my heart was beating had I not been wearing the puffer coat.

"Did I miss something?" We both turned to Taylor. I was grateful for the distraction. "Are you two dating?" she asked.

Okay, maybe not *this* type of distraction.

I expected Wade to snort at the thought of being with me. Liking me at all. Instead, he walked away, sprinted up the stairs, and slammed his bedroom door.

The silence that followed felt electric.

"Snow is going to make travel a bitch tonight. If you want to take the truck, be my guest, but Trini and I are staying." Link sprinted up the stairs, and a few moments later I heard a door creak open, then shut.

Was the fucker with Wade?

Like, *with* Wade?

Why the hell did I care?

"Are you leaving?" Theo asked.

I wanted to. Damn, I really, really wanted to. I knew being here with Wade was going to fuck me up. "I don't drive."

Theo snorted in disbelief. "Really?"

I dropped on the recliner with a wince. "Not every seventeen-year-old drives, Theo." My stats were probably wrong. One in a million seventeen-year-olds didn't drive, me being the one. I tilted my head back and closed my eyes.

CHAPTER 10

I fell asleep.

And woke up swatting a fly attached to an arm of a giggling girl. I struggled to lift my heavy lids until finally I opened them fully and started to stretch. Then I remembered pain, and it greeted me with party bells. I winced, pulled my left arm closer to my body, and struggled to my feet. I was drenched in sweat, having slept with the coat on.

"Wade didn't want to wake you up but—" Piper put her hand to her lips and whispered, "His parents are almost here, and I thought you might want to hide with the rest of us."

Still working in lagging mode, I didn't quite catch her words. Then the front door opened, and she startled. "Too late."

A tall blonde woman walked into the room, stomping her boots of the still-spilling snow. The first thing I noticed was that she had a dead animal over her shoulders. I blinked a couple of times and realized it was a fur scarf, and I didn't think it was fake. She stiffened as her eyes landed on me. Thankfully, Piper jumped into action.

"Mrs. Wilson," she squealed.

The woman jolted back to normalcy and smiled. A smile that reminded me of Wade's, although it didn't quite touch her eyes. Piper hugged her and kissed the air near each cheek. "Piper, dear, how good to see you." Even the woman's voice exuded elegance. Low and seductive, like a black widow. Lure them in and kill them.

Jesus, I needed a real night's rest.

After they did their thing, Mrs. Wilson returned her attention to me and snapped her fingers. "You must be Mr. Tapas's new employee. The snow is making a mess of things. You should hurry and start shoveling before we get caved in."

Ouch.

I heard someone at the stairs and caught Wade with Lincoln, wearing tuxedos. I shook my head trying to get the fuzz out. "This isn't real," I said to no one. I was still dreaming. Except people weren't dying in this dream. *I* wanted to die in this dream.

"Mom." Wade approached his mother and performed the same fake kiss to the air. Then he turned to me as I stood at the center of a vortex coming to sweep me back to my reality. Didn't happen. "This is Xander Morales. A friend. He's not staff."

Lincoln passed by me and chuckled because why the hell not. Since, you know, I was brown folk.

The woman cupped her chest as if she'd been offended. I couldn't quite tell if it was that Wade used the term friend to describe me or that she messed up and thought I was staff. Probably the former. Which totally, yup, pissed me off.

"We're really not friends," I clarified, glad that my voice sounded deeper than usual. Still sexy sleep mode. I shook my head. "No, more like arch enemies trying not to kill each other."

The woman arched a brow, her face paled, and she now cupped her neck as if I were going to launch myself at her and strangle her with the dead animal she wore.

Wade chuckled, something that sounded totally fake. Even he couldn't make that sound real. "He's kidding." He glared at me.

"Nope," I said. "Totally not kidding."

Wade gave Piper a look that had her jolting into action. I wondered if she had one of those pull strings on her back that brought toys to life. She took my arm. "You're such a jokester. Let's get this coat off and get you cleaned up."

Because, apparently, I looked like a mess. I let her push me away from them but not before I totally got the last word in. "Looks like Rikki lost the fight there."

Piper broke out in laughter, then tried to swallow it but failed.

We ended up in an indoor pool house. Because, why not. The house was big enough. She turned to make sure no one was following us, then started to laugh and punched me lightly in the arm. "You are so bad," she said.

"Ouch." I rubbed the tender spot. She had a good punch.

"You plan on sleeping in that thing?" Before I could tell her I was plastered to the coat, she unzipped me and pushed it off my shoulder. The action made me wince again. "Are you hurt?"

I wasn't sure until I pulled up my Henley and revealed my very purple bruise on my left side. She gasped. "Xander, what happened?"

"Wade saved my life. His life-saving skills suck."

"Are they broken?" She pressed her fingers carefully against my skin, and I flinched. She squealed and pulled her hand back sharply.

I laughed at her reaction.

"You are terrible," she said, huffing away from me. "I'd never seen Wade so scared. Do you have any idea how many people have died in skiing accidents?"

I opened my mouth to agree, but she kept talking.

"You could've landed on your head. Are you sure you don't have a head injury?"

Her hands were nowhere near my head. She totally copped a few feels before finally looking up at me. "I'm fine. I didn't hit my head." And thankfully, neither did Wade. As a professional snowboarder, he would've known if he had to be rushed to the hospital. Right? I felt horrible at the thought of him hurt because of me. Too late to say anything now. Didn't matter anyway. What's done is done.

"Go shower—you're all icky," Piper said. "There's a robe in all the bathrooms and a laundry room over there." She pointed past the pool. "All the rooms are on the second floor. The only one left is the one near the stairs. Sucks to be you."

I rolled my eyes. At least I had a room and wouldn't be sleeping in the igloo I'd have to make after I shoveled the snow.

I started back toward the living room. Thankfully, the critter assassin was not there. I took the stairs as Wade was coming down. I felt a tinge of relief that he was okay. I hadn't killed him. At least until he spoke. "You are unbelievable," he breathed out as he passed me.

Yeah, the devil himself wouldn't want his ass. "Just remember I'm the reason you got your man this weekend, and I'm not shoveling your fucking snow." I didn't wait to hear any more of his shit and just headed to the room I'd been given and slammed the door. Hard.

Even I was allowed a tantrum once in a while.

CHAPTER 11

I called Carmen to let her know my predicament. She was fine with me staying over, but I had to fork up Trini's phone number in case I never made it home. Carmen was not overbearing and gave me enough space the size of the Grand Canyon. I loved and resented her for it. She hadn't eased into my upbringing; I'd give her that. But everyone, even me, knew that teenagers needed reigning in. She didn't. I had hoped she would've hauled ass to pick me up. But the thought of her driving in this snowy weather made my chest hurt.

So, I stayed.

I dropped the phone and undressed in the room. Sucks to be me meant that I didn't have a bathroom in my room. I had to use the one out in the hallway. After trial and error, I found it. I'd also found a new toothbrush and packaged toiletries. After the shower, I dunked my clothes in the laundry and stayed with a towel wrapped around my hips. Everyone else was in the pool house so I had free reign of the house.

A dozen or so bedrooms, six bathrooms, and an inside pool. No one dared to use the master bedroom. The room took a quarter of the second floor, with floor-to-ceiling windows. Yeah, I looked. A few family photographs dotted the flat surfaces. Most of them were of a young Wade with a snowboard. But others had him with what I figured was his younger brother. They looked exactly alike. They looked happy in the picture. A perfect family on top of a snowcapped mountain. The date on the photo read five years ago.

Five years ago, I was in seventh grade, Bea was graduating eighth grade, and Katie was just starting school. I still had my family alive. I walked out of the master bedroom promising myself never to return.

I found Wade's bedroom, which was cleaner than I'd expected. The bed perfectly made, his clothes perfectly folded and in their place. The room looked like a museum. I almost expected to see *Do not touch with your dirty fingers* signs all over the place. He had an anteroom gutted as a trophy room, and there were loads of that. Medallions hung on the wall, trophies galore. A couple of used snowboards as decoration pieces were spread throughout and photos of his friends and him, some of him with family. All the time he wore that smile. Newspapers called him the golden boy because of his blond locks and light blue eyes. But it was the smile that made me realize how different we were. I couldn't remember when I felt the desire to smile. Not like that anyway. Since he'd been with me, all I'd seen was his scowl, sneer, and genuinely angry face.

That I suddenly cared how *I* made *him* feel made me realize that I, too, was drawn to that radiant smile. Just like everyone else, and I hated the feeling. I preferred pushing people away. The closest I had to a best friend had been Jace at Boys Home. That had been the last attempt at trying to acclimate with friends. All I wanted now was to graduate high school and see how far the blood money would take me. Fuck it. I didn't owe anyone anything.

"What the hell are you doing in here?"

I spun around, almost losing my towel, to see Wade in the doorway. Honestly, I hadn't expected him back so early.

His bow tie was undone but everything else seemed perfect. He took a step inside and closed the door, leaving all the air out in the hallway because now I couldn't seem to draw a good breath. His eyes lowered to my torso, and then the scars, then back to the bruises. He hissed.

"Did I do that?" He took a step forward, as if he meant to touch the bruise, but stopped and dropped his hand. Part of me wanted to feel that touch to see if I'd feel something. Another part was relieved he stopped himself.

"I'm good." I started for the door, except he was in my way and didn't move. "Do you mind?"

He ran his hand through his hair, tousling it to perfection like only rich assholes could manage. "Listen, I'm sorry for what my mom said."

"What?" I hiked up my brows. Didn't expect *that* apology. "I don't look like the help to you?" His eyes speared my own and I didn't want to move. I was being a dick. I knew it but I couldn't stop. Didn't know how.

"Jesus, why do you make this so damn hard," he said.

Whatever happened at this tux event did not seem to have ended well. He didn't carry himself like the happy guy I'd seen in his pictures and in public. He looked tired, sad. Raw. "Make what hard? Please, do explain."

His eyes roamed my face, and I got that sinking feeling in the pit of my stomach again. Then he came to a conclusion and shook his head. "You know what? Forget it." He started for his dresser and pulled out a tee and shorts and tossed them to me. I caught them before they fell on the floor. "And put some clothes on." I could've sworn a splash of color sprung onto his cheeks as he walked into his private bathroom.

Dismissed again.

I walked toward the door and wondered about Lincoln missing. Why hadn't he followed Wade to his bedroom? A little spark of hope circled the dark part of my soul. Then I stomped it out like a raging fire on my shoes. No way. No way. I was not attracted to Wade Wilson and this shit with

Lincoln was *not* making me jealous.

Told you. Just like Papi said.

No. Fucking No. I'd never felt this way before, so it was hard to pull apart the emotions rambling for attention inside of me. Being a label freak, it drove me insane. Maybe I should add OCD to my list of attributes.

I didn't move to leave. Instead, I stood waiting for Lincoln Chan to make his move and show up. He'd come inside and I'd leave. At least I'd know Wade was off-limits. *Why* I needed to know didn't matter. Only that I did. It wasn't like I was Wade's type anyway. If the look on his mother's face when she saw me said anything, it was that I was less than. No surprise. Hell, my ethnicity had been struggling to surface among the vast of white waters since forever. Why I thought Wade would be different made me an idiot.

I didn't know the guy, and he sure as hell didn't know me.

And, right, I wasn't gay.

I hadn't realized I was still staring at the door when the shower stopped running. Cowardice pushed me out of the room as if I were being flung by a bungee cord. I made sure not to slam the door this time.

CHAPTER 12

Dressed in Wade's clothes, I met everyone in the pool room. While I ignored Wade in the pool with Nick, Theo, Taylor, Piper, and Trini, I headed toward Lincoln, who sat on one of the lounge chairs, looking pleased with himself, as if he didn't know how to relax and have fun like teen morons in the pool dunking each other for a chance to toss a small ball inside a small hoop. I'd learned to swim at the Y, but I wasn't very good at it. Dad used to take us to the beach, but I'd stay in the shallow end, watching my cousins swim deeper. Something about the slime and the darkness under my body didn't sit well with me. I always thought I'd get swallowed by something. The perks of an overactive imagination.

I sat next to Lincoln and stretched out in the chair at the edge of the pool. My fingers itched to draw something. Wade saving me from the drop. Wade on that lift, our shoulders brushing. Wade in the pool with the water glistening over his pecs.

Shit. I looked away and shifted in my seat.

Lincoln leaned closer to me. "May I tell you a secret," he said and sipped his wine. "Wade didn't accost my sister for a meet because of some desire to have sex with me."

"TMI, dude. TMI." Not the image I wanted in my head. Ever.

He chuckled. "He wanted to propose a job collaboration in the food sense."

I wasn't all that keen on what food sense he meant, and he picked it up because he elaborated.

"Wade wants to extend the services of the resorts to include restaurants." He pointed at himself. "I am a chef. A joint venture would benefit us both. I'd run a kitchen and he'd get out of his father's thumb. No intimacy involved."

I remembered Wade's foul mood when he returned. "And it didn't go well?"

Lincoln turned back to where Wade had shoved Theo into the water and lunged for the ball. "No. His father's a moron, I'm afraid. Doesn't see the value of his son's ideas. They want him to be their athlete, always have."

I wondered what it would've been like to have my parents make every decision for me. While we didn't have money, and home life sucked sometimes, I didn't know enough about what options I had to even consider my future. But to be like Wade, to have the know-how to be more and still not be enough for his parents had to suck. I wasn't sure what was worse, being ignorant about the possibilities or knowing and not being about to do shit about what you wanted.

"He is handsome though," Lincoln said beside me, tearing me from my thoughts and apparent staring contest with Wade, because he and I were suddenly shooting lasers at each other. I hadn't even realized he was looking at me. I quickly turned my eyes away from him to Lincoln, who was now looking at me weird. "I can see the appeal."

"What appeal?" I asked.

He smirked and took another sip of his wine. "Not very smart though."

Laughter led my attention to Wade in the pool and Theo dunking Piper.

"So you guys aren't, like"—I felt my cheeks flush—"a

couple."

"No. We are not, like, a couple. He's too young."

I almost felt relieved, but then I remembered … right, I didn't care.

I heard Beatrice's snicker in my head, but gratefully she remained silent.

I looked at Wade again. He looked too young to be going into any type of business. "Why are you telling me this?"

"Because I believe Wade may have an interest in you."

That made me almost swallow my tongue. *I'm not gay*, I almost said. "Yeah, right. I could be the help, remember?"

Lincoln smiled as if I'd given him confirmation of something. "Usually, men claim not to be gay when faced with a proposition, so is it safe to assume you have similar interests?"

I snorted, though I felt like my heart decided to run a marathon without my body. "I'm not gay," I said. "And he used me to get to you. I don't think that makes him trustworthy. And he doesn't even know me."

"Sometimes, you don't need to deeply know someone to feel something for them. It's instinctual, something under the skin, rooted in the soul. Despite what you know of the person, it changes your perspective of them. It's called attraction," he said with that slimy voice of his.

"God, you've been living under a rock for way too long. Attraction makes people do stupid things. For instance, your sister." We both turned to Trini in the pool, laughing and splashing Piper. "She's with someone who hit her because she thinks she loves him. How do you justify that?"

He scowled. Yup, something I was deeply familiar with causing in people. "Trini has to learn to make her own choices."

"And what? We wait and hope that he doesn't kill her?"

He sat up and almost growled. The guy was not taller or bigger than me, but angry people were dangerous people. "Don't presume to believe that I would let anyone harm her. But Trini has to figure out what she wants. And if that

fucker lays a hand on her one more time, I will handle it."
Seemingly tired of me, he walked to the pool and expertly
dived in. I hadn't expected that response from him and felt
better to know that he would protect her. Maybe I didn't
have to feel compelled to kill Chad and hide his body under
the snow.

Lincoln popped up near Wade, who tossed him the ball
they'd been playing with and swam closer to him. Too close.
I wouldn't mind killing Lincoln and shoving *him* under the
snow though. So much for not being a couple. I had the way
of the cupid. Shoving people together and away from me.

I pulled out my sketch pad, which I took everywhere,
and started drawing.

The movement felt familiar, and the sound of pencil to
paper soothing. Everything else became background noise
as the image started taking shape before me. First the face,
then the eyes, nose, lips. The hair, shoulders. All of it elegant
until I got to the animal fur around her neck. I made sure
that was bloody.

Trini was the one to approach me as I completed my
artwork of Mrs. Wilson and her errant bloody mongoose. I
closed the notebook. "Are you still mad?" she asked with
that pout that always turned me into an idiot.

"Where's Chad?"

She shrugged. "We're just talking."

"I'm not mad at you, Trini. But don't expect me to get
along with him."

"Fair enough. Are you going to swim with us?" she
asked, wrapping a towel around her pink bikini.

"Didn't bring swim trunks."

She shrugged. "Swim in undies."

I leaned closer to her. "I don't have any on. They're in
the wash."

She blushed and looked cute. I willed my body for a
reaction to her, got nothing. Didn't mean anything, right?

I waited for my sister's reply and got nothing.

"Well, I'm sure Wade has an extra pair."

At the mention of his name, my body felt taut. I looked at him in the pool and caught him looking at me. He broke contact first. Not sure what that meant. If anything. One thing was for sure, I didn't trust myself in the pool with him. I'd touch him and have to deal with the repercussions afterward. One thing Lincoln got right. Attraction was visceral. Didn't have anything to do with love or even needing to know anyone. It's what made babies and divorces. "Nah, I think I'm going to check out the media room."

"Cool, I'll go with you." She didn't let go of my hand and led me through the house, picking up a bottle of booze on the way to the TV room, which was fitted like a real theatre, with sound system and all. I hadn't been to the movies since Dad had taken Bea and me to watch Avengers. I rubbed my chest at the memory. Which also reminded me that I had one long night ahead of me. If I had a night terror here, everyone was going to freak out.

Trini put on a movie and climbed into the chair next to me. Lifting the armrest and scooting closer into my side, she wrapped one bare leg on top of mine. The lights dimmed, an action flick started as she slipped her cold fingers under my tee and caressed my bruised ribs softly. This was really nice.

She sat up briefly to take a pull of the bottle, then handed it to me. I hated booze. I hated the smell of beer. It reminded me of everything wrong with the world. But maybe the alcohol would knock me out. Maybe, it would erase any night terrors, so I took a long pull and the shit burned its way into my stomach.

She giggled again and lowered herself into my arms. "You are one big question mark, Xander Morales."

"Why do you say that?"

"You act so badass, but you also act like a big teddy bear."

"No," I said dryly, remembering Wade calling me cute. "Just no."

She giggled again, and I found myself running my thumb up and down her back in a lazy movement. I couldn't get my thoughts in gear. I took a few more gulps of the hard liquor until I felt my skin tingling. The movie ran for about five minutes when the door opened and everyone else started creeping inside. Wade shot me a glare of death. No hint of his shiny smile in sight. It made me feel sad in a way. Made me wonder if the smile he put on for the world was fake. If, deep down, he was actually an angry boy who had plans to get out of his father's thumb. To do something on his own.

Without me.

That last part made me snort. Trini patted my chest as if soothing the bear inside of me. The liquor in my bloodstream didn't help to settle my thoughts, which were now sluggish.

Wade made a point to sit in front of me with Lincoln beside him. Lincoln, the asshole, lifted the armrest and leaned a little too close to Wade.

Not a couple my ass.

And why would I care? I didn't. At least that's what I told myself while I wanted to punch Link in his face. The booze didn't help. It actually made things worse. I hated the feeling. The spiraling sensation suddenly took hold of me, making me sick. I had to get out. I couldn't breathe. Trini noticed and pulled away from me.

"Are you okay?"

No. I wasn't. I got to my feet and the world turned in on itself. And I with it. Face first.

CHAPTER 13

I couldn't move. Cold. I felt so cold.

I blinked my eyes open, unable to focus. Unable to see.

Cold wrapped me in its vice grip. I clenched my teeth, willing myself to remain awake. Stay awake. Don't give in to the darkness at the edge of my vision. I wouldn't come back, and I needed to find my sisters. My mom. They were somewhere like me, in the snow.

Cold. So cold.

And wet.

I felt myself sinking as the ground opened up and swallowed me. Gravity no longer made sense. I couldn't tell which way was up, which was down. My chest caving in, hurting to breathe until I couldn't breathe anymore.

I was floating. Listless.

Then I saw bodies in the water above me. The small frame of my sister. Then Bea's long hair fanned out, masking her face. Then Dad. Curlicues of blood like flames outlining his body. Then something splashed in the water. Something with large teeth.

My mother appeared in front of me. Pale skin, waxy eyes, her dark hair swaying in the water behind her. Her mouth moved, but I couldn't hear what she was saying. I couldn't breathe. I couldn't scream. I couldn't wake up. I needed to wake up.

"Lo siento, mijo."

Then I screamed. Breaking through the crack of my psyche and to the surface.

Blessed oxygen filled my lungs. My body in motion as I struggled to move, to run, to get away from the dead surrounding me. Hands were on me. Pushing me. Pressing me down. Trying to take me back into death's embrace. I swung a fist. Heard someone curse.

"Stop it, dammit. I'm trying to help you," a familiar voice broke through the darkness. Broke me. I clung to him, fisted his T-shirt, and drew him into my body. I needed to feel something, to live beyond this recurring nightmare. I breathed him in, taking in the scent of cedar and cleanliness. Not death and rot. Wade. I wanted to be in the glow of his light, the reason for his smile. I wanted to be found. I didn't want to be alone anymore. A terrible sob ripped out of me, and I clenched my teeth to keep more from spilling out.

He wrapped both arms around me in a tight hug as I quietly cried into his chest. "It's not real. It's not real." And for the briefest moment, I believed none of it was real. My sisters were alive and playing in Katie's tent in the living room. Mom cooking in the kitchen and Dad working. The smell of sofrito in the air. The sound of something sizzling in the frying pan while the television competed with Mom's music blasting from the speakers. Home. This had been home.

Gone.

All of it gone.

I'd been left behind and I couldn't find my way back.

"They're dead," I breathed out. "They left me behind. I should've died with them. They left me behind." I closed my eyes and let the dark take me.

I woke up on the floor, wrapped in a blanket, sporting the largest headache the size of the moon. I grumbled and sat up. My body hurt. My teeth hurt. Then my head started to spin. I jumped to my feet and launched myself to the bathroom, which, thankfully, was in the room because I wasn't in my room. I was in Wade's room. I spewed into the toilet until nothing was left in my stomach.

I heard him behind me turn on the sink and handed me a paper cup with water. "You are a bad drunk."

Wearing pajama bottoms and a rumpled T-shirt, his hair every which way, he still looked good. I took the cup and rinsed my mouth, then spat the water into the toilet before flushing it. I didn't bother getting up. Instead, I leaned against the tub and drew my knees into my chest. I remembered falling in the media room. Voices around me and Wade settling me onto his bed. Water. I'd drank a shit load of water afterward before passing out again. Then the nightmare. I wanted to disappear. To cease to exist. I asked the first thing that popped into my head.

"Where's Lincoln?" I knew that was the wrong question to ask when he glared at me. Or narrowed his eyes, which made it look like he was glaring at me.

"How should I know?"

My temple pounded in time with my beating heart. "Well, you two were all over each other last night."

Wade snorted, his eyes darkened. Yeah, I was pissing him off. Great work, Xander. "And you and Trini until you passed out."

"Is she okay?"

"Yeah. After we assured her you were still breathing." He sighed, a nervous twitch, and ran his hand through his hair. Having straight hair, he could get away with doing that without making it worse.

The memory of the night terror made me cringe. I didn't remember exactly what I told him last night, but I knew I'd been rambling. I lowered my eyes away from him, unable to look at him. "Did I hurt you?"

"You almost punched me in the face, but I deflected. I'm fine." I was waiting for him to ask for an explanation. The silence stretched way too long. "Bad Dream?"

I licked my dry lips. "Yeah, something like that." Okay, queue in the guilt trip. "I'm sorry," I said into my knees. A long moment of silence followed, and I looked up to make sure he hadn't snuck out, but no. He was leaning against the door, arms crossed against his chest, looking down at me on the floor with an expression I couldn't read. "Say something."

"I'm savoring the apology. You think I could record it."

I lifted my middle finger at him and he chuckled. Then he offered me his hand. Reluctantly, I took it and got to my feet. I stumbled and he held me steady. For a moment we were standing toe to toe, and his touch sent electricity jolting through me. This was pure visceral attraction. Yup, I couldn't deny that shit. I could ignore it though. I could regain some semblance of control. I wasn't my dick. I pushed away from him, smelling my own vomit now. A mood killer.

"Thanks. I should probably shower."

"Yeah. Your clothes are clean and dry on top of the dresser. Come down for breakfast when you're ready." He started to leave, and I wanted him to stay.

"Wade," I called him back. He turned, and I hated the expression on his face. Pity. Poor, broken Xander. It was unfair for me to think that. Not his fault I was a broken piece of shit.

"What?" he said when I didn't say anything.

I shook my head. "Nothing, forget it." I slammed the bathroom door, breaking whatever hold he had over me.

After I showered and changed, I met the others in the kitchen, and I wasn't the only one nursing a hangover.

Piper lay spread out on the sofa, moaning. Theo and Nick were at the counter, and Taylor was sprawled on the floor. Lincoln and Trini were missing. Wade handed me a pink liquid I eyed suspiciously.

"Pedialyte. Rehydrate."

I drank the sweet nastiness, hoping that my headache would go away. "Where's Trini?"

Wade shrugged as if he didn't care. Of course he didn't care. Why would he? "I'm not her keeper."

I scowled at him. "You're such an asshole."

"Hey," Theo scolded. "Keep your voice down."

I wanted to thump Theo in the head. Nothing quite like fear to get the juices rolling and the pain dissolving. I pulled out my phone and dialed Trini, walking away from the kitchen and sprinting upstairs. She picked up on the third ring. "Are you okay?" I quickly asked, bypassing the greeting.

"I'm fine, Xander. You should stop worrying about me. I'm a big girl."

"I never said you weren't."

She sighed. "Do you have a ride back?" she asked. Her soft voice still sent needles through my heart. It confused the shit out of me. "I'm heading home with Chad. Lincoln got a call, so he had to leave. Do you want a ride with us?"

With Chad and Trini. No fucking way. "Nah, I can get a ride with Wade." I wasn't sure, but I could hope.

"Okay, then I'll see you at school. Okay?"

I shut my eyes. The next question hurt. "So, you broke up with me to go back with him? Is that the story you want to spin to conclude our fake relationship?"

"It's nobody's business, Xander," she said. Sometimes, Trini surprised me with the glimpses of the tiger inside of her. The one people should fear. "And we're still friends. If anyone gives you shit."

I chuckled. "I'll send them to you."

She snorted. "We protect each other. Right?"

"Always." Because that was the truth.

We ended the call. We hadn't been a real couple but we had become friends and I didn't want to mess it up.

"Breakfast is done," Wade called out.

I shoved the phone in my pocket and walked back to the kitchen. He eyeballed me as if I were going to grow a pair of horns. "You okay?"

Nope. Thinking about Trini with Chad made me want

to punch something. I also realized I had no ride back. I was at Wade's mercy. "Yup. Can I hitch a ride with someone?" I said just to the room. I didn't care who. I just needed off this mountain.

"I'll take you home," Wade said quickly.

"Thanks. Does that mean we're leaving now?"

"I actually wanted to hit the slopes for a few hours first."

I rolled my eyes. "Jesus, don't you know how to do anything else?" Something less dangerous. I left out.

"Oh, oh," Theo grumbled beside me.

I ignored him. "I mean, really? You already perfected the sport, get another dream."

He slammed the plate of food in front of me. "I love this sport. It makes me happy. You should find something that makes you happy and stop being a dick all the time."

I took hold of the plate because it smelled amazing, and my stomach growled from hunger. "I do have something that makes happy." I shoved a spoonful of scrambled eggs into my mouth, watching Wade lift a brow. "Making you pissed off makes me happy, see." I smiled, forcing bits of eggs out of my mouth and back into the plate.

I caught a hint of a smile before he turned away. Why that made me suddenly warm inside? I had no clue.

We were driving down the mountain later that afternoon. The sky clear of clouds, the roads full of snow, and just Wade and me in his SUV. The others had gone with Theo. White-knuckling it down, I focused on my breathing. Good thoughts. At least until Wade took my hand in his. The light touch startled me out of my panic mode, and I turned to look at him, then to his fingers gently gliding between mine.

"I hope this is okay," he said without looking at me.

"Uh," I managed to lose my vocabulary. "Maybe it'd be better if you kept both hands on the wheel." Because I was an idiot.

He gave me a sideways glance with that smile all for me, and it jolted something in my chest. "Trust me," he said.

"I do trust you. I don't trust this car or the snow or anyone else on the snow."

"Fair enough," he said and placed his hand back on the steering wheel. I realized I wanted his hand on mine. I wanted him to distract me. "So talk to me," he said. "What's your future look like?"

"You mean if we survive this mountain?"

"When we survive this mountain. When."

I didn't know how to answer that. "Honestly, I've never thought about my future. Mrs. Rashard seems to think I should consider art school." He arched his brow and gave me a glance. I panicked. "Eyes on the road."

He complied.

"I would've never guessed you had some art in you."

"Yeah, well, I'm full of surprises."

"Yes, you are."

I didn't like the way he said that, as if we weren't talking about the same thing. "What about you, Mr. Perfect? Lincoln told me about your plans for your father's business. Is that what you plan on doing? Getting out of snowboarding and into the family business?"

He shrugged. "It's a safety net."

"Nice to have one of those. What's your future look like?"

"I'm going to Harvard. I'll study business and maybe go to law school. Then, I'll take over the family business."

"What about snowboarding?"

He clenched his hands around the steering wheel harder than necessary. "It's just a hobby."

"A hobby that gave you sponsors and acting gigs. You don't want to keep going with that?"

"Nah. It gets old after a while."

"I could just imagine. Having my life in everyone's eyes would force me to live in some cave."

"Is that why you left me at the café? Because of everyone

taking pictures?"

I shrugged. "I didn't realize you came with a few million nosey followers."

"Is that a deal breaker for you?" he asked quickly.

I wasn't sure what he meant. Did he mean to be friends? To talk? To be together in other ways? Since it was a no to all, I didn't ask him to specify. "No. Though, I would prefer not to be your sidekick."

"That role is already taken by Theo," he said.

That made me a little bit tense.

"Look," he said, his eyes gleaming ahead of him. I turned to the windshield to see the open road. "We made it down the snowy part of the mountain and you haven't tossed your breakfast."

Surprise. Surprise. The distraction helped. Talking to Wade helped. "It must be easier going down than going up."

He made a sound like Yeah right, buddy.

We made it to my house in one piece. Wade leaned over to get a view of the house. "What?" I asked.

"Nothing. It's nice," he said. "Stop feeling as if you have to be defensive all the time. Friends can be a good thing for you, especially now that you've been dumped by your fake girlfriend."

I knew I would regret telling him that. "Because friends are sooo much better than fake girlfriends."

He smirked. "They can be if they're real friends. Not fake friends."

"Like you?"

"Like me."

"And what benefits do friends like you come with?" I asked, realizing what I said too late.

"I want to give you skiing lessons. Safe skiing lessons."

Something about this seemed more like a date than friendly lessons. "I hate snow," I said.

"Then, I'll teach you how not to hate snow."

I raked my hand through my hair. The moment I'd been dreading. Trust or scram. Friends or risk turning into Trini's stalker. Be safe or take a risk.

Fuck it.

"Okay. Sounds good."

Except it didn't really sound good. It sounded scary as shit, and Wade had no damn clue.

ELIZABETH ARROYO

CHAPTER 14

"I'm sorry, Mr. Morales, but Wade Wilson will be unable to mentor you this semester. Mr. Wilson spoke highly of your progress these few weeks, so I'll allow detention rather than expulsion for your infraction." Dr. Newman had said when she called me into the office Monday morning. The Monday morning after the skiing trip. After he had held my hand and called me cute. After he offered to teach me to ski. After he made me feel shit I'd never felt for anyone else.

All of it had been a manipulating lie. I hated him for it. I hated myself for believing being friends with him could even be possible. I'd been a joke.

Fucker got what he wanted and had cut me loose. And I felt *violated*. That was the word I was looking for. "Violated," I said to the group. "He got what he wanted and dropped me like a sack of shit." I usually refrained from speaking in group, but I was pissed. I couldn't stop my knee from bobbing up and down, and I kept rubbing my palms against my thighs. Itching to hit something.

I hadn't felt this wound up since … since Boys Home.

Everyone in the group was silent, watching me, waiting for me to burst into flesh and muscle. Anger pushed against the inner wall of my skin, a living, breathing entity inside of me, begging to be released. The group around me knew all too well what that felt like. They knew better than to speak or move, better than to look away. They were as coiled tight as I was, ready to spring to their feet in a moment's notice should I go nuclear.

"On a scale of one—"

"Eleven, okay." I leaned forward, trying the breathing shit and failing to fill my lungs. The only good image I could conjure up was of Wade. And that quickly dissolved into darkness every time I remembered my convo with Dr. Newman.

"*Why?*" I had asked her.

"*Wade took on more than he could handle*," she'd responded. *Me.*

I was more than he could handle. I was a broken piece of shit unworthy of him.

I was nothing to him.

"Well, why do you think he would've done that, aside from his deal with Trini?"

I snorted a laugh and wiped my cheeks. "Who knows? Because he's an asshole who uses people is my guess."

"How did he use you?"

I blinked a few times. Okay, Dr. Reyes was pissing me off. "Haven't you been listening?"

"I heard that he helped you get out of trouble. A mutually beneficial transaction. It sounds like you used each other."

I opened my mouth and snapped it shut. I hadn't told them about Wade offering me lessons, or how he had held my hand in the truck. Or how he had made me *feel*. Only to tear me down by using Dr. Newman. He hadn't even had the balls to tell me face-to-face.

Dr. Reyes had no clue what the hell he was saying. I scanned the room. Sage and David both were watching me, as if looking at a rattlesnake waiting to pounce. Jack's lips were a tight line on his face, quite possibly resisting the urge to count the lines on my face. They were getting on my nerves.

They were all rich assholes who were here because they wanted daddy's money. That's all they cared about. Fame and fortune. Then I realized something, and I started to laugh. "Fuck me," I said, trying to keep my shit together. "We *are* a bunch of losers."

Sage snorted. "Speak for yourself."

I ignored him. "Our family doesn't care about us. They don't care about you." I pointed at each of them. Even Jack stiffened. "Why the hell would they put you up with a Latino doctor instead of some white bread who could actually help you?"

Okay, so I was being a big dick. A defensive big dick, because now Dr. Reyes was getting on my nerves. I was known to push people away. Why not? Maybe he'd give me a clean psych eval and set me free. All I needed to do was piss him off, right? "You are white rich kids, privileged. Don't you think Mommy and Daddy could afford someone not south of the border?" I turned to Reyes, who'd gone back with that stoicism I wanted to knock out of him. "No offense."

"Do you think my ethnicity makes me inferior to my Caucasian counterparts?"

"Don't *you*? I mean, come on. We're brown folk. People will always look down on us."

"What people?"

"White people."

"Is that what happened to you? Did this person look down upon you because of your color?"

I almost said yes. His mother did. She thought me the help and wanted me to shovel the fucking snow. I pressed my lips together.

"I don't think it's a matter of being *brown*," Sage said. "But of being *different*. I'm hated for being gay."

"I'm hated for not being smart," Jack added.

"And I'm hated for having a big dick," David said.

I was kind of shocked at David. Not so much for what he said, but for speaking at all. His voice was thick and very masculine. And yeah, my eyes glanced at his crotch to see if he was sprouting his self-proclaimed big dick. So had Sage and Jack. David shifted in his seat.

I shook my head of those thoughts and slid back to the present issue. "Why do we even give people this power over us? Who cares if they hate us for our differences? We've survived more shit than they could ever know." Not sure where that came from, but the others nodded. Except Jack, who went back to searching the room for odd sequences.

"I agree. I don't care what my family thinks of me. I am not a broken thing to be fixed," Sage said.

I pointed at him, fueling something stirring in this shit show. "You're right. Fuck them."

David went back to being quiet.

"On that note, how do you think you could 'fuck them,'" Dr. Reyes air quoted the words. "Let's use the word empower. How can you empower yourself so that they don't make you feel broken?"

I narrowed my eyes at Dr. Reyes. Fucker turned this back to therapy.

"I guess pissing on their shoes won't cut it," I said dryly. Sage blushed and chuckled.

"Or gluing their dresser drawer," David added.

"Or stripping their napkins," Jack offered shyly.

Dr. Reyes leaned forward. His dark eyes swept the room. I felt more exposed than ever. "I'm afraid not. It's a Band-Aid. Makes you feel better for a moment, but nothing changes. What changes do you think you can control?"

We all stayed quiet.

"That's what I want you to work on in your journals for next week. Bring back some ideas." Dr. Reyes looked quite satisfied with the direction of the group despite that I had meant to discredit him.

They all nodded and jotted inside their journals. I did not.

Time up. We started to scatter. I remained behind. Yeah, I'd been a dick, though it had turned out okay. I was the last one to head out when Dr. Reyes called me back.

"Mr. Morales, please sit."

The *sit* was an order. I'd never tested the boundaries here and figured it would be a good idea to listen to him since he could have me committed. I sat.

"You seem particularly agitated today. I understand the stress of being in a new school. Forming new friendships. After your release."

"I don't want to talk about it."

"You lost your friends abruptly. Jace Chambers specifically."

"I didn't lose him. He went home."

Dr. Reyes lifted his chin as if he understood the difference. I wasn't sure if he was bullshitting me, but I didn't want to test that theory by talking about what happened at Boys Home. "And you went home too."

I bit down hard. "I don't have a home."

"What about your aunt? Are things not going well there?"

"I don't know. Like you said, I've just returned. What's your point?"

"May I see your journal?"

I flinched. No. I didn't want him to see my journal.

"It is part of our therapy agreement. You do remember."

"You mean you are my warden, right? Let's call it what it really is."

"If that's how you want to view it, then yes. Let me see it."

I reluctantly pulled it out and slammed it onto his palm. He thanked me and started to flip the pages. He paused at the ones I did about Sage, Jack, and David. I thought he was going to say something about the NDA, so I beat him to it. "I didn't draw their faces. You can't tell who they are, so it violates nothing."

"These are really good, Xander," he said. And he did sound impressed. He flipped to the last page. An empty white one. "You see them as what? Heroes?"

I felt heat brush up against my neck. "Something like that."

"Why?"

"Because they did *something*. Something that made them feel better."

"I don't see one of you."

"Duh," I snapped, unable to hide my anger in my voice. "I haven't *done* anything."

"If memory serves, you punched a certain individual who hit a girl."

Chad.

"Yeah, and she went back with him." I pulled my notebook away sharply and shoved it back inside my bag. "Meaning, I did shit to protect her."

"Is that why you did it? To protect her?"

"Yeah, you think I like hitting people?" I didn't. I really hated it. "But in the end, it meant shit anyway. She's back with him and I can't do shit."

"You can only do what you can *control*, Xander. You can control what you offer her."

"What can I offer her?"

"Friendship. You can always choose to be friends."

Like a slap to the face, we came full circle. "I have to go."

"I have another question for you, Xander. Before you go." He paused and I inhaled sharply, waiting for the questions. "If you don't like hitting people, why did you hit Mr. Lawrence Whitman?"

I bristled when he said the name of the man responsible for sending me to Boys Home. Except, I hadn't told them everything. Not even Reyes. "It doesn't matter anymore. I was punished for it. I'm still being punished for it."

"So, being here is a punishment for you?"

I ran my hand through my hair. "If I had a choice, I don't

think I'd be here." That was the truth. The only one Reyes was getting right now.

He nodded. "I'll see you next week, then."

I nodded and started out but paused at the door and turned over my shoulder to look at him. He had already started to pick up some of the discarded cups and papers left behind. "Doc." He lifted his brown eyes to mine. "I'm sorry about what I said. About you not being good enough because you're not white. I didn't mean it."

A tight smile formed on his lips. "I know. And it takes a very brave person to apologize for their mistakes, Mr. Morales. I fear there is hope for you yet."

I rolled my eyes. "You would," I mumbled.

I could've sworn I heard him chuckle as I walked out.

CHAPTER 15

I lost my fake girlfriend weeks earlier than expected, and Wade had pretty much blew me off too. I had to remind myself that we weren't friends and that his friends were not my friends. During lunch, I headed for the familiar weeb table where Maury and Alejandra were discussing the upcoming anime convention and their cosplay costumes. I missed the deadline and hadn't been able to get tickets. The easy banter actually felt like home. Although Carmen's place wasn't loud, home had always been loud. My mom spent her time usually on the phone with one of her sisters talking loud while cooking. Katie usually made a racket with one of her toys while watching *Barney* with the TV on louder than hell, and Beatrice and I discussed how we could get Mom to let us go to the library without an escort. The house always felt full. Noise and chaos made everything less stagnant.

"What do you think?"

I lifted my eyes to Ale, who had asked me something. "What?"

Maury rolled his eyes. "See, no one cares about them."

The people at the table across from us busted out laughing, and I couldn't help but to turn to see Wade with his minions. I suddenly felt sick. "I'll catch ya later," I mumbled and dropped my food in the garbage, leaving the tray on top. As I headed outside to the quad, Trini and Chad walked inside holding hands. Now I really felt sick. Like, *I'm going to vomit on his shoes instead of piss on them* sick.

Surprisingly, I didn't feel angry as much as worried about her. She deserved better. Chad would never change. It'd start with a slap now and escalate to something worse. I'm pretty sure that's how it started with my mother and that scared the shit out of me.

She lifted her brown eyes to me, and I saw nervousness and a little bit of fear. Was it for me or Chad? I didn't want her afraid of me. We were friends. I smiled at her as I passed, to reassure her that I would be here for her just as Chad grew a pair of balls and rammed into my shoulder.

I stumbled, earning snickers from his own group of friends. I had to swallow the need to ram my fist down his throat.

"Hey," a deep voice said behind me. "Everything okay?" I'd recognize that voice anywhere.

"Hey, Wade," Chad said, as if he and Wade were besties. Give it to the want of popularity and rainbows to pacify a dick.

"Hey, Chad," Wade said, equally as pleasant.

I couldn't stand to listen to this shit, so I gave Trini one last nod and walked away. The best deterrent to chaos I had ever found. One foot in front of the other. Move. Get away. Run. I itched to run anywhere but here and breathed instead. I made it to the furthest spot while still on campus when I heard him behind me.

"Xander," Wade said.

I spun, and he had to skid to a stop or slam into me. "What the hell do you want? I thought you washed your hands of me?"

He looked at me as if I'd lost a few screws in my head. The reference to Pontius Pilot washing his hands of sin was a famous one in my household. "*¿Perdiste las llaves? Me lavo* *las manos. Espera que llegue tu papá."* Meant Dad was going to kick my ass for losing the keys and she would not feel guilty about it.

"I wanted to catch you before Dr. Newman did. I just have training ahead of me. Doesn't mean we can't still be friends."

The anger from being *violated* returned in full force. I had to clench my hands into tight fists to keep from hitting something like the bench I had been heading to, so I shoved them into my hoodie pocket. "So you forgot about your training when you offered to be my service dog and teach me how to ski?" Wade shifted his light blue eyes from mine, guilt written all over his face and it slammed into me like a bat to the gut. The lie. "Right, mommy dearest caught sight of me. Doesn't want you hanging around the maid's son or the landscaper's son, which one?"

"I'm sorry about that."

I flinched because he did sound sorry. "You are unbelievable. You know that?" I started walking away. At this point, I'd reach the running tracks and circle the damn school to get away from him.

"Why?" he said behind me, incredulously. "Because I care?"

I spun back around and this time he did slam into me. Instead of pushing him away like I should've done, my hand reached around his waist to steady him from falling. Just inches from my own face, I could see the slight scar on his left brow, a small freckle on that same cheek. My chest tightened. I was going to bust like a balloon with all the strange emotions fluttering inside of me. I reached for anger and clung to it like a baby monkey on its mother's back. "Bullshit," I said and took a solid step away from him. "I don't need you, want your pity, or your concern. Didn't ask you to stick up for me or save me. You have no idea who I am." I wasn't so sure either anymore. "Your mom is right. You should stay away from me. You don't know me." I glanced behind him and realized we had an audience.

Practically, the whole school stood out in the quad watching us. Wade didn't seem to notice or care.

He narrowed the space between us, and I fought the urge to bolt. I didn't want him to think I cared that he was too damn close to me. I didn't want him to think he made me uncomfortable or had the upper hand. "Do you even know the concept of friendship? We hang out, talk, get to know each other." His full lips lifted in one corner. His version of a smile that had me clenching my hands into fists to avoid reaching out to him.

"Great, sure. Meet me after school in detention. You'll have my dedicated attention between the hours of three and five." I arched my brow, waiting for his response. Got nothing. "Exactly. You and I are not friendship material, Mr. Wilson. Go back to your friends and stay away from me."

Please don't follow. Please don't follow.

I brushed past him, back into the school. I had to ignore the shocked faces around me. Even the weeb table looked at me as if I'd suddenly sprouted wings.

Or horns.

It felt more like horns.

CHAPTER 16

Mr. Yancy, the head football coach, believed that scrubbing the locker room and sports equipment would create responsible adults so that's what we were to do for the two hours of detention. The other three students in with me had dropped a stink bomb in the History Department. Though my infraction paled in comparison to the stink bomb, in my honest opinion, everyone looked at me as if I were the anti-Christ.

The stink bomb masterminds—Roger, Mike, and Emir—hadn't considered the ventilation grate linking the boy's bathroom to the history office. So when the bomb went off in the bathroom, it stunk the offices and pissed off the teachers.

"And that's how demonstrations go wrong," Emir said.

"And wars begin," Mike added.

Roger just shrugged.

Just then, a fifth person entered the room, and my heart did that familiar thing that made me want to yank it out of my chest.

Mr. Yancy scowled, clearly displeased as I was with the late arrival, only for different reasons. "Mr. Wilson, thank you for gracing us with your presence. Since you and Mr.

Morales were the last to arrive, you get the cage." He pointed his thumb toward the equipment cage. "I'm sure Mr. Morales will catch you up on what you need to do. Go change into your gym uniform and start your jobs."

The three other guys rolled their eyes and headed toward their locker to change. I shook my head and headed for my corner, where I changed quickly. Anger and curiosity made me fast. Rounding the corner to Wade's locker just as he was lowering his T-shirt, I caught sight of very trimmed smooth skin. I ignored what it did to my body. I was at war with myself right now.

"What the hell did you do?"

He slammed his locker closed, looking as if someone had sat on his cat. I wasn't sure if he had a cat. Sorry, for whatever the hell he did to earn his way to detention with the losers. It made me feel all sorts of guilty.

"None of your business," he snapped out.

"What happened with training?"

For a brief moment his cold expression slipped into something regretful. "Postponed."

I raked my hands through my hair, not caring how it probably looked. I needed a good sharp pair of shears to cut it. I didn't generally care what people thought about me. Until now. "Please tell me you didn't get here because of me." If you spend enough time with people, you get to know their tells. Body language spoke volumes on what someone really thought. I had learned that at Boys Home. While the staff could sprout smiles to burn the sun, their eyes played to a darker tune. Their hands often clenched, and their body rigid meant someone was going to get messed up.

After what happened with Wade's mom, which hadn't been his fault, I could tell how uncomfortable he'd become when he shifted his stance. I also knew when he looked away from me that whatever was coming out of his gorgeous mouth would be one big, fat lie. "Don't flatter yourself, Morales," he said angrily.

Without waiting for me, he headed toward the cage.

We worked in silence for the most part.

Scrubbing the equipment silently left me with too much time to slip into my own thoughts. Something I did not want and avoided by watching the guy trying to avoid me working in the opposite corner.

Wade Wilson was a puzzle box I hadn't figured out the question to. He'd used my situation to get to Link for a business deal. He'd cared enough about me not to let me fall to my death. And I could never forget how he held me as I sobbed into his chest after the effects of the night terror. He hadn't even brought it up, knowing that it would make me uncomfortable. Then he'd been so touchy-touchy and feely-feely during the ride down the mountain. Wanting to spend more time with me.

The reason Newman's words had hurt so much was because I had believed we could be friends. All that was confusing right now. Then after our argument on the quad, he gets detention. No way that was a coincidence. What the hell did he want from me now? There had to be something. So much for trying to reel my thoughts in. They were all over the place now.

I watched as he made a face scrubbing the basketball a little bit too enthusiastically and almost got water on his face. "What lesson do you think they're trying to teach us by scrubbing balls?" he finally broke the silence.

"To stay in school. Shit could always get worse." I grumbled.

There was a long pause with nothing but splashing and heavy breathing between us as I decided to call it and try to figure out Wade's motive for being so interested in me. *If* he was interested in me. "So, what are you training for?"

He looked relieved by the distraction. "I have a competition in February. Just a PR thing." Deciding he'd had enough of silent cleaning, he pulled off his gloves and sat on the dirty floor next to where I was working, his back against the chain link, his wrists on his knees.

I did the same, only took the seat opposite him so my back was against the shelf. "How long have you been skiing for?"

"Since I could walk. Then I picked up snowboarding, and I have been a goner ever since."

"You love it?"

"I did," he said quickly and scratched his nose. A movement so child-like and endearing. "I did when it didn't feel like work. I think my mom sucked all the fun out of it."

My chest clenched at how easily I could go from pissed at him to gooey. That's the only word I could think of that expressed my feelings at the moment. As if I were about to turn into a liquid puddle on the floor. "You're amazing at it," I admitted before I realized how gooey it sounded.

A hint of a blush speckled his cheeks. "Thanks," he said.

I felt a smile tug at my lips. "You're blushing."

"No, I'm not," he said. A lie. He totally was blushing.

"Yes, you are." I chuckled.

"Snowboarding without the competitive edge feels different. Out on the snow when no one really expects anything, I feel like myself. Like nothing in the world could stop me and I am in control." The gleam in his eyes slowly darkened as he looked away from me. "It's just different during competitions." Looking anywhere but at me, Wade got to his feet. He turned to pick up the water bucket when I threw him my dirty rag. It slapped the back of his neck with a wet plop before falling to the floor. He quickly jumped and squealed. "Ew, you fucker," he said, pressing his body as far away from the dirty rag, as if he wanted to meld through the cage to the safety of the other side.

I laughed. "You're a germaphobe."

"No, I'm not," he said, shivering.

"Yes, you are. You look as if you're about to faint."

"And that's why you do not have any friends."

That stopped the banter and silenced me. He wasn't wrong. "Are you serious about this friend thing?"

He sighed, still rubbing the back of his neck, as if the

dirty rag had attached itself to his skin like a sticky bomb. "Yeah."

I got to my feet and dusted the seat of my pants. "Okay, well, Trini's my only friend, and I had to punch her boyfriend to become friends with her, so how does it work?"

He arched a very perfectly trimmed brow. "You really have no clue."

I shrugged. "You're right. I've never had friends before." I realized I sounded pathetic. I didn't need or want his pity and was glad when I didn't see it in his expression. Just a blank curiosity.

"Well, I could use your help," he said. "Friends help each other."

Okay, here goes. The reason why he was stalking me in detention. "What do you need?"

He sighed with a guilty look on his face that pinched his features. "I might need help getting my best friend to talk to me again."

That wasn't what I expected him to say. "Theo? Why?"

"Because I may have punched him in the face to get here."

I blinked my eyes as if that would clear my ears. Then I threw my head back and laughed. And laughed some more.

"Not funny."

"And you're teaching *me* about friendship?"

"Don't rub it in." He nervously raked his hand through his hair, and I could tell he was serious.

"You punched Theo, your best friend, in the face to get detention with me? Why?"

Wade lowered his eyes to my lips, then quickly lifted them back to my eyes, and I saw something there I hadn't expected either. Wade Wilson wanted to kiss me, and that wasn't the terrible part.

I wanted to kiss him back.

CHAPTER 17

Wade picked me up on Sunday for our first skiing lesson. On snow. Not water. We went at the crack of dawn, and he promised to bring me back that evening. I trusted him. I had no choice. I did well as we drove on smooth roads. The fear didn't start until we stopped to put on the required chains on our tires. Then we continued into snow territory. I managed to hold my spewing until we stopped in front of his house. Wade gave me a moment. He didn't ask questions or baby me. I appreciated that.

Afterward, we slipped on skis and headed toward the small hills at the back of his house. Not the mountain. "This is where I learned the basics," he said with a hint of pride in his voice. That damn smile was so bright I wanted to catch it and put it away in my pocket for later.

"Okay, so teach me."

I had no clue what I had walked into. Wade spoke and I tried to listen. I really, really did. Really hard. But it was all so distracting. *He* was distracting. And cute when he'd get mad. His ears were red and he'd narrow his eyes while his nose scrunched up.

"Are you listening?" he asked.

"Yeah, you said flock. I'm supposed to see a flock of

geese or something on my skis." I smiled.

He really tried not to smile and succeeded. "Stopping is important, Xander," he deadpanned. "You are not taking one step on my mountain until you master the stop. Got it?"

I rolled my eyes. Did he not know that I only did this for him? I never, ever intended on skiing on my own. I didn't tell him that. "Yes. Stopping is important."

With that, I took his lessons very seriously and managed to stop my descent perfectly. He laughed, proud of himself. I didn't tell him that stopping going two miles an hour was nothing compared to going faster. I didn't want to rain on his parade.

The lesson ended up with us in his steaming hot tub. I'd never been in a hot tub before and moaned when I slipped inside. "Oh God, this feels so good," I said with my eyes closed. He was staring at me when I opened them, as if I had turned into Aquaman. "What?" I asked on the defense.

"Nothing," he answered. A lie I didn't push. If he didn't want me there, he would've said something, right?

I poked his calf with my big toe. "Friends don't lie."

He snorted. "Where did you hear that?"

"*Stranger Things*," I answered.

He snorted again. "Friends lie all the damn time."

"So you're lying and something is wrong with me?" I pressed my lips together to keep from smiling, feeling goofy.

"There's nothing wrong with you."

"So what's wrong with *you*?" He quickly turned to look at anything but me. "Hey," I said, drawing his attention back to me. "We're friends. You can tell me anything. You know that, right?" The truth of those words struck me harder than I thought they would. On the one hand, I wanted to know everything about Wade. Like if he still had feelings for Caleb—which seemed prevalent, considering my confused emotional chaos right now. Which led me to my other hand—everything inside of me was telling me to run. Get away from him. Friends be damned, just run. I hoped he didn't see any of that shit in my expression.

"I've been snowboarding for so long that I forgot what I actually liked about it until today, being with you."

The sincere and straightforward way he said that had me totally believing it. I was sure it was the hot water and not my own rushing blood that had me feeling really hot inside. I was grateful that he kept on talking. I learned his brother swam like a fish and wanted to be the next Michael Phelps. Wade made me guess who Michael Phelps was, and after I guessed wrong the first time—I thought he invented the screwdriver—I got it right. Wade talked about his snowboarding teammates in the Olympics. The grueling training schedule. Winning gold. All of it part of him, except he didn't have that proud gleam I'd seen when he had talked about it in the cage at school. "There's no shame in leaving the sport with a gold, Wade."

"You don't know my mother." He gave me a sad smile I hated to see. "I've talked your ear off. What about you?"

"Why the sad face?" I ignored his question.

He scowled, and I felt his leg brush up against mine. We were wearing swimming trunks and nothing else. Wade had an athletic build. No surprise. I'd barely tapped the skiing thing and my arms and thighs were already burning. I was tall and had a fast metabolism. At least that's what Carmen always told me. I wasn't ripped and muscled the way Wade was. I was more huggable. At least if I'd let anyone hug me. "Why are you deflecting?"

"Why are *you* deflecting?"

"You are annoying, you know that?"

I shrugged. "It's one of my many flavors."

Wade's smile broke my words. This one wasn't meant to be seen in public. This one was meant for me. This one made me feel as if I were suddenly near a predator wanting to swallow me whole. "I wouldn't mind tasting your other flavors."

Shit. Shit. Shit. Flirting via text while I was lost on top of a mountain and drinking coffee was way different than flirting for real, in a hot tub, half-naked. I didn't like this flirting for real. I couldn't get my brain cells to work. "I bet you say that to all your friends," I said, thinking of how he looked at Theo during lunch. Yeah, I deflected. "What's up with you and Theo?"

Smile gone. "We're just friends."

"Does he know that?"

"Yeah, he's into Piper. Haven't you noticed?"

I had noticed, but then I saw how Theo looked at Wade and realized Theo was very confused.

"Besides," he said. "Theo and I tried once. Didn't stick."

I wanted him to stop talking. I hated being right about people. He didn't stop.

"We were better off as friends."

"Who did the breakup?" I asked, though I already knew. "I did."

"Not your type, huh? You prefer them older."

He splashed water on my face. "Fuck you," he said. "You don't know shit about me."

He was right. I didn't. I got to my feet. This talk was getting way too deep for my sensibilities. "It's late and you promised to get me back home tonight." Yeah, I was running. So what?

"Yeah, yeah, big baby," he mumbled behind me.

CHAPTER 18

It'd been almost a week since I'd spent detention with Wade, and Theo still hadn't responded to any of his apologies. After we dusted the sports equipment, Mr. Yancy had us watch the destruction of 9/11.

"Why are we watching this?" Wade asked, wiping a tear. I wanted to hold him and make him feel better.

"To remember we're human," I responded. "To feel empathy."

I handed the tissues to the guys. I'd already seen this video. It'd been played on loop at Boys Home to remind us of all of our very own mortality.

Wade and I had spent the week after school treating each other out to eat. We'd gone to the Pancake House every evening when he wasn't training. The other days he had to be at the gym or drive to the mountain to practice. He had a very rigid training schedule.

We were sitting at the Pancake House when a couple of girls from school had come in and looked at us, then they started to giggle. I knew something was wrong the moment Wade flushed pink.

"What?" I asked, waiting for the other shoe to drop. The banter and time with Wade all one big joke coming to an end.

"Don't get mad."

That got me mad, and he seemed to realize it when he sighed and stabbed the burger he ordered with a fork. "We were recorded," he said to the burger.

I didn't say anything unsure what the hell that meant. We hadn't done anything wrong to end up in prison. He lifted his eyes to mine. "That afternoon in school. When we were arguing. Someone recorded us and put it online. The media, um, thought that we were together. They're speculating that we, uh, might be boyfriends."

I scrambled to pull out my phone to check Google but he snatched the phone away from my hand. "Give it back," I whispered, trying not to cause another scene. Everyone was a photographer nowadays.

"My parents took care of it. We got a good PR person. And after our little argument, speculation shifted to me having a nervous breakdown."

The guy was talking alien. "What?"

"I hit Theo right after our argument. That was recorded too and sent everyone speculating about my mental state, not my sex life, so you're in the clear."

Why did that not make me feel better? And why did I want to know about his sex life? I raked my hand through my hair. "Shit, how could you live like that? You're not even safe in school from those leeches."

He shrugged. "My mom wants me to go back to being homeschooled."

It'd only been a few weeks since I'd met Wade but being without him in school made me already feel lonely. "That would suck."

He snorted. "Yeah, it would. I'm holding it together. I am."

It sounded as if he were trying to convince himself. "Why do you still do it? Skiing?"

"Because I love it." He sounded as enthused as a Lab getting spayed. I didn't believe him but didn't push it either.

It wasn't my business.

The following week, I had my round two of ski lessons with no hot tub afterward. This time, he had me talking about my aunt Carmen and Moe. He didn't ask about my parents or the night terror I had in front of him. I told him about my art journal and how drawing made me feel as if I were putting a lid to anything negative inside of me. Thankfully, we were on the snow in skis and gravity had taken that moment to drop me on my ass after I hit an ice patch before we got to anything else deeper. Wade laughed until I tackled him onto his ass too. Then we just spent the rest of the lesson throwing snowballs at each other.

After detention, Wade drove us to his parents' beachfront property. We had to change things up or risk more media exposure. Not that I'd gotten any coverage. Apparently, his PR person was able to keep me out of the drama and keep the attention on Wade's mental state. I couldn't imagine being him. Having all my skeletons out for the world to see. That was scary as shit. I found myself more at ease with him. Living in a secluded bubble with just the two of us and our ramblings about how I lived under a rock and not ever learning to ski.

"Let's swim," he said. I realized Wade was always in motion. As if sitting still would force the planet to swallow him whole.

I watched the wave crash in and didn't find it appealing. "Nope. I'm fine being a land mammal. And one activity a week with you is enough. Just ask my bruised body."

The scan he gave my body made me regret that I'd mentioned it.

He dropped on the blanket I had spread out on the sand. I had made myself comfortable, laid back and stared at the clear blue skies. I couldn't remember when I felt this relaxed. My mind numb without thinking of upcoming shit in my life. The looming court date, how Trini was doing, graduating high school and figuring shit out after that. I climbed into a safe space in my head and pushed all that shit back. Only me, the sky, the sound of the ocean in the distance and the feel of Wade beside me.

I'd done more observing Wade than he knew. Like I knew he smelled of fresh outdoors, like the smell of wood with a cinnamon aroma underneath it—which was weird. Yeah, I knew what wood smelled like. It was a heady scent and all Wade. It did things to my body I had to struggle with. Like when his hands shook slightly when he held his ski poles. As if he were nervous of me or the snow. I still couldn't tell which, but there was something definitely off about him. Or like when his nose crinkled whenever he got pissed.

I felt him nudge my ribs with his elbow. "Come on. Live dangerously."

I opened my eyes and wanted to tell him exactly how dangerously I have lived. Instead, I said, "I don't have a swimsuit."

He waggled his eyebrows three times, irritatingly adorable. "I have an extra pair in the house." Deciding for me, he got to his feet and reached down to help me up. "Come on. I'm bored as fuck."

Uh. The guy was relentless. "Fine, but I get a pass on skiing this weekend." Although I actually looked forward to being with him almost seven days a week, I needed to stop this or risk actually really liking Wade Wilson. And I still didn't trust in our friendship. Why be friends with me when I had nothing to offer him?

"Fine. I'll give you a week break."

I snorted but took his hand so he could help lift me up. The contact sent heat throughout my body. Swelled the parts of me I tried to hide in these thin-ass boardshorts. I suddenly felt the need to get as far away from Wade as I could.

I usually hated touching people. And for a Latino who had a gazillion family members who hugged and kissed each other on entry and exit, it was hard not to be seen as the arrogant one. Too good to be with them. Too good to say hi or bye. They had no idea that their touches made me want to crawl out of my skin.

So this new emotion rising out of a simple touch from Wade started to make me think deeper about what I had really craved. A soft touch. A simple smile. Something warm that centered at the base of my soul to absorb that dark presence always out of focus around me but hovering there. Just waiting for me to accept it and snap the way I had almost snapped when Wade had ditched me, and Dr. Newman had forced me into detention.

That anger felt almost as good as whatever the hell this was. At least I could name it, label it, put it away. I couldn't do that to this feeling Wade pulled out of me. I had no name for it yet.

A gentle breeze slithered down my spine as he released my hand and I shivered. Thankfully, he was already walking to the house and didn't see how he affected me. At least I hope he hadn't. Didn't matter. It wasn't like I would act on any of it.

I changed into a pair of swimming shorts and followed him out to the pool. "Now, answer me this, why the hell would you have a pool, pool," I gestured to the pool, "when you have the ocean in front of your freaking house?"

That got a chuckle out of him. "They may both be water but used for a different purpose and containing different elements."

Okay, not the response I thought would come out of his mouth.

"Pool is safer, now get inside."

I felt a tingle along my skin at his blatant command of me. "Don't get too bossy."

That smile of his seemed to go on forever. Yeah, the prick knew how bossy he was. After floating in the pool for an hour—which was the only thing I managed to do, we changed back into dry clothes, locked up and he drove me home.

"This is cute," he said about my small home. I'd never

seen his home but the one he had on that mountain was bigger so I could imagine.

"I thought I made it clear about that word around me."

"You said not to call you cute. I'm not. I'm calling the house cute."

I tried not to roll my eyes. "Great. Thanks for the ride."

"You're not going to invite me inside?"

"Hell no."

He chuckled. "See you tomorrow then."

We didn't have detention tomorrow and I almost regretted it. "Yeah," I said dryly. As if my heart weren't pumping wildly with the anticipation of it. I was just at my door when I heard him call my name. I turned to look at him as he leaned out the window.

"And you *are* cute, just so we're clear on that." He winked at me.

Fucker.

I turned away quickly before he could see the blush on my face.

CHAPTER 19

Wade had been shunned from his JB table so he sat with me at the weeb table during lunch. Everyone looked at us suspiciously, as if I were a doppelganger and Wade an interloper. It took a few minutes for us to settle into anime conversation, especially with the convention in a few months. We talked about cosplay ideas, our favorite scenes, and even Wade got comfortable with the group. Although clearly he preferred to be with Theo. They kept snatching glances at each other, as if their distance affected them more than either of them had realized. Which left me with a sour feeling in my stomach that made me wonder again why the hell Wade had risked Theo's friendship to be with me in detention.

I didn't trust him. And I didn't trust my feelings for him.

When I walked into Dr. Reyes's group room after school, I wasn't thinking clearly. I stopped just inside, wondering if I'd gotten the rooms mixed up today. Adam Brody stood next to the sweet table, pouring himself some juice. My body went into full hyper mode. The others were already waiting, so I took my regular seat and waited.

Sage sat straighter and shifted in his seat as Adam walked toward the empty seat beside me like some sort of Adonis to be worshipped. Okay, that thought was just plain weird. I was not visualizing the six-foot-four man with dark, tousled hair and buzzing blue-green eyes as a worship-worthy god. Nope.

I shifted in my seat, earning a Sage glare. Jack and David didn't mind holding Adam's gaze. Jack counted the number of steps it took for Adam to reach his seat while David remained planted as always, an immovable object. Dr. Reyes walked in, greeted Adam, and took his seat.

"I'd like to introduce Adam to the group. He generously agreed to share his story today."

The room was silent. Everyone stared at Adam like an outsider. He rubbed his palms down the length of his thighs. "I hope me being here is okay."

"Did you sign an NDA?" Sage asked.

"Yes," Adam answered quickly. "Everything said here is said in confidence." Although he looked like a god, he squirmed like a human. Like all of us.

Dr. Reyes had us all introduce ourselves. Sage gave a shy wave, Jack nodded, David tapped his foot, and I just stared. I wanted Adam gone. He seemed to realize it and kept his eyes on me when he asked if we were okay that he was here.

No. I wasn't. He knew my story. Well, not all of it, but most of it. Having him here felt too overbearing. I hated the Brodys. He was one of them.

"Xander?" Dr. Reyes brought me back from my thoughts. "Are you okay that Mr. Brody is here today?"

I shifted uncomfortably. All heads turned to me.

We'd been in group for four weeks already. We knew the worst version of ourselves and expected nothing. The reason this little group worked so well. We hadn't charged down each other's throats. Just tolerated the forty minutes to get this bullshit program over with. At least that had been the mindset until Adam joined us. The group dynamic shifted because of the odd man out. The drifter who drew upon everyone's curiosity, and being curious meant we cared, on some level, about the structure already in place for the group. We all knew Sage needed attention. Jack needed direction, and David needed something to listen to. On occasion, he'd participate too. I needed to disappear.

But what did Adam need? Why had he invaded our space, *my* space?

I seemed to be the only one who knew him outside these four walls. I suddenly realized I was staring at him for too long. My eyes fell to my feet. "Yeah, whatever. I don't care."

Yeah, right. So why did I have the sudden itch to bolt? My eyes even lifted to the exit, which I always had in my line of sight.

Always.

"Thank you," Adam said kindly.

Adam spoke as if he were outside of his body looking in. He spoke without inflection, no slight tremble, even when he got to the hard bits. It wasn't hard to realize that his experience shadowed my own. He'd lost his parents in a car accident that led to his deafness. He'd been shunned by a family who required everyone to be perfect. He'd been broken and pieced back together through his experiences in the streets. Homeless, until finally finding a foster parent who took him in and cared for him. When he finally silenced, we all just absorbed it all. Surprised that someone who looked so well put together, actually wasn't. Someone like me.

Except Adam hadn't killed his family. Hadn't lied about what happened either.

"Any comments or questions for Adam?" Dr. Reyes asked.

"Yeah," Sage said dryly. "Did the shit get better when you left home?"

Adam's smile was kind but also sad. "No," he said honestly. "I had to learn to live with myself first before anything got better, and even now, it's still a struggle."

"Well, that sucks," he said.

Adam chuckled. "Leaving the toxic environment did help me see things differently, Sage. It was how I perceived others, how I allowed them to influence me that shaped me into something better. Or at least I'd like to think I'm better than I was before."

"Well, I certainly think you're handsome," Sage said with a smirk.

"Thank you," Adam said with a hint of blush.

"Any other questions?" Dr. Reyes asked, breaking Sage from the conversation before the guy started having across-the-room sex with Adam.

"So what helped you deal with all of it?" David asked with a voice that always sounded as if he'd just woken up.

Adam got to his feet. "Glad that you asked." He pulled out small business cards from his pocket and handed each of us one. I was the last to get a card.

Sage snorted. "You're kidding, right?" he said in his usual high voice opposite David. "Isn't this counterproductive?"

Dr. Reyes leaned over. "Actually, I know Charlie Cox very well. He's helped mentor a great deal of young people over the years. It isn't therapy, of course, but it is something you can do if you are interested."

David looked like he fell back asleep, and Jack looked like he wanted to say something, so he did what he always did: he looked at me, which gave me courage to say what was on my mind.

"When?" My question seemed to hang out there in limbo. "When can we check it out?"

"How about next week?"

"Sounds like a plan." I nodded to Jack.

"Can, um, we go together?" Jack asked.

"Sure," I said quickly, feeling a bit more courageous when needed to step up. Funny how that worked out for me. "I'll meet you here after school."

Jack gave me an appreciative nod.

Great. Meant we were all going to be training to box.

CHAPTER 20

Wade and I were separated during detention. I worked the library with Emir. The guy was a history buff and with AP US History under his belt, he gave me the rundown of WWII. The guy's eyes brightened just talking about it. It made me realize I lacked passion in my life. Sure, I liked drawing. I drew away the darkness inside of me. Projected it on white space and closed the book on it. I hardly ever went back to it to see that darkness. I didn't *love* art. It was more a compelling need to draw out the insanity inside me. I'd never talked about art the way Emir talked about history, or had that gleam in my eye like Wade on that mountain. As college careers loomed closer, I had no clue what the hell I wanted to be when I grew up. And the growing up part was fast approaching.

I met Wade outside as always after detention and climbed into his sporty car. Our time together already fitted into a sort of schedule. Ever since his friends shunned him, he'd been spending more time with me. I had to own that and the reason behind it. I wasn't a fool to think I'd be his first choice.

"Are you okay?" he asked as he started driving toward our familiar ground—his beach house.

I had too much on my mind right now to think about a good answer to that one, so I just claimed I was tired. Nothing big. Move on. We listened to music in the car—he liked Panic at the Disco and I didn't care.

"Can we just go to the beach?" I asked. I didn't want to swim today.

"Yeah, sure," he said with a careful undertone I usually heard from my aunt after a night terror. I ignored it.

I got the blanket from the house and spread it on the hot sand. Then we sat. Silence made Wade uncomfortable. I was used to it. He finally sighed, got to his feet, pulled off his T-shirt, and dropped it. Without looking at me, he sprinted to the water and disappeared under a wave. My heart did a little jolt until I saw his platinum blond hair pop over the surface. We weren't alone on the beach, and he quickly started a conversation with two other guys I assumed were his friends. They must live around here. And Wade was Wade. He knew everyone. That shouldn't bother me, but it did.

"Get over it, X. You can't control everyone."

The sound of Bea's voice in my head startled me. It'd been a while since I heard her voice. The sassiness in it always made me defensive. "I'm not trying to control him," I whispered, feeling off in talking to myself. I shoved an earbud into my ear to at least seem as if I was on the phone. I wonder if other people did that. The ones I saw always talking on their headphones, carrying conversations. They could be talking to the dead too.

"Yeah, you are. You always try to control people. The reason your friends are smaller than you."

I snorted. "Everyone is smaller than me."

Wade turned to where I was sitting, and our eyes met and held. I couldn't move my lips and wished Bea would not talk. *"He's cute. And you like him."*

I snorted again. "He's just a friend."

"You can lie to yourself, but not to me. I know what's inside of you."

Pain shot through me, and I looked down to see knives

sticking out of my chest. All of them. Bea and I had tried to hide the knives so Dad wouldn't kill us. He'd killed us anyway.

I inhaled sharply and my body jerked in response. I jumped to my feet and stumbled back. My eyes were glued to the space I'd been in. To the space my sister haunted searching for the knives.

Breathe, Xander. Breathe. I rubbed my chest, the echo of pain still raw. The blanket empty.

"Hey."

I spun to Wade standing behind me, dripping wet, looking at me as if he expected a meltdown. Without thinking, I flung my arms around his neck, hiding my face in its crook. "It isn't real. It isn't real." I needed to know my sister wasn't sitting on that blanket with the bloodied knives on her lap. I needed to know that they were dead. That she was dead. That what lingered in my nightmares wasn't real.

I felt his arms circle around me, his cold wet body pressed against me, and his lips near my ear. "You just fell asleep. It was a bad dream."

My legs felt like jelly, and I would've fallen had he not been supporting me. My body began to tremble. Cold. I felt so damn cold.

"Let's go inside," he said softly.

I didn't want to let him go. Unable to move my arms away from the safety he provided. I feared if I did let go, he'd just float away. He gave me a moment.

"I don't mind this, but, um, you know I'm gay and we're in public."

Shit. I didn't want to be in the media as his boyfriend. I didn't want the attention. I quickly pulled back. If I didn't know any better, I could've sworn I saw a hint of disappointment in his expression before he looked away and grabbed the blanket. He didn't look at me as he started for the house, and I followed.

He left me in the kitchen to change into his dry clothes and came back soon after. He handed me water, then we made sandwiches and ate.

"So, have I breached the friendship zone?" he asked.

I shrugged. "If you mean, are we friends, yeah. I think if I had to introduce you to my aunt, I'd introduce you as a friend. Why?"

"Well, because I'd like to know where you go when you sleep. I'd wanted to ask you about your scars since I saw them. I'd hoped you would give that information willingly, since we're friends."

I suddenly lost my appetite. "Is that why you're with me? To get deets on the psycho?" Okay, I was pissed. Didn't realize it until he asked me the one question I couldn't answer.

"What's that supposed to mean?"

"It means the only reason you've been at my hip is because you're friendless since you can't even face Theo and force him to take your apology in person. You feel all sorts of guilty, and I'm pretty sure it's not only because you punched him. I see the way you look at him."

"He's my best friend."

Ouch. Why did that hurt? "Then go be with him. Why are you slumming with me?"

"You are such a dick," he hissed out. I avoided looking at him. He was handsome even when angry, and it made me feel all sorts of things I didn't want to face. "All you have to say is that you're not ready to tell me anything about yourself. To mind my business. You don't have to get all defensive as if everyone's out to get you!" His voice rose, and I could've sworn the ground shook from it.

"If I'm wrong, then why am I here?"

"Because I care about you, asshole!" He slammed his sandwich into the garbage, half-eaten, and spun around, giving me his back. I itched to run out the door. To leave. All of it. Things didn't add up. Why the hell would he care about me?

But I didn't move. I just watched him grip the sink, as if it was the only thing holding him up. He dropped his chin.

I needed to say something, but words wouldn't come. I was a fool with words. I didn't know how to communicate in words. I'd only fuck shit up.

"Should I leave?" I asked, my voice hollowed out, stripped of whatever emotions I had burrowing under my skin right now. I couldn't let loose.

"No, I'll take you home."

The next day at school, I met him at his locker. It took finagling with Piper to get his locker number, but after a few pouts, she released that information. Leaning against his locker, I pushed myself off as soon as I saw him. He was talking with Theo. Apparently, they'd gotten back together. My chest clenched and my stomach warred against me, but I stood my ground. He said something to Theo, who glared at me as he walked past me, and Wade slowly started unpacking his things into the locker.

Though he couldn't ignore me, he didn't say anything either. I took a moment to reconsider what I'd planned to do to apologize for being such a jerk with him. He closed his locker and looked at me. Yeah, I was doomed with this guy. "Come on," I finally said.

I turned away from him and started walking through the hallway, secretly hoping that he wouldn't be behind me when I finally reached the art room. That he decided I was a broken piece of shit, and he didn't really want to be friends with me. But when I reached the basement-level art studio and turned to look behind me, there he was.

"What are we doing here?" he asked.

"You want to see me? You want to know?" I swallowed the lump in my throat. "There's no turning back once we go through this door."

His light blue eyes never left mine. "Show me."

Jacked full of nerves at what I was about to do, I led him inside and to my tripod. I lifted the drop cloth off my art piece and wanted to look away from his reaction to it. I didn't want to see him laugh at me or ridicule me, but he didn't. His eyes widened like two blue saucers with a series of emotions I couldn't even try to pick apart.

The piece was dark, with an edginess that held an echo of death. But there was also light casting down from the darkness. I let him study it in silence. The mismatch of light and dark shadows. The element of a dark soul. The perception of raw fear. What I felt when I had woken up from that hospital bed to find out my parents and sisters were dead. "My family died in a car accident a few years ago. I still have nightmares," I managed to croak out. I couldn't tell him about Bea or the knives. I couldn't tell him about the snow or my drunk Dad.

Wade's eyes gleamed, and one tear slipped out of his left eye to trail down his cheek. He didn't bother to brush it away, and I didn't move. He seemed to need this more than I did, and I needed to know why. "I'm afraid," he finally whispered. "I'm afraid of snowboarding. I'm afraid of getting hurt. I think about it all the time during competitions, and for me, that's dangerous. One slip and I'm eating more than just snow." He pressed the heel of his palms to his eyes, making a frustrating sound. "This is so stupid. This place feels like a holding cell of lost dreams."

"That's very depressing. But not totally wrong."

He chuckled, but the sadness remained in his eyes, and I wanted to help him with that. "Sit," I ordered. This time, he cocked his brows at me, already wanting to argue. "Please," I added.

Wade reluctantly sat down on the stool. He looked uncomfortable and regretted the truth he'd just spilled. I, on the other hand, felt a sense of pride that he needed me. The feeling allowed me to brush off my own insecurities. It freed me from fear and consequence. The feeling allowed me to shoulder someone else's pain and act. To do something about it. I had a hero complex. I realized that when I couldn't leave Jace to suffer in that place. When I had hit Chad for hitting Trini. I grew a pair when someone else needed help, while I shriveled when it was me who needed saving.

Another label to add to my ever-growing list.

I positioned myself behind him and started kneading his shoulders. I pressed my thumbs just at the base of his neck and liked the moan he let out. It did something to my body. I didn't say anything but kept kneading his shoulders, enjoying the soothing sounds he made under my touch.

"I shouldn't have said that about snowboarding. I love snowboarding. The only thing I'm really good at."

I walked around him, so I was facing him. He had to lift his head to make eye contact with me as I leaned down into his space.

I wanted to kiss him.

I ignored my lizard brain and hovered my mouth over his ear. "Don't lie to me," I said. My words made him stiffen. "I can see you. I know you feel as if you have to prove something to everyone, but you don't have to prove anything to me." I felt his breath on my cheek.

"You probably think I'm a coward," he said.

"You're the bravest person I know," I responded, not shocked by that revelation. He was brave. "You shoot into the sky as if it's nothing, performing those tricks. You won Gold. *Gold.* And you came out during the Olympics, risking your endorsements and your friends."

"Someone is trying to get into my good graces," he joked.

"Don't do that," I said. "I'm not like everyone else, Wade." He shivered under my fingers when I said his name.

"I know you're not like everyone else." His eyes were glued to mine. "And I saved your life," he said finally, lifting me out of whatever trance he had me under.

"Oh God, you'll never let me live that one down, will you?"

"Nope."

"I should get you a Superman suit."

"I have a Cap costume I can wear for you."

Hell yes. I would like to see that. Instead, I snorted. "Don't let this moment get to your head."

He took my hand and pulled me in between his legs. Shocked silence had me moving where he wanted me. "My turn," he said. "No bullshit. Do you want to kiss me?"

The world seemed to snap out of existence while his eyes turned into two deep pools of light that threatened to suck out my soul. My mouth moved, but I had no idea what I said. I knew when he smiled that it must've been yes. I had wanted to say yes. *Yes. Yes. Yes.*

He leaned in, cupping my waist, pulling me closer. The hungry look on his face promised all sorts of things I couldn't imagine. And I had a pretty good imagination. I wanted that so much.

Don't trust him.

Don't trust him.

He wants something from you.

The negative thoughts pushed through my needs like a battering ram. I didn't want him to have control over me. I didn't want my father to be right. The last words he'd said to me, to be right. In a blinding panic, I pushed him away. He startled, looked hurt, and I hated myself for putting that look there. I lost the ability to speak. I did what I always did. I ran. I didn't stop at my class. I ran straight for the exit doors and pushed myself out into the pouring rain. By the time I got home, I was soaked. I dried myself and hid in my room, calling Carmen to let her know I left school before they called her.

I couldn't think of anything but Wade and how I had denied myself the one kiss I craved for. Fear had pounded right through me. I learned early on not to trust anyone. Wade had to be hiding something, because why the hell would he want to spend time with me? Why would he want to kiss me when he could have anyone? I couldn't lose myself to the light pools of his eyes that wanted to drown me. I couldn't let myself go. I'd done too many bad things, had too many secrets festering inside of me. I couldn't let myself feel anything else. I'd explode.

Having to tear a piece of my soul out, I started to sketch Wade in a Superman suit, and I was the monster he destroyed.

CHAPTER 21

I avoided Wade the next day at school. He made it easy since he wasn't waiting for me at my locker. I didn't know if I felt disappointed or relieved. A bit of both, I suppose.

I did catch sight of him with Theo at lunch. And, of course, Wade had ignored me.

I met Jack after school in front of Dr. Reyes's office to go to the boxing gym. Jack drove a bright yellow Jeep. Not what I'd expect him to drive. I had pictured him in something small and foreign. "Hey," I said as I hopped inside and strapped in.

"Hey," he said timidly. He didn't move right away but kept looking at me for confirmation. I realized this was the first time he actually wasn't counting anything. His lips weren't moving, and neither was the car.

"I'm good, whenever you are," I prompted.

"I don't know. Me in a boxing gym. With other ... men?"

That struck me as odd. "I'm sure they'll be women there too," I encouraged.

He nodded, his lips forming a thin line on his face. "Okay. Okay. I can do this."

"We can do this. *Together.*"

He smiled at the word together and I felt a kindred spirit.

Charlie's Gym was located close to UCLA. Jack parked in a spot, and we started for the entrance. He looked like a schoolteacher in khaki pants, white shirt under a dark sweater, belt, and Chucks. His shaggy strawberry blond hair covered most of his face, which was the point.

"You're going to be fine," I said at the door. "Ready?"

He nodded, sweat gleaming on his forehead.

I opened the door for him and followed him inside.

A bigger place than I had expected and the training grounds for Lassiter-The Beast-Parker. The guy was working his way up the slums and had a big fight coming up. Okay, I may have had a slight interest in the guy.

I didn't see any of the others yet. The reception area was flanked by a security wall made of glass so we could take in the room beyond it. Jack's eyes widened, and I thought he was going to faint.

"Are you here with Adam?" the dark-haired man asked from the desk. This place was not for those trying to lose weight. This was a serious boxing gym, and everyone seemed to be made of the same composite—hard, lean muscles, and sweat. A lot of sweat.

"Yeah," I said, trying to sound tough. Yeah, sometimes I acted the part. Most times I felt it. Not so much here.

The guy buzzed the glass door and swung it open for us. "Sal is already at the mats with your friends. Go ahead."

I turned to Jack, whose lips had started to turn blue as he counted under his breath. "Hey," I said roughly, snapping him to attention. Jack had a compulsion to count everything. Too much stimulus and the guy would get sick. Like real sick. It helped him concentrate on one specific theme—a color, a shape, in this case I thought a set of machines. "The treadmills. Count only the treadmills."

He licked his lips and nodded. That seemed to work. Although he seemed pale when we reached the others, he was no longer searching out the room or mumbling.

Sage looked irritated when he caught sight of us but kept

his mouth shut. Sage had been the unlucky one in front of Jack one time when Jack had a panic attack that had him spewing like the exorcist right on Sage, who had then fainted on the vomit. After that drama played out, Sage preferred tough love therapy for Jack. Indifference and avoidance. Except the kid always sought out Sage, as if the guy were his lifeline. Sage moved to the left and Jack followed.

I sighed, hoping this wasn't a mistake. I didn't want to clean up vomit or pick up a douchebag from vomit.

Sage clutched his satchel close to his body as if it were his soul as Sal flanked him to greet us. A big muscly man with shaggy dark hair, brown eyes, and a smile so wide I thought he'd won the lottery. "Welcome," he said. "My name is Sal. I'll be giving you the tour today before you meet with Charlie."

Adam came up behind Sal and smiled. It did something to my stomach to see him. Sage turned to Adam, as if pleading to be saved from the burly man. "Has he signed an NDA?" Sage asked.

I pressed my lips together to keep from laughing. Adam's cheeks peppered in a blush. "Uh, no. This is a public place."

It took a moment for that to settle into Sage's mind. I thought the guy would either pull out the document for everyone to sign or leave. He did neither, though he did look for the exit and seemed to think better of it.

Sal clapped his hands, making Jack jump. His muscles bulged under his shirt. "Okay then," he said with a smile. "Let's get started."

Adam left us to go to the locker rooms and we followed Sal like lost puppies.

I'd never been in a boxing gym before and everything here was meant to be hit with a fist or a knee or a foot. Sal took us through the equipment and let us hit things. As pissed off as we were at the world, we were pretty pathetic. Sage tumbled after trying the speed ladder; Jack got tangled on the jump rope and would've eaten dirty gym floor if David hadn't been watching him very intently and caught him before he fell. David just stood there with his arms folded across his chest and a *hell no* expression. And I got a blowback from the punching bag right in the forehead.

"Does Adam train?" Sage asked.

Sal turned and led all our eyes to the MMA cage and the two guys battling inside. I heard Sage take a deep surprised inhalation. I felt the same way, and more. Much more. Adam wore nothing but shorts. A tattoo covered his left side from shoulder to ankle. I couldn't make out the details, but even from this distance, the artwork looked amazing. His hair had been pulled up in a tight bun. No hearing aids. Fists lifted, ready for an attack. I suddenly didn't want to see Adam get hurt, but I couldn't look away. The guy was all lean muscles and sweaty. Not overdone like Sal, just perfect. I suddenly felt hot under the collar.

"That guy is delicious," Sage said.

I quickly turned away, feeling my cheeks blush. I hadn't been thinking that. No, I hadn't.

Sage gave me a *yeah right* look, although I hadn't spoken. Thankfully, Jack took that moment to bolt for the nearest garbage can to spew.

"Well, at least he didn't vomit on me this time," Sage said.

"Leave him alone," David defended in his deep sleepy voice. "He's trying."

David rarely spoke and yet ... I turned to Sage, who turned to me at that exact moment, and we both lifted our brows. *Yeah, these two had something going on*, our look said. If Dr. Reyes had chosen us all because he knew we would work well together, did that mean ... Sage's lips quirked in a smirk. *You're gay too*, that look said.

"Okay." Sal clapped his hands and rubbed them. "Let's call it. Why don't you three go upstairs and I'll get the little guy?"

Thankfully, Sage turned to lead us. I was the last to fall

in line and couldn't help but glance back at Adam. At that moment, his eyes lifted and caught me watching him. Something definitely passed between us. I was held in his focus. Adam did look delicious.

Shit.

I broke contact first and paid attention to my steps instead. I suddenly felt boiled from the inside out.

Sal brought us water with Jack in tow. "Charlie will be right in." With a smile I'm sure made him famous, he walked out.

I couldn't think. Couldn't breathe. My mind buzzed with unspoken truths.

X, deal with it. You're gay. Papi was right.

My sister's voice invaded my mind. I leaned forward, my elbows digging into the tops of my knees. I didn't need this shit now. I didn't. There was too much swelling inside of me already. Guilt. Fear. Anger. I didn't need this shit.

And you want to kiss Wade and Adam. You've become a closet slut.

I shot to my feet.

Sage startled and clutched his satchel tight with a squeal as if I was going to hurt him. Violence didn't quite make the cut on how I felt. "I'm gay," I shot out. "And if you fucking say anything, I'm going to pull your intestines out of your ass and hang you with them."

With that said, I ran out.

CHAPTER 22

I did it. Fuck it, I did it. I gave myself one more label. Leaning forward, I stared at the floor. Dr. Reyes sat in front of me, giving me time to settle. My body jittery at my announcement that I was gay. The threat of the intestine-hanging thing may have been a bit much. I admitted that to Dr. Reyes after I had time to settle my nerves.

I finally leaned back to look at him. "I'm not going to pull their intestines out of their ass and hang them, if that's what you're afraid of."

"I'm not afraid of that," he said. "I'm afraid you need to talk about what's been going on with you these past weeks. Does this have something to do with Wade?"

The sound of Wade's name in therapy had me cringing. I regretted telling Dr. Reyes about how his mother had treated me. How I felt lacking. I regretted a lot of things about Wade Wilson.

"It's not about him. It's about me."

Dr. Reyes nodded. Good. I was doing good so far. I bobbed my knee up and down and clasped my hands together, unable to stay still. My nerves jacked. I couldn't work with not knowing what was crawling inside of me that made me feel so damn pissed. Dark. Broken.

"I am proud that you came forward to let us know you're gay. That was very brave, though we could've done without the threat."

"Yeah, sorry about that."

"Do you want to talk about what led you to reveal your sexuality?"

"I've never—" God this sucked. Shit I should've been able to tell my dad, not the doc. "I've never been with a girl or a guy. I'm still a virgin. Maybe the oldest virgin in the state." I chuckled. "Maybe, I should, you know, try with a guy or something. I don't know. I fucking don't know, but if I don't do something I'm going to explode."

"Masturbation is also an option," Doc said.

That he said it with a straight face made me respect the guy. "I don't mean explode in *that* way," I said. I rubbed my palms along my jeans again. "Do you think it's weird? That I'm just thinking about it too much?"

He gave me a small smile I didn't take to be anything but compassion. The guy had been there. "No, I don't think it's weird. I think you're in a place of self-exploration. It's okay to explore your own body. To explore your own feelings."

"Right," I said. "Okay, well, if you're not going to arrest me for the threat thing, I think I'm done."

"Would you like to talk about how removing intestines through the ass is possible?"

It took me a moment to realize he was joking. I chuckled, then laughed out loud. He laughed too. It was a good nervous laugh.

As I walked out, I thought about the huge labels hanging over my head. PTSD, intermittent explosive disorder, opposition defiant disorder, and now gay. The taglines went on and on. I thought about how being gay made me different. I didn't *feel* different. I didn't feel the need to jump up and down and yell that I was gay. It was more intimate than calling it out. My connection with Wade and Adam confused me, sure, but it didn't change who I was. Good or bad. I didn't want any type of connection.

Liar.

Yeah, a total liar. I did want to feel something because it pushed every other fucked-up feeling out of the forefront of my mind. I had too much in my brain to figure out and I was especially curious as to where it would lead me. Did I want to be tagged with the LGBTQ crowd? Hell, I didn't even know what half that shit meant. Did I want to seek likeness in other gay people? Maybe I'd learn something about myself in the process. I don't know. I didn't really want to be with the straight crowd, the geeky crowd, the brainiacs. I didn't want to be anywhere with people. Being alone was safe.

That thought slipped by the dark side when I saw Adam's bright smile aimed directly at me, shooting invisible light beams at my solar plexus. The only way I could describe the sudden burning I felt behind my ribs. The guy had this rugged, sweet, handsome veneer touched by something dangerous that I found curious.

I wanted to *be* him.

And kissing him would be nice.

I was going insane. My fingers itched to draw, my sketchbook in my pack always with me. I shoved my hands into my pockets, wishing I could zap out of existence and not be blindsided by the danger Adam promised beyond that smile. "Hey," he greeted. "Great that I caught you. Wanna grab a bite to eat?"

This looked like a set-up if ever I saw one. Okay, so he knew my therapy session day and time. At least that meant Dr. Reyes hadn't ratted me out. I'm sure the other guys had. We were in a public place when I had my freak-out, after all. They didn't have to uphold their NDA rules. Sage was rubbing on me.

Being homeless at one point had trained me never to say no to food. "Sure."

Like me, Adam didn't drive, but unlike me, he had his own personal driver. A big guy got out of the car, and I could've sworn the car groaned and then sighed at the relief of him outside. Eskinor. The guy reminded me of Eskinor from *Seven Deadly Sins*.

Yeah, I was a weeb.

Eskinor opened the door for Adam, who slipped inside and scooted over. I gave him a sheepish smile and climbed in behind Adam. The car instantly cooled my skin. The air set at freeze-your-balls-off.

"Wow," I said dryly. "You have a car and driver. Must be nice."

"Bubbles is nice," Adam responded as we headed into traffic.

"Bubbles?"

Adam leaned closer to whisper, and I felt myself jolt to attention at his nearness. I'd never get used to that. Ever. "Lilo and Stitch?"

Recognition dawned on me, and I couldn't help but laugh. "The guy was black. Wrong color," I reminded him.

He shrugged. "Still reminds me of him."

Yeah. I couldn't argue with that.

We reached a diner near the UCLA campus. "Are you a student here?" I asked.

"Yeah. Third year."

I followed him to a corner spot where he sat with his back against the wall and his eyes to the door. The spot held by those of us who expected trouble. Adam hadn't been bullshitting about his homelessness story during group. The effects of it still hovered over him. It didn't bode well for me.

"Sit down," he said kindly.

I took the seat opposite him, and he waved to a pretty waitress, who quickly came to take our orders. "So is this a date?" As soon as those words left my mouth I wanted to crawl into the earth and die. "I mean, a friend thing, or a therapist thing."

Adam smirked and his eyes shimmered. Yeah, I figured I must look like a beet right about now. How the guy could be a badass fighter and adorable like a puppy still had me gooey inside. I settled my eyes on the drink menu. "Unfortunately, you're too young for me. Right now."

The *right now* had me lifting my eyes to his. We were only three years apart. Then I realized I was a guy. A guy. It was my turn to lean in and ask a very inappropriate question. "So you're into dudes?"

"I'm gay, if that's what you mean."

More heat and more blushing. I shrugged out of my hoodie before I internally combusted right there on the bench.

"Does that make you uncomfortable?"

Yes. But not in the way he probably thought. "No," I said instead. "I'm not a homophobe, if that's what you're implying." I didn't mention that I was gay too. It was too new for me to announce openly.

"Good that we got that out of the way."

"So why are you stalking me?"

"Right," he said without malice. "Get to the meat of it."

I shrugged. "Why drag it out, right?"

His green eyes seemed to reach for something I wasn't sure I could give. "I just wanted to touch base. You left in a hurry Thursday night. Missed Charlie's speech."

The waitress brought us our drinks and he took a sip. I played with the rim of my cup, unsure how I felt about Adam being here to try to fix me. Everyone I'd known had tried to fix me at one point. My mom by limiting my playtime with my sisters. My dad by drilling into my brain what it meant to be a real man. Society trying to shape me into a productive member of society—whatever the hell that meant. I wasn't even sure I could be fixed anymore. Adam watched me, and I realized he was waiting for my explanation. "I'm sorry," I said, feeling like a total asshole. "Was there a question in there somewhere?"

The smirk didn't leave his handsome face and the glimmer returned to his eyes, as if I'd just challenged him and he liked it. "Why did you leave?"

"Not my scene," I lied. Adam knew I was lying. I had

liar written on my forehead.

"Fair enough. So, what do you like to do?"

"Draw," I said quickly. "Beat people up," I added to soften the surprise.

He chuckled. "I draw too, and I also beat people up, as you saw in the cage."

I did not want to remember a sweating Adam in a cage fight. "We seem to have some things in common."

Adam kept his eyes on my lips. I knew he was reading them, but it sent all kinds of thoughts running through me, and I didn't want to look at his lips. "A lot of things in common, it seems." That smirk made my stomach clench. I had to get back control. I was losing my mind.

"What do you draw?" I asked.

"Monsters."

"How long have you been seeing Dr. Reyes?"

"Two years. Since I came to school here."

The food came and we started to eat.

"You know, I first thought Charlie was full of shit. I met him when I was fourteen. I broke into the club through a window." He chuckled at the memory.

"So what happened?"

"Well, he found me asleep under his desk. Sal had forgotten to set the alarm, so he was more pissed at Sal than at me. Which I thanked God for."

I remembered Sal taking care of Jack. Remembered how patient he was with Sage's paranoia about NDAs. I hoped the others found Charlie helpful. "How did the group respond to Charlie?"

Adam ate slowly while watching me. "They all said they'd come back. I guess we'll see. You care a lot about them."

I never considered myself caring about them. "I hardly know them."

"You know them differently than anyone else. That's a bond no one can break."

I thought he was wrong. Bonds and friendships beak all

the time. I just had to think about Jace for that.

"You can come back to the club whenever you want."

A nudging feeling burrowed inside me, as if I'd swallowed a chipmunk and it was now scratching me on the inside trying to get out. Accepting the invite meant accepting people into my life. Forming friendship bonds or some shit.

And we know how much you'd love that, Bea's voice in my head again. This time sarcasm oozed in her words. My words.

"Nah, I'm good."

"Alone?" Adam asked.

The word and what it meant felt like a thousand knives through the sternum. I'd been alone since my family died. Left behind. The truth of that hurt like the knives Bea pulled out of my chest every time I dreamt of her.

Alone.

Lonely.

Coward.

I swallowed the food but tasted nothing. Finally, I called it. I got to my feet. "I should go."

Thankfully, Adam didn't try to stop me.

I was able to catch my breath outside and move. I didn't run but walked away. Unsure where the hell I was going, probably the wrong way. My sense of direction sucked.

My mom had hung a portrait of two kids crossing a dilapidated bridge on my bedroom wall. Behind them, a glorious angel hovered. Its beautiful golden wings spread wide, ready to catch them should they fall. I had always felt safer in my bed, knowing that my guardian angel would protect me. The reason I hadn't been the one hiding the knives. I'd told Bea to relax. Dad would never use the knives on us because our guardian angel would protect us.

She had snorted in derision. *"There's no such thing as angels, X, help me."*

To ease her mind, I had helped her hide the knives.

But Bea had been right. There were no such things as

angels or a God who protected children. Children suffered just as well as adults. I stopped believing in angels and people. Nobody really cared about me. They all wanted something in return. Money, a warm body, someone to save them. Something. Adam, Trini, and even Wade weren't any different. Better to be alone than have your soul ripped out and have only the dark wraiths left behind.

Once I was far enough from the diner, I dropped on a bench and pulled out my sketch pad. I drew furiously. Instead of an angel, I drew a demon with dark wings. It wasn't until I heard a car horn and looked up to see Adam that I realized the sky had begun to darken with cloud cover. It would rain soon.

"Come on," Adam said. "I'll take you home."

I lowered my eyes to the image staring back at me, and my chest tightened. My sister's wide brown eyes stared back at me.

CHAPTER 23

I'd done everything Dr. Reyes had asked. I remained friends with Trini despite her asshole of a boyfriend. I hadn't gotten into a fight in weeks. I had made friends with Wade. And on impulse, allowed myself to feel something more. To hope.

For shit.

I wasn't the pre-accident kid anymore. I'd never be that kid. That kid died when my father forced us into that van. I wasn't the kid who drew images of strangers and pretended they were friends because I didn't have any real ones. I wasn't the kid who settled, who could look away when someone was getting hurt. To ignore all the warning signs of abuse around me. Guilt shattered my ignorance and my innocence.

We should've died together that night.

I'd been nothing but a shell since, and I couldn't find my way back.

Things were bound to get worse. It was only a matter of time.

Coerced to go to my cousin's quince party with Carmen and Moe, I found myself among people I didn't even know. Extended family only seen at special events like weddings, *quinceañeras*, and funerals. The men were hanging out at the bar, the underage teens hanging off their hips, waiting for the liquor to change hands. When they came around to me, I had refused and was called a *puto* for it.

A bitch.

Peer pressure at its finest.

I took to the shadows, away from the dance floor and people. When Mom married Dad, she had moved to Chicago. We hardly ever saw her family. We'd had no one to take us in whenever Dad had thrown us out of the house, or whenever they fought. Dad had been careful not to send Mom to the hospital during his binges, but it'd been close a few times. After their death, when I saw the number of people at her funeral, I resented them all for it.

They, in turn, resented that I was now considered a rich bastard and gave them nothing. I paid Carmen to take care of me. They talked about that too. What they didn't talk about was how my family died. How my dad was an abusive drunk. How they did nothing to try to help my mom get away from him.

I didn't belong here. I didn't belong anywhere.

A loud crash made me turn to see Moe with Carmen in the lobby. Moe was drunk. And he was a violent drunk. He'd never laid a hand on Carmen before, but there was always a first time. A couple of the uncles helped walk him out and I followed behind. Carmen shot me a nervous glance.

"He's just drunk," she said.

As if that made it any better.

We made it to her car, and he refused to get into the passenger seat. He even shoved the uncles out of the way. Benicio lifted his hands. "*Cálmate, cabrón*, and get in the car. Your woman will drive."

Swaying, Moe looked angry. "I can drive. Give me the fucking key." He tried to snag the key from Carmen, but she pulled it out of reach. "Bitch," he slurred. "Give me the fucking key."

I felt bad for Carmen. By that time a few more people had come out to watch Moe make a fool out of himself. He was used to that, if stories about his drunken episodes were true. "No, Moe. Just get in."

He took a wobbly step toward her, and I stepped in the middle, hoping that seeing me, knowing how my own family died, he'd relent and get in the passenger side.

Nope.

He shoved me back. "*Dejame, maricón,*" he said.

I lifted my hands and realized they were shaking.

He pointed his finger at me. "You think you're better than us, keeping all that money to yourself, man. You're nothing but a *puto mamaguevo.*"

I lost it. I swung first, hitting him on the side of his face. He seemed to sober up quickly because he tackled me onto the ground. My head hit the pavement and a burst of pain rushed down my neck, branched out along my spine, and tingled the tips of my fingers. He slammed a fist into my ribs, spewing some Spanish curse words. I'd heard them all from my father when he'd gotten drunk. How they could've figured me out before I even came to that realization didn't matter. Whether they said it to hurt me, or because they feared it, didn't matter.

Nothing mattered because my family was already dead.

Someone lifted him off of me, and adrenaline allowed me to get to my feet despite the sway in the world.

"I don't want him in my fucking house!" Moe screamed.

Carmen was crying, pushing him away from me. Then he slapped her hand and got into the passenger side. She turned to me. Not angry, but guilty. The same look Mom gave me when Dad would throw us out.

Sorry, mijo, just leave for a little while. Walk around the neighborhood and come back when he's sleeping.

I didn't wait for her to say anything.

I just stormed off.

It didn't matter anyway. They weren't my family. My family was dead. I chanted that in my head for five miles before Bea's voice overruled me.

They do matter because they're the only family you have left.

CHAPTER 24

Carmen called me a few times, but I knew even that would eventually stop, and it did. Trini called me too, but I ignored it. I hadn't known much about Santa Monica when I'd been forced here, but I learned quickly. The best thing to do was find a hidey hole alone, trust no one, and sleep with one eye open. I already had a spot I navigated to whenever I needed to get away.

The abandoned warehouse I had squatted in in the past. A chain-link fence warded vagabonds away and signs of *no trespassing* and *private property* made it look as if someone actually cared about the place.

Not.

I found a weak spot in the fencing and slipped underneath. I quickly scanned the place and found nothing but shadows and quiet. Empty. Like my perception of killer snow, the place felt *evil.* As if what had happened had seeped into the walls and floorboards. As if I were poking at chance just being here.

The place even had juice, so I was able to charge my phone. I made myself a pallet with anything dry I could find and plucked a steel pipe from the floor before lowering myself onto it, my back against the wall facing the door.

I thought about the fucker who tried to hurt me. Lawrence Whitman. I had erased him from thought after I'd been forced into Boys Home. The place had looked nice when I had first arrived. There were even stables and horses. Though we never got to use any of that type of therapy. Not the kids in the East Wing. We were the violent ones, the ones that were like perforations to society. The ones people could just tear away.

Everything that happened to me felt as if it had happened to someone else, not me.

I listened to the stillness for any break in the silence but heard nothing. Loneliness had been a deal breaker for my sanity when I was younger. Especially after the accident. The feeling of being the only person in the world, allowing my mind to take over, thinking too much all had been detrimental for me. It led me down a dark path, unable to see anything good in my life and wanting *more*.

Over the years, I learned to dull that craving by reminding myself that I didn't deserve anything more. I was on borrowed time. I either survived it or would do something stupid that would get me killed. I wasn't suicidal. I'd get my blood money soon, and then I'd figure shit out.

I watched the darkness turn to light as the night turned to morning. My phone buzzed with a text. I thought about ignoring it, but I hoped it was Wade asking about our missed skiing lesson.

Be careful what you wish for.

Wade: Where are you?

I imagined the sneer on his expression as he typed that question. It boiled my heart.

Me: Did you know my calc tutor was born in the Philippines? I always wanted to visit there.

Wade: I didn't know that. I'd never been either. Maybe we should plan a trip?

Planning a trip meant a future. With him. I did what I did very well. I deflected.

Me: Did you know that rats communicate to each

150

other through grumbling noises like raptors? I think they are plotting against me.

Wade: Xander. Where. Are. You. I know what happened with your uncle.

Shit. I deflected again.

Me: I went to the art museum with my class. It was the first time I stepped inside someplace so grand. I felt so small. My pains felt shallow compared to those that came before me. I don't know how to feel about that. Did you know most artists are batshit crazy?

It means if I become a famous artist, my own depressing story will be added to theirs. It'll read something like: Xander Morales, lived in silence while those he cared about perished. A coward of his own making. A sad, gay man who died because he never learned to ski.

Just as I hit send, I realized I just ousted myself to Wade. My pulse quickened as his response pinged on my phone.

Wade: I'm not an artist but I bet I can top that. Wade Ashton Wilson, lived a fake life, through a fake smile, and loved by everyone but himself. Unable to silence the fear in his head, and unable to give voice to his shallow needs. He died alone, buried with a gold medal.

I let out a relieved breath. He hadn't mentioned the gay thing, and his story was depressing.

Me: Ashton? Your middle name is Ashton?

Wade: Really? That's all you get from my depressing eulogy.

Me: I know depression. I don't know Ashton.

Wade: Well, tell me where you are so I can show you Ashton.

The order made my body vibrate. Why the hell did I like him giving me orders? There was something really wrong with me.

Duh, dude, you're squatting in your worst nightmare. There is something wrong with you.

I didn't want Wade to see me here. I didn't want him to know about this place. But another part of me wanted him here. I wanted someone to look for me. To find me when I was lost, and I was totally lost.

I sent him my GPS coordinates.

I fell asleep waiting for his confirmation text and woke up with a blade to my throat.

CHAPTER 25

The metal against my skin felt cold. I saw the man over me, felt his hot breath on my cheek, smelled mold on him, and my body reacted. Grunting, I spun my body into the asshole over me and clamored on top of him, ready to punch him in the face.

I blinked away the haze in front of me. Instead of oily, inky black hair and deep brown eyes, the person under me had platinum blond hair and light blue eyes. Not Lawrence Whitman.

Wade.

His hands were up near his face, wearing fear like a mask. Fear of *me.* I quickly jumped off of him and slammed against the wall at my back. "What the fuck?" I asked, breathless, adrenaline pumping through my veins, cupping my neck.

He got to his feet. "Sorry, I was just checking for a pulse. You were knocked out."

There was no knife.

I breathed away my panic and raked my hand down my face, letting my body uncoil from the threat.

"Are you okay?"

"Yeah, yeah." I leaned back and closed my eyes, appreciating the silence he gave me for a few minutes while

I collected myself.

"What is this place?" He dusted off an old, ruined desk and leaned on it to watch me.

I slid to the floor and folded my knees to my chest, resting my hands on them. I needed to spill something. To share the burden I carried with someone else. I'd drown if I didn't. But he wasn't asking the question I knew he wanted to.

"It's an abandoned warehouse."

I could tell he didn't like that answer, but too bad. He wasn't asking the right question. "Yeah, I can see that, but why did you choose to come here?"

Choice? A fucking choice? That pissed me off. Wade didn't know shit about me, about my life. Something must've registered on my face because he looked uncomfortable. "Why don't you ask me the question you really want to? The reason why you stopped being my mentor. Just *ask*."

He shifted on his feet and cupped his mouth. I could see the indecision on his face. The want to believe more about me, but there wasn't much more to me at all. "My mother said you were arrested." When I didn't offer anything up, he added, "Why?"

I met his eyes, and I wondered what his mother had told him about me. It hadn't sent him running from me, that's for sure. He deserved to know. "I was arrested for beating up some homeless guy," I said dryly.

"Why?"

"Because that's what cops do. They arrest people who hit other people."

Wade bit his lip to suppress a smile. "I meant, why did you beat up some homeless guy?"

I ran my hands along my thighs, realizing I was still wearing dress slacks instead of jeans. I could imagine how awful I must've looked. "I told you. I hit people."

He sighed angrily. "Jesus, everything with you is a damn tug-of-war."

"Okay," I said, licking my dry lips. "Tell me why you

can't just tell your mother you don't want to ski anymore?"

"Because I don't know if I really want to stop skiing, and I don't want to break her heart. Now, why were you arrested?"

"I'm sure your mother told you."

"I want to hear the truth from you."

I'd never told anyone the whole story of what happened that night. Not even Dr. Reyes. I lowered my eyes to Wade's shoes, finding it easier to talk without looking at him. For the first time, I wanted to tell someone. I wanted someone to know, to be on my side. To believe me. I knew it was a risk. Wade could simply scoff and say yeah, right. Give me the same look the cops gave me when they found me, but I needed to know that too. So I told him. All of it. The words spoken fast before I could think of pulling anything back. "I was sleeping in here when this guy just grabbed me. He was stronger than me. I was half asleep and didn't figure shit out until he had me pinned to the floor." I leaned my head back and closed my eyes, seeing that night so damn clearly as if it happened yesterday. "He was so heavy behind me, it hurt to breathe."

I heard Wade gasp but didn't look at him. I couldn't.

"I couldn't get him off. I tried. I even tried to scream, but he kept pressing his body into mine, and I couldn't take in enough oxygen into my lungs to shout. I was fifteen at the time. A skinny idiot thinking I was tougher than the world. He said I was pretty. That I'd fetch a good price on the market."

"Xander—"

I ignored my name. I needed to get this out fast. "And he wanted a taste. We weren't the only ones squatting in the warehouse. I heard voices. Close. He did, too, so he stopped moving. That's when I took a chance and jerked up hard. I hit his nose with the back of my head. He fell off me, and I scrambled for anything I could find to hit him. I just picked up the first thing. A broken-off piece of wood and hit him with it twice before I ran into the street and into some cops who stopped before hitting me with their car. The guy was behind me, bleeding, and the cops looked at me as if it were *my* fault. I knew they were just going to arrest me, so I ran. They caught me and arrested me." I chuckled. An ugly sound. "They took the guy's information and asked him if he wanted to press charges. They took him to the hospital. I don't know what happened to him afterward. They arrested me for assault, curfew violation, breaking and entering, and running from the scene of a crime. It wasn't my first offense. I'd been picked up for curfew violation before. The judge gave me an ultimatum: jail or the Boys Home, which is a prison for kids like me." The silence felt like a living, breathing thing in the room.

I didn't tell him what they did to us at that place. Some things were so buried I couldn't unearth them without consequence. This was my burden to carry. I couldn't share it with anyone, especially not Wade Ashton Wilson. The lies I told myself to survive. The fear I buried inside of me of being broken. Of losing control of my sanity, my heart. I was afraid of becoming my father. Carmen had fought tooth and nail to get me out of that place, until she finally did. I never planned on going back. Ever.

"I spent eight months in that place before I was released. I went to public school for a little while, but I tend to fight, so Carmen thought it'd be better to put me in some rich, fancy school, and you know the rest." I opened my eyes and hated the look on his face. Pity, maybe.

"Okay," he said dryly. "I concede. Your eulogy is way more pathetic than mine." He pressed his lips into a thin smile I just had to return. Then I let out a relieved breath.

That hadn't been what I had expected him to say. I expected him to ask why I hadn't tried to tell the cops the truth. Why I hadn't fought harder to make them believe the truth. I still wondered if that fucker hurt someone else. That would be my fault too. Wade didn't ask. I got to my feet and dusted my hands on my pants. They were still dirty. "Well, you're still alive, so that means you still can beat me in the pathetic category if you truly want."

He chuckled. "I guess we'll just have to see, won't we?"

The thought of having a future with Wade made all my insides crave it to the point of pain. "I guess."

Wade sighed. "Well, I'm not leaving you here," he said. "So you have two choices. Come stay with me. Or make amends with your aunt, who's worried about you."

I snorted. "Do you even know what happened?"

"Yeah, she explained it to me."

"Then you know what he did."

"And he's gone."

I startled. "What?"

"Your aunt threw him out of the house. She thought you needed time. She thought you'd come back after a few hours of cooling off. She cares about you."

All I could think about was that she threw out her husband for me. Unlike my mom, she chose to protect *me*. Then I felt guilty about it. "She shouldn't have done that for me."

"Why? Because you don't deserve it? You deserve to be here? Is that what you believe?"

Yes. I did. But I snapped my mouth shut. "What the fuck is this? Your version of tough love?"

There was something that flashed in Wade's expression, then he started to laugh. It was a sweet sound, considering where we were. I chuckled with him, unable to help it, then lowered my eyes to my hands. The space silenced again. "Maybe things will change when she learns I'm gay." *When she learns I let my family die.* I didn't say the last part out loud, and I let the gay thing hang out there.

Wade took my hand and pulled me gently into his embrace. I went with it not realizing how much I needed the contact. I felt safe. "Then we'll see where we go from there."

"We?"

"Yes, asshole. *We.* I'm here to help you."

"Why?"

He chuckled and shoved me away in play, but he didn't let go of my hand. "Damn, you don't trust anybody."

"No. I don't."

"Maybe, I want to help you because I committed myself to you when you threatened Purdy, and I take my role as mentor very seriously. Maybe I want to help you to get into heaven, if heaven really exists, which I'm not totally sure. What the hell does it matter? I want to help you, so let me." This time, he raked his hand through his hair and shivered. "So, what's it going to be? Are you going to return to the land of the humans or stay with the mold people?"

I rolled my eyes. "Ha. Ha. You are so funny." After I got my things, we headed to Carmen's house.

Wade stopped the car in the driveway, and I couldn't find the nerve to get out. He waited with me, giving me all the time I needed. "I've always known, you know?" I said into the quiet car. "My dad used to say these nasty things about me being too sensitive, too much like a pussy, too girly. I wanted to prove him wrong out of spite, but deep down I always knew." I chuckled and turned to Wade. Though his face was hidden in shadow, I could still feel the weight of his eyes on me. I wanted to be brave for him. For us. Whatever that meant.

"I'm here for you, Xander. You don't have to do this alone."

"How did you do it?"

Wade smirked. "I got caught. Not my best moment."

Of course. And I was stalling. He didn't push it. I finally collected myself and my nerves, and walked inside, feeling a little braver that Wade had my back.

Carmen's eyes were bloodshot, and I felt guilty for worrying her. Without warning, she threw her arms around me and hugged me tight. I stood there, dumbstruck. All the other times I'd run away and was brought back by the cops or out of hunger she'd simply sit me down and feed me. She had never cried to my face or hugged me. "I'm so sorry," she cried.

"It's not your fault," I whispered into her hair, feeling like the lousiest nephew on the planet.

"I shouldn't have let you go," she said. "I should've taken you home."

Home. It's been such a long time since I felt I was home. "But it's true," I blurted. She pushed me to arm's length, her hands squeezing my shoulder as if fearing I'd run if she let me go. That had crossed my mind. "It's true. What he said. I'm gay." My heart took that moment to shatter into bits and pieces. Fear took over every part of me and it took every strength I had not to run.

She cupped my face, her brown eyes so different from my mom's. Hers were more warm, kinder. "Xander," she said. "I love you. *You.* And everything that makes you, you."

I wanted to see the lie in her expression. Feel the lie in her words. But I didn't. My dad had been right, but it didn't make me less than a person. It hadn't given him the right to say the things he had said to me, to make me feel worthless.

Awww, X, I love you for who you are. You know that.

I did know that. Bea and Katie loved me to the moon and back.

Hearing the conversations I would never have with Bea in my head, knowing that I'd never get to know my little sister, Katie, made me crumble, and I couldn't stop the tears. I hid my face in my hands and sobbed. I hadn't realized how much I needed to let it all out. My shoulders shook, snot ran down my nose, and I felt about to burst, literally.

I didn't know whose hands were on me. Carmen or Wade's or both. I felt protected. A feeling I'd never felt before. A feeling I had craved for so long.

When I finally looked up, Wade was gone.

ELIZABETH ARROYO

CHAPTER 26

It'd been days since my breakdown and I hadn't heard from Wade. He hadn't been in school either and hadn't answered my texts. I even almost called him. Almost. Then the world really got tilted on its head. After school, Chad walked out with Piper, holding hands. Piper! Not Trini.

"She's a slut."

I turned to Trini beside me, my mouth opening and closing like a dying fish. She linked our arms and led me to her car, walking a lot straighter while ignoring the couple so that they knew she was ignoring them. "I left him before he started dating *her*, let's get that cleared up. He was a dick. You were right."

"Wha—"

"Whatever," she cut me off. "I have Wade news," she said, giving me whiplash. "Well, actually, Theo news that Wade gave him to give to me to give to you. That's how the grapevine works, apparently."

We reached her Jeep, and I quickly slipped inside. She looked way too small to be driving such a rugged thing. "What'd he say?"

She smirked. "Don't you have something you want to spill first?"

I pressed my lips together. "No," I said. "Maybe," I amended when she glared at me. "You're driving." Thankfully, that deterred the conversation for a few minutes until we reached Dogs. The place was buzzing with students but, thankfully, she didn't hop out to have this conversation in public.

"I thought we were friends."

"I know."

"I thought you liked me."

"I do like you." I threw my head back and pressed my palms against my dry eyes. Frustration settled smack dab in the middle of my shoulder blades. "Argh! I hate this. Feelings suck. Why do we have to have feelings?"

She laughed, warming up all my insides. "Comes with being human." I felt her poke my stomach. "Yeah, you're human. And you're in looo—"

I glared at her.

"—like, with Wade." She said that as if it were the best thing in the world. I still wasn't sure yet.

I lowered my hands, deciding to ignore that statement. "So what's the Wade news."

She scratched her nose as if trying to decide whether to wrench the truth from me. Thankfully, she didn't push it. "His mother pulled him out of school so he could concentrate on training. No technology. No phone. No friends."

"Just Theo," I blurted.

She smirked. "Is that jealousy? Are you and him—"

"No. We are not. And don't say anything, Trini. Please."

She snapped her lips together. "Not my place to say."

I believed her and trusted her to keep my secret.

The following day, I met with my school counselor, and we talked about college options. I didn't want to study art. I'd been starving for way too long. Starving as an adult and insanity did not appeal to me. The good news: I didn't have to select a major yet. She explained I could go into college as undecided and chose then. I had also applied to the Navy just in case I failed to get into a college. My schooling over the years had been untraditional at best. If I wanted to get into a decent school, I'd have to study my ass off and take the SATs again before I applied for colleges. Using Wade's tutoring schedule, I delved into it until my brain felt fried. I realized I had an aptitude for numbers. Expressing myself in words was a bit harder.

While I missed Wade, I had to keep my emotions in check. I was too volatile and a control freak. Every time Nick and Taylor mentioned Wade, I wanted to jump across the table and force Nick to take me to him.

Instead, I exhausted myself with schoolwork.

My final group session with Sage, Jack, and David went off without a hitch. We all got certificates signed and everything. "This doesn't mean you're done with individual therapy," Dr. Reyes explained.

Sage pouted. "Rain on my rainbow, why don't you."

Jack was the first to offer up his phone number, writing the digits on the whiteboard. He flushed as he spoke. "In case," he said, leaving it all hanging. In case we wanted to remain friends. David wrote his, I followed, and Sage wrote his with a flair and hearts and baby unicorns.

It felt bittersweet but safe to have their contact information.

The following week, my court date arrived. After Dr. Reyes testified to my sound mind, sort of, I was free. No more anchor of therapy or prison around my neck. The decision to continue with Dr. Reyes was mine and mine alone. I even thanked him after the hearing, and we went our separate ways.

Moe had started to reach out to Carmen, and I hated seeing her in pain. She worked all hours, and I could tell she was sadder than she let on because of the breakup. I tried to talk to her about it, but she told me she had already made her decision. It was the last straw, and she was tired of his violence when he drank and how he treated her. She was done. No going back. Kaput. Let it go. Then she broke out in Elsa's song, because why not. I sang with her, because if anyone knows anything it's that you don't let anyone sing Elsa's song alone.

The Christmas holiday came way too quickly this year.

"You should invite a friend," Carmen said as we were shopping for groceries.

I thought about my list of friends. The weirdos in therapy who I'm sure didn't want to be reminded of therapy. Adam, who I wasn't sure was really a friend. Wade and his group, which were more his friends than mine, and Trini. "I think Trini's doing something with her family."

Carmen nodded and looked away. "What about Wade? You haven't said much about him anymore."

"He's staying at his resort now. I don't drive."

"I can take you."

"It's two hours. One way."

She shrugged. "I can still take you."

"In snow. No. That's okay."

She didn't mention it again.

My phone buzzed when we got home.

Trini: Be ready in an hour. Going to Wade's Bash to celebrate. I got a place.

My stomach felt tied in knots thinking about seeing Wade.

Me: Can't. Sorry. Find some other nut.

I didn't want to see Wade. Not after his silent treatment and the way I was feeling.

Trini: Stop being a drama queen. I'll be there in the hour. Be. Ready.

I think I made a monster. Though it was nice seeing Trini stick up for herself.

An hour later, Trini arrived. I held her at the door. "I didn't pack. I'm not leaving my aunt. It's the Christmas holiday and she's alone."

Trini narrowed her eyes at me and almost bowled me over walking inside. "Hi, Mrs. Soto. How are you?"

They greeted each other with a kiss to the cheek.

"I'm fine, Trini. I'm glad you're here."

They both gave me matching evil grins. They knew each other better than I thought, and I suddenly felt as if I'd been played.

ELIZABETH ARROYO

CHAPTER 27

"I packed you a bag," Carmen said. "And you'll still be home for Christmas, so don't feel so bad."

"*Tramposas,*" I said, making her and Trini laugh.

"I don't know what that means, but it sounds horrible," Trini said.

I sprinted up to my bedroom and quickly scanned my room to see if Carmen forgot to pack something. I plucked my sketchpad and some drawing pencils and shoved them into my satchel.

I heard Trini downstairs talking to Carmen, as if they'd been friends forever. Trini didn't sneer at my small living space. She didn't turn her nose up at being offered some *pasteles* to eat later. She took it all in a grocery bag and Tupperware.

"You people are going to make me fat."

"A little meat doesn't hurt anyone," Carmen said. "Only the cow."

"I heard something about chopping up a cow?" I interrupted.

"Ew …" Trini said and playfully slapped my arm. "Now I have a visual."

"*Deja tu tontería, nene.*" Carmen sounded so much like

Mom at that moment. Only Mom had never called me *nene*. I liked the sound of it. I gave her a fat, sloppy kiss on the cheek and a hug.

"*Manejen con calma*. It's supposed to snow this week up there. If you need a ride back, call."

I felt a moment of panic at the mention of snow but nodded.

Carmen gave Trini a hug. "Please take care of him," she whispered into Trini's ear.

Yeah, my heart cracked a little bit.

"I will," Trini whispered back.

Then we were driving up the mountain on a Tuesday afternoon.

"You have a nice aunt," Trini said.

I did. "What happened to your family?"

She shrugged and kept her eyes on the road. "They tried to drag me to a family thing, but I told them I was going to hang out with Link." She gave me a mischievous smile that somehow didn't make her look all that mischievous.

"They let you get away with murder because you're too cute."

She snorted. "Well, I get to hang out with my BFF."

"Who? Piper?" I joked.

She snarled. "You do not want to mess with me while I'm driving."

No. I did not, so I stayed shut for most of the way.

Trini nudged me awake with a poke to my ribs, and I mumbled something like *blashmeer* before I said something coherent and opened my eyes to snow.

I couldn't see the cabin through the thick falling snow. *Shit. Shit. Shit.* We'd driven into the storm. The hazy clouds above us gave me no sense of time. I started to breathe hard as she stopped the car in front of a two-story cabin on the side of the mountain. We'd already made it. *Don't panic. Don't panic.*

"Xander, don't vomit in my car."

Thankfully, I didn't. I managed to push open the door

and tumble out on hands and knees and didn't spew, though I came close.

She turned off the truck, then walked to the front door. "Holy, shit. This is nicer than I thought." She unlocked the door and a security system before returning for me. "Hurry up before we freeze out here." She helped me pull our bags out of the trunk and I opened the door for us. The place was nice and warm. I didn't even know how to start a fireplace, and there was a huge one in the center of the loft-like living space.

The place was really nice.

"For some reason, when your aunt mentioned she got a cabin, I thought something like *Cabin in the Woods*."

"My aunt got this cabin?"

She shrugged. "I may have mentioned Wade's birthday party and she thought it'd be good for you to come. And she has a hook-up with Adam Brody—which you never told me you actually knew. But whatever. This is his cabin."

Okay, I wanted to hit the rewind on her. I didn't. I just let her play out. "Wait a minute. You thought *Cabin in the Woods* and still brought me here?"

She innocently shrugged. "I was desperate to get out of my house. Haven't you ever taken a risk for the possibility of an adventure?"

I rolled my eyes. "You'd be the first to die in a horror movie. I'm just saying."

She quickly perused the area and found a breaker box she used to turn on the lights and lift up the long shades covering the floor-to-ceiling windows that spanned the two levels. I felt so damn exposed.

"Not a lot of privacy, huh?"

She smiled. "It's one way. We see out, no one sees inside."

I had to admit, it was kind of cool.

"And if the owner of the place is smart—" She sprinted behind the kitchen area, and I heard a loud squeal. I ran to see her jumping up and down in glee, though I didn't feel the same.

Two snowmobiles were parked side by side in the garage. "Yes! No driving and no walking!"

I've never driven one of these. I'd never driven a car. "Do you need a license to drive one of these?"

"Good question. Just don't crash."

Right. I wanted to tell her if I did crash, it wouldn't be intentional, but I didn't want to snow on her parade.

CHAPTER 28

While I checked provisions—like food and water in case we were snowed in for the remainder of our stay, which seemed likely because like hell if I was going out in the snow, party or not—Trini spent the whole time on the phone. I caught some of the convo she had with Taylor. She talked about the cabin and Adam Brody with giggles. I almost rolled my eyes. I didn't want to shatter their hopes by telling them Adam played for the opposite team. My team. Like me. The thought made me smile like an idiot. They also talked about Wade's Olympic ski team, who apparently were at the party. I knew when the convo turned to Piper when Trini made a face.

I reheated the food Carmen gave us, trying to ignore her loud conversation, and started to eat.

She caught me looking at her and cupped her phone. "It's Taylor. She wants to know if we're going to go over for the party. Wade has a full house."

I cocked a brow. "Have you seen outside?" Okay, I never said I was brave.

"We can take the snowmobiles."

I cocked my head. "I don't drive."

"It's easy. I'll show you—all you have to do is follow

me."

I wanted to say no. But I also wanted to see Wade. Though I leaned more on the no. Then she put Taylor on speaker.

"Pllleeeeease," Taylor shouted on the phone. "I'll owe you forever."

Shit. "Fine."

They both squealed. I felt about to regurgitate Carmen's *pasteles* but swallowed them and chased them with some soda instead. I reconsidered my position as I started to put on my snow gear.

"It's dark," I said.

She searched through the garage and pulled out a couple of flashlights and handed me one. We checked to make sure they worked. I shoved mine in my coat pocket. She found helmets and goggles. "We're going to be fine," she said. "There's a lot of homes along this stretch of mountain, and we have less than a mile of mountain to trek to get to Wade's. I know this place like the back of my hand, so just follow me."

"Yeah, okay," I said.

She went through a crash course on the controls, on turns, and where I should keep my eyes: ahead and on the track she'd make for me. Then we were outside under the dark skies. The clouds gave the whole area an eerie green color.

"We're screwed," I whispered.

"We are not," I heard her in my ear and forgot we decided to keep communication through our phone. My earbuds under the helmet. "Just follow me and let me know if you lag behind, but don't lag behind."

We headed off.

The only thing I could see was the speck of our lights in front of me. Everywhere else was pitch black. I tried not to veer my eyes into the woods. Nothing to see anyway, why get creeped out? "Did I mention how you'd be the first to die in a horror movie," I said, my voice shaking.

"Yeah, and you'd be right behind me since you *are* right behind me."

Yeah. Which made me an idiot.

"Why do you hate snow so much?" she asked.

Snow killed my family. Thinking about it now as I rode on snow, I found that thought ridiculous. Snow wasn't a serial killer. Snow wasn't some enemy waiting for some unsuspecting asshole to end. Snow was snow. My father had been the one to kill my family. The snow was inconsequential. That thought didn't make it any better. "It's cold. I hate the cold."

She snorted. "Didn't you, like, live in Chicago? Hate to break it to you, but Chicago is cold."

I rolled my eyes and almost ran over a gnarled root. "How about we keep quiet and just get there, yeah?"

"Chickenshit."

I did not argue.

Just before my balls froze, we reached an area I recognized. We came out from the backyard of Wade's estate, the tall windows ahead lit bright and the house drummed with music. A party.

I did not want to be here.

I released the gas and let the thing coast to a stop. Trini got out of her mobile elegantly and pulled off her helmet, also elegantly.

She gave me her dazzling smile. "You'll thank me later."

I doubted it, but I wasn't getting back to the cabin alone. Not in full dark and with no sense of direction, so I followed her inside. I was sweating as I pulled off my winter gear in the mudroom. Thankfully, I had clean socks. I wasn't dressed for a party; I had my worn jeans and a black Metallica T-shirt I'd found in the lost and found at a previous school.

The house was packed with people. I recognized some faces from school, but others were strangers. Trini leaned into me and whispered in my ear, "Just be nice. Enjoy yourself. We'll head out in the morning." I wanted to be mad at her, but it was hard when she kissed my cheek and walked deeper into the house, heading toward the pool.

I'd never been to a party, not even a high school dance. I had never allowed myself to have friends. I'd been in recovery for my injuries in ninth grade. Tenth grade I'd been all about fighting anyone who looked at me wrong. And I'd spent eleventh grade at Boys Home. An oversimplification of my life. I couldn't stop wondering what the hell I was doing here. The thought exasperated when I headed toward the kitchen and caught the attention of most of the people standing along the way, including Piper with Chad. I didn't know Piper very well, but she definitely wasn't Trini. She was the opposite of Trini. Piper'd beat Chad's ass if he ever laid a hand on her. I caught her give Trini a look. The same look I had often given Wade when I saw him with Theo. A little bit jealous with a lot of interest. Okay, I wasn't going to try to even get into them waters. Nope. Trini ignored them both and disappeared in the crowd.

As I passed the living room, a group of people was cheering, watching highlights of the Olympics when Wade had won gold. I'd seen this reel over and over after he told me about his fear of faceplanting. I hadn't believed him at first. He'd been majestic on the halfpipe. Had almost flown in the sky, making it look so damn easy.

Then I remembered what he had said about how it would be dangerous for him to feel afraid as he performed, and I saw all the ways he could get hurt or die. I turned away from the TV and headed into the kitchen. I pulled a water bottle out of the cooler and eagerly drank it. I didn't plan on getting drunk. I was here to see Wade. To tell him how I felt about him. To just let this shit driving me mad go and see how it all fit. It stung that he hadn't reached out after he had front-row seats to my breakdown with Carmen and I told him about getting arrested, but I also knew Wade wasn't like me. He'd do what his parents expected of him, and that didn't include me. Fine. I would deal with that. Maybe I deserved it after sending him mixed signals about the kiss in the art room. I'd spent the weeks without him trudging through my revelation of being gay and liking him. I was trying to hold on to my sanity of graduating high school and going to college. I was trying to keep my shit together and burn through my anger through productive means, like art. All of that crashed when I saw Wade stumbling drunk, laughing, in Caleb's arms, as if ... as if they were together. I recognized Caleb Knight from the picture in the magazine.

I shouldn't have come. I'd been the idiot to believe in something I didn't deserve. I couldn't hide who I was from fate or God or the damn universe. I had promised myself when I woke up that night alone in the hospital that I would always follow my gut instinct. I would never succumb to peer pressure. I wouldn't be that kid, unable to stick up for his mother and sisters.

I learned to fight until I bled.

I learned to curve the appetite that longed for a deeper connection with someone. Someone I could tell all my darkest, deepest secrets to and who wouldn't judge me. Someone who saw me worthy of more than just ridicule and indifference.

I was a fool to think I could've found it with Wade.

His cheeks were blushed, his hair tousled, his pupils blown. High as a fucking kite. The guy behind him wrapped one arm around Wade's waist, pulling his back into his chest. A possessive move. A controlling move.

"Xander," Wade said in a brush of air.

"Who's this?" Caleb asked close to Wade's ear.

Wade made a move to pull away from the guy, but Caleb didn't release him. Wade shifted, as if blowing in a breeze. Too damn drunk to stand straight. "He's a friend," Wade slurred and smiled. "When did you get here?" he asked.

"Just now. Came with Trini."

His eyes lit up. "Right. You and Trini." He kept the smile on his face. I walked closer to him and everything about him seemed off.

"There is no me and Trini." Out of all the reactions I

had imagined when we finally spoke, this jealous coiled shit inside of me had not been it. But there it was.

Control freak.

"Who the fuck is this?" I was taller and bigger than the prick behind Wade.

"Excuse me?" The guy blanched.

Wade patted his hand. "It's okay, Caleb. We're just friends."

I couldn't tell if he meant he and Caleb were just friends or if he and I were just friends. Or both. Again, Wade tried to move away from Caleb, but he held Wade firm.

"Let him go." The warning in my voice was very clear.

"He'll fall on his face if I let him go," Caleb said and kissed the top of Wade's head, his eyes boring into mine. "Besides, he doesn't want me to let him go."

Wade blinked a few times and again licked his lips. Dehydration setting in from drinking too damn much. "I think you should let me go, Caleb. You already hurt me once." Wade attempted a forward motion, but Caleb didn't release him.

Caleb stiffened. "Let's go talk."

"You're not taking him anywhere. Let him the fuck go."

"Who do you think you are?"

I fisted my hands. I wasn't letting Wade go anywhere like this. "I am the guy who's about to fucking rip your tongue out of your mouth if you don't fucking let him go," I said it so low that the threat was potent enough to have him releasing Wade.

Wade stumbled and reached out for the counter. I reached to help him when a fist slammed into the side of my head. Bad move. I had a hard head. I managed to still catch Wade and move him away from the fight as I ducked the second blow and slammed into Caleb, tackling him into the hallway and to the floor. There was a crashing sound around us. A few shouts and screams. I landed two solid strikes before someone hauled me off of him. Theo shoved me back and pointed at Caleb. "Get out of here, or I'm calling the police."

I had expected Theo to tell *me* that, not the fucker with the busted lip. Caleb got to his feet and searched for Wade, who hadn't come out of the kitchen. "We're together," he said, forcing my blood to boil.

"The hell you are. Get. Out." Theo's point was made. Shivers coursed through my spine at Theo's threat, and he hadn't even made one.

"I'll call him later," Caleb said.

The fucker had to have the last say before he stormed out.

I turned to Theo for an explanation. Didn't get one. I was pretty sure Theo's expression mirrored my own, and I had to push that thought out of my head. We found Wade sitting on the floor, hugging his knees in the kitchen. "Why is he here? He shouldn't be here."

I opened my mouth and closed it, unsure what to do or say.

Theo turned to me. "He doesn't mean you. Help me carry him upstairs."

I didn't need Theo's help to carry Wade. I carried him myself as Theo cleared the way so I could take him to his room. Wade wrapped his arms around my neck, and I felt his breath on my skin. He was crying silently. Both Theo and I helped Wade out of his clothes and into pajamas. Then we tucked him into bed. Theo looked beside himself, ran his hand through his hair. "I didn't know he was even here," Theo said with a painful expression on his face.

Wade waved at him. "'Tis okay," he slurred. "I hate him."

I wanted to ask more about Caleb but didn't. "Go make sure no one destroys the house. I'll stay with him."

Theo nodded, handed me a lined garbage can, and walked out. Just then, Wade had started to spew. He almost missed the can, and I got splattered. Human waste, disgusting. I swallowed back the bile rising to my throat and pulled his hair back. When he was done, I helped him back to the bathroom—made sure he didn't fall in the toilet as he pissed and helped him brush his teeth.

Theo came back and covered his nose. "Ugh, it stinks."

"Take the trash with you."

Theo made a disgusting expression as he took the trash and left me some Pedialyte for Wade.

I helped Wade back into the bed and sat on the floor, my back against the bed frame. The room was silent with Wade in bed and my own thoughts scrambled. My intention of figuring this thing between Wade and me not going as planned. I knew from my dad that people were usually more honest when they were drunk. Alcohol lowered inhibitions. It was also a depressant, which explained Wade's crying. It hadn't been because he still liked Caleb. At least that's what I told myself.

"I'm sorry," Wade whispered.

I didn't want to look at him. Not the way I felt. "Who is he?"

I heard him wipe his nose. "My ex. I hate exes."

"Are you still in love with him?" I couldn't help it. I had to know. I couldn't play games with my jacked-up emotions. I wouldn't survive it.

The silence between us stretched too long. "That's not a fair question."

I snorted. *Fair! Fair! Was it fucking fair that you made me fall for you?* "Just go to sleep," I ordered, angry at him for being such a handful and angry at myself for expecting him to wait for me to figure out my life before hooking up with someone else.

"Well, stop asking me stupid questions."

I wanted to tell him that wasn't a stupid question. It was a fair question that would've put things in perspective for me. I said nothing. Just let the silence stretch.

"Why do you hate snow?" he asked.

I felt his fingers dig under my hair and touch the back of my neck. It calmed me. I was pretty sure he wouldn't remember any of this tomorrow. "The car accident that took my family had been in snow."

"I'm so sorry."

"Not your fault," I said back.

"Lay down with me?"

I turned my head slightly toward him and caught his eyes as he searched for something in my expression. I wanted to ask him what he saw, what he wanted. I would give him anything. *Anything*. But he didn't say anything. I got to my feet and fed him some Pedialyte before I pulled off my vomit-speckled shirt and dropped my pants to remain in my tight briefs. As he watched me, I slipped behind him under the covers and laid on my back, my hand on my stomach, staring at the pale ceiling. He remained curled on his side, his back to me. I didn't reach for him. A few moments later, I heard his deep breaths and soft snores.

I'd fallen for a guy who didn't give a shit about me. A guy still crushing on his ex. And that Wade was the only guy to bring me to this point made everything one big damn joke.

Did Wade prefer Caleb?

Doesn't matter, Xander. You are out of his league. Wade deserves someone like Theo.

Anyone but you.

I silently prayed that I wouldn't dream as I felt my body fold in on itself and drifted into sleep.

CHAPTER 29

Night terrors were different from nightmares. In night terrors the dreamer knew it was a dream but couldn't wake up. It felt like a breaking point in reality. It felt so real, and it was usually terrifying. The dream that accosted me during the night hadn't been terrifying, but it had felt real. My pounding heart rushed oxygen to all parts of my body, inflating my dick to a painful erection. I smelled mint and soap, and then soft warm lips pressed against my mouth. The kiss exploratory before it became something deep and desperate. A need so great broke from me that I didn't know where I began or ended.

Wade. I knew it was him even without opening my eyes. I'd dreamt of him before; this dream was so much better. I felt the soft strands of his hair under my fingertips. His leg over my hips as his hand ran down my chest, my stomach, and lower to cup me. I jerked into his hand, needing to feel more. More of his mouth on me, more of his scent on me, more of his skin against mine. I didn't know what I wanted, what I needed. I just knew I needed *more*. So much more.

I felt his teeth nip my lip and I moaned. The sound so loud to my own ears. Then I spun on top of him. He spread his legs open, and I felt his hardness against my own as I rubbed against him. The friction felt so damn good. The feel of his heated skin, his tongue and mouth on mine felt so damn real.

Real.

I blinked open my eyes and blinked again. Wade under me. His beautiful eyes half-lidded, pupils blown, a hungry expression on his face. His lips swollen and damp, parted as he moaned. His hands trailing up and down my bare back.

"Is this real?" The moment those words left my mouth I knew the answer.

Every cell in my body paused and his eyes widened, and I saw regret there. So much regret.

This *was* real. "Fuck." I jumped to my feet as if he were on fire. My body coiled tight. *Oh God, did I take advantage of him?* I cupped my lips as he watched me pace, confusion and regret bounced back at me. He quickly sat up.

"Oh God, Xander, I thought we ..." He jumped off the bed as if burned by it, too, and pointed to the bed. "You woke up next to me, and I thought we already ... I thought this was okay. I couldn't remember."

Fuck! I wanted to roar. I bolted to the bathroom and slammed the door, only able to breathe when I wasn't so close to him. I palmed the door and leaned my forehead against the cool wood. My heart wouldn't stop galloping in my chest. I hadn't wanted it to go this way. Wade drunk. Not knowing what he was doing. Using me as seconds!

I punched the door hard enough to leave an indentation, and pain zipped up my arm. My knuckles bruised. Then I turned to the sink and ran the water. My dick still hard. My body cried out for the guy's touch. I washed my face and my hands, allowing myself time to calm the fuck down. This was what I wanted. This was what I came for. But after Caleb, after Wade drunk, I hadn't wanted it to go this way. I had no clue what I was doing. I preferred to stay in the bathroom forever, but instead, I walked out, not knowing what I was going to do now.

Wade had been sitting at the edge of the bed and he

jumped to his feet when he saw me. His hair tousled, lips swollen. So damn beautiful. "I'm sorry. It was totally—"

I didn't let him finish. Before I could think of how fucked up everything would get, I invaded his space, cupped the back of his neck, and smashed my mouth against his. He stiffened for a moment, and I expected him to push me away. He didn't.

He opened his mouth to me. Our tongues warred for control. I nipped his lips, retreated and repositioned, then took him harder, faster, deeper. His hands lowered to my ass and pressed me against his body. Shorter than me, I felt his erection on my hip. I wanted to feel it somewhere else. I wanted to finish what we started.

My hands reached under his tee and I pulled it up and over his head.

"Xander," he started.

"Shut up," I responded and fused our lips again. I didn't want to talk. I didn't want to think. I wanted this. Wanted him. Somehow, we made it to the bed. We undressed and he was on top of me, grinding me, taking control. We were fused. A tangle of limbs and kisses. My own life floated out of existence. Everything else didn't matter. Everything else turned to background noise. The world at the edge of my peripherals. Inconsequential. Only Wade mattered at this moment.

He broke us apart and reached over, grabbing something from his side table. Then his hands were on me again. I felt the condom in my hand, rolled it on as he continued to dominate my mouth. Lube came next as he touched me in ways I'd never been touched. Made me feel things I'd never felt. I became a sensory pit. All my nerve endings firing at once. On the tinkering slope of pain and pleasure. Trumpets roared. Fireworks exploded. I was in total bliss. It crested and slammed into me like a wave, leaving me drowning and breathless until I surfaced, gasping.

I threw my arms around his neck, pulling him into me tight as I trembled from the intensity of it, unable to move, feeling the rapid beat of his heart against my own. His breath on my neck where he whispered words of passion, words that helped me draw back into myself. He patiently held me as my body came down from the high he'd just put me through.

I didn't want to let him go, but I didn't know what to do next. He gently pulled out of my almost chokehold, and I thought he was going to get out of bed and leave my ass, but he curled against me. I pulled him in closer to me, his head on my shoulder, our legs tangled as he ran his hand up and down the scars on my left side.

Wade knew what to do, and I had so many questions swirling through my head. My sexuality was no longer in question. I *was* gay. And I wanted to know what he liked. What I should do, how I could make him come totally undone the way he was making me. I wanted to see the lust in his expression, the want of me in his face. I wanted to control him. Make him beg for me. I wondered if someone could fall in love this fast, or was it just the pheromones?

"That was unexpected," he said, breaking me from my thoughts.

His eyes were lighter now, his hair rumbled, his lips swollen from kissing so much, and I placed a soft kiss on the small mole on his cheek. "Really? That's the word you came up with for what just happened?"

"Well, mind-blowing sex doesn't seem to cut it."

Mind-blowing sex. Did I just have sex with Wade Wilson? *Duh, asshole.* "Was that … okay? I mean." Shit, I didn't know what I meant. "Did I hurt you?"

Wade chuckled beside me. "No, you didn't hurt me, and yeah, I think that was better than okay." He propped himself up on his elbow to look at me. "Why are you talking as if you've never done this before?"

I felt my cheeks heat up. "I've never done this before," I said.

"With a guy?" Wade's hopeful expression was adorable.

"Uh-huh," I answered. "Or with a girl."

If I had a camera, I totally would've memed his expression right now. That moment you realize you banged a virgin. "Xander, I didn't know." His babbling was cute, but he was making me blush even more. "Was it okay? I mean, shit. I thought … I mean, you are gorgeous. I don't—" I couldn't take any more of it. I cupped his face and pulled him to my mouth, cutting off his words with a kiss that turned deeper and slower until we stopped kissing. Exhausted, he fell back into my arm. "I should've been more careful," he said.

The concern in his voice warmed my heart. "It was perfect. Not that I have anything to compare it to." He poked my side, making me giggle like an idiot.

I wanted to ask what happens now but didn't want to ruin it.

"I'm sorry about brushing you off these past weeks. My mom is evil incarnate." He yawned, sleep dragging him under.

"I'm sorry too," I said. "I should've kissed you in the art room."

I waited for his response, but it never came. His breathing deepened and a soft snore escaped his lips. I kissed the top of his head and willed myself not to think about morning.

We lay in a tangle of limbs. The bed all kinds of wet at our backs. Sex was messy as hell. The scent of musk and sweat mixed with soap in the air. My brain fried. I pulled out the condom, tied it, and tossed it into the trash near the bed. Then I crashed. Too tired to move. I had no night terrors, and I woke up alone with a note on Wade's pillow.

Went snowboarding. You are still not allowed on my mountain. I'll see you later.
—Wade

I slid out of bed with a cheesy smile on my face. I showered and wrapped my hips with a towel and gathered my clothes. Yeah, vomit. I headed toward the laundry room. The cleaning crew was already cleaning up the party left behind. One of the women smiled at me as if she knew what Wade and I had done this morning. I blushed, slipping into the laundry room. I shoved my clothes into the machine to wash. Twenty minutes later, I shoved the clothes into the dryer. That's when I heard the front door.

"Mrs. Wilson," one of the maids said. "We are almost finished."

"Oh, that's okay, Maria. How is my son?"

"He's already on the slopes."

"Of course he is," she said. Her voice was too high, too snotty. I couldn't believe she'd raised such a beautiful, kind person.

I heard some dishes rattling and waited for my moment to escape back to Wade's room. Hearing nothing for five minutes, I opened the door and slipped out into the hallway. I just had to sprint upstairs and lock myself in Wade's room until he returned. Good plan. Be silent. I sprinted, almost made it to the stairs when a door opened, and I slammed right into it. I fell on my ass and then heard a scream that pierced through my eardrum just as I passed out.

I woke up to the cops putting me in handcuffs and shoving me in nothing but a towel into the back of a squad car.

My fucking luck.

CHAPTER 30

I felt cold. A mind-numbing, dick-shriveling cold. I couldn't stop my teeth from chattering despite the car's heater set on melting. Mrs. Wilson reported that I had attacked her. The maid I'd seen earlier mouthed *lo siento* to me. She didn't want to risk her job, confirming what I already told the cops. I'd been invited to the house. Wade let me stay. I was a guest. It fell on deaf ears. I was the vagrant in this situation. My legal status was questioned despite me telling them that I was Puerto Rican. To white folks, we were all the same. Gum stuck in their shoes. I didn't even have the energy to fight.

Three squad cars sat in the driveway, including the sheriff. I remembered the last time I'd been arrested. When I'd been assaulted, and the cops had arrested me. *Me.*

My luck hadn't changed.

Trini appeared on the snowmobile with Wade behind her. I didn't want to look at them as they sprinted toward me. All I needed was to see Wade's expression when his mom told him I assaulted her. I didn't want to see the anger in his eyes when he believed her. Trini argued with the cop near the car. They knew each other.

"Rickman, he is a guest. Wade invited him."

More chaos ensued when Mrs. Wilson met Wade in the driveway, sobbing. A good actress. She should win an Academy Award.

"Mom, he is my friend," Wade said.

That hurt. I had stupidly thought we were more than friends, considering how we spent early this morning. Idiot didn't begin to define how I felt.

"I invited him. He stayed over."

"Mrs. Wilson, he's a friend of Adam Brody. We're staying at the Brody cabin," Trini chimed in. "He was here before. Don't you remember?"

She did remember. The reason I was sitting in the squad car. But the mention of Adam made her think twice until recognition finally slammed into her and she cupped her mouth. An Emmy. She should win an Emmy for dramatic effort. The sheriff, a tall thin guy, seemed less than happy.

"Mrs. Wilson, was this a mistake?"

I held my breath. My life in the hands of a drama queen.

"Mom, please."

I heard the desperation in Wade's voice. He still hadn't acknowledged me as anything but a friend.

"Perhaps I misjudged the young man."

The sheriff rolled his eyes, as if this wasn't the first time she'd misjudged someone. Rickman pulled me out of the car. My bare feet already numb from the cold pressed into the snow. The guy shoved me around and released my cuffs just as Wade wrapped me in his coat and glared at Rickman.

"Asshole," Wade said to the young cop. "You could've at least let him dress."

"Not my job, Mr. Wilson."

I really wanted to punch the fucker. Thankfully, Wade held me tighter and led me back into the house. Wade's kindness was like a double-edged sword. Once he let me go, I headed straight to the mudroom, intending to get out as quickly as I could. I didn't bother to get my clothes out of the dryer. I pulled on my snow pants bare underneath. Shoved my feet into my boots with no socks and threw on my coat, hat, and gloves. I heard Wade and his mother arguing.

"What is he even doing here?" she chided. "And where is Caleb?"

"*You* invited Caleb?"

"Of course I did. You've been nothing but a ruined mess since he left you. Evidenced by your bad performance on the snow. He was good for your career, and now he's out and interested."

The silence that followed tore through my heart. Of course Wade was considering it. The love of his life. "I don't want Caleb," he finally said, less than convincing.

"Well, I won't allow you to throw your career away over a violent travesty of a boy you find cute today only to discard later."

I rubbed my chest at the pain there.

Idiot. I was a one-night stand. Nothing more.

It was good while it lasted.

For five damn minutes.

I didn't want to hear any more. I rushed out, found Trini, and ordered her to take me back. We made it somewhere between here and there in the middle of nowhere when I pitched to the side, forcing her to stop. I couldn't hold back the sobs that tore through my body. The tears that burned trails down my cheeks. If I had anything in my stomach, I knew I would've thrown it up, too, but I didn't, so I dry heaved. I felt *used*. Dirty. A discarded piece of shit who deserved nothing better.

Trini dropped on her knees beside me and hugged me. I wished she were Wade. No, I wished I were someone else. Anyone else. Someone who hadn't allowed a kiss to give him hope. Someone who hadn't wanted more of life. Someone who deserved kindness. I wasn't that person. I would never be that person.

After a few self-deprecating moments, I lifted myself to my feet and we started riding again. When we arrived at the cabin, Taylor and Nick were already waiting for us in the second snowmobile. Without a glance their way, I sprinted inside and into my room, slamming the door behind me. I needed to be contained. Away from everyone. I rushed into the attached bathroom and dropped inside the bathtub, clothes and all. I hugged my knees and tried to condense myself into a speck of nothing and closed my eyes. So damn tired. I felt the heavy weight of my body drift away.

"You can't hide in the bathtub," Beatrice said.

"Why not? The bathtub is the safest place to be in a tornado," I responded.

"This isn't a tornado."

A loud crash exploded in the next room. Beatrice smoothened out the towel she had on her lap. "Sorry, X, but I have to hide the knives." She reached forward and pulled out a knife from my chest. Pain exploded through me, and I shoved my fist in my mouth to keep the scream from tearing out.

"Shhh, they'll hear you." She pulled out another, then another, and placed the bloody knives in the towel. She slowly rolled the blood-soaked towel with the knives. "I'll keep them safe so no one hurts you," she said. "That's what family does. We keep each other safe."

I jolted awake.

My breath stuck in my throat as I patted my chest, searching for the knives still embedded there. "Not real. Not real."

A dream.

I rolled out of the tub and sat against the wall, willing myself to calm. To remember my time and place. To imagine something good. I thought about Carmen and the way she called me *nene*. Good. I was good. I anchored myself to that until my breathing eased. I took a few more moments before I undressed and showered until the dream faded.

I had one moment of weakness with Wade. It couldn't happen again. I had six more months before I got the rest of the blood money. Six months before I graduated and got out of town. I was going to go to college. Somewhere as far from California as I could get. New York, maybe. High school would be forgotten. People left behind. The only hope I had to starting over.

CHAPTER 31

I decided to leave before any more shit came my way.

If Trini didn't take me back, I planned on calling Carmen.

Man up, bro.

I really had to take my sister's advice on that one. So what if my first time ended up being with a rich, arrogant prick who still hung off his mother in a vice grip? I'd finally lunged into a different stage in my life. No longer curious about my sexuality. Cross that one off my bucket list. So why did I feel like shit? Why did I feel used and in need of a scalding shower and ice cream?

Growling, I shoved the last of my things into the bag and dropped onto my bed. I plucked my boot off the floor and shoved my feet into it, trying not to think about this morning. I'd lost all sense and control. Gave it willingly to Wade. And the fucker hadn't had the decency to even be there when I woke up. Left me to go ski on a mountain. Left me to face his mother alone.

The conversation I'd overheard played in my mind. She had wanted Wade with Caleb, the drunk fucker handing off Wade at the party. The asshole who had broken Wade's heart. While I was just a boy toy. The thought of those words—*boy toy*—forced me to grind my teeth. Had I been an intermission for Wade? A prelude to the main course? I felt sick.

I'd learned to bottle up all my feelings during my stay at Boys Home. I had built a safe space in my head that I could go to whenever I was at risk of being hurt. A place no one could touch. I had slowly created it. Four walls, thick windowpanes overlooking the Falls. The only real good memory of my family had been on that spontaneous trip to Canada after my dad's drunken stupor.

I imagined the sound of crashing waters. The feel of cool mist on my face. And Bea's giggling as she skipped around me singing one of her made-up songs about me going over the falls in a barrel. Katie strapped into her stroller, laughing, too, while my mom and dad held hands as if they were in love. An echo of that memory. A tableau I kept inside my heart where no one could touch it. My safe space no one could take from me.

I kept myself locked in that room. Didn't allow any other emotion to well up and spill out of me. I sighed, hoping the great curtain walls I'd built around my heart would hold.

I heard heavy footsteps out in the hallway, then a knock on the door. "Xander," Wade said. "Please let me in."

Just the sound of his voice cracked my resolve, forced me to swallow the wedge in my throat. This wasn't something I could just ignore. I couldn't run away from myself, although I had tried.

He may have inserted himself inside my heart, but it didn't mean I had no control. Actions and emotions were two different spheres in my universe. My dad taught me the two faces of the serpent. One—the sober, kind one who would take us to the movies and on spontaneous trips. The other, a red-eyed demon who beat my mom and hated us. Of his blood, I should be able to do the same. Shove those emotions I had for Wade into a closet behind my curtain wall and never let anyone see them.

I got up, unlocked the door, and returned to the bed,

shoving my foot into my other boot as Wade took a hint that I wasn't going to open the door for him and let himself inside. I almost peeled out of my skin as I caught his glimmering light blue eyes. His platinum blond hair longer in the front fell across his eyes, and he flicked his head to look at me, then to the bag on the bed. He wore dark denim jeans, a knit turtleneck that hugged his broad chest and narrow waist, and boots that were unlaced. I gave him a quick once-over before paying attention to my bootstrings. Looking away from him gave me more willpower to not slam him against the door and kiss him.

He leaned against the door and watched as I finished tying my boot and stood up, wiping my hands on my thighs. "What?" I snapped with pure venom behind the word. "Came to stare at the brown boy?"

He sighed. His eyes never leaving mine held the apology I did not want to hear but had to anyway. "I'm sorry."

"For which part," I snapped. So much for not letting him inside my safe space. Anger, I could deal with. I could lead him into anger as easily as I could shove him against that door and toss his ass out. "The kiss? The fuck? What exactly are you sorry for, Wade?"

"You're upset."

The fact that he said that so damn calmly got me riled up. Hell yeah, I was upset. I was livid. I snorted. "I'm not upset. I'm pissed." He took a step closer to me and on instinct I took a step back. I wasn't sure if I could hold up the walls if he touched me. I already felt them cracking and letting the floodwaters in. "Don't," I warned.

"She's my mother."

As if that made everything she did okay. I knew about deadbeat mothers too. Mine had allowed us to be tortured by my dad. "So what are you doing here? Go be the good little boy and call Caleb like she wants you to. Keep risking yourself on that damn mountain because it's what she wants. Do you even know what the hell it is *you* want, Wade?"

He clenched his jaw, grinding his teeth. Didn't need experience to know there were still some feelings for his ex there.

"Look, Wade," I started before he spoke. "I don't need this shit right now." I had to end this before I drowned. "Thanks for the fuck. Really clarified some shit for me. Now we can move on." I should shut up, but I wasn't that smart. "Besides, you made it very clear that we're just *friends*. Hell, you didn't even bother to wake up with me. Left me a damn note." Okay, that last part sounded angrier than I intended.

Again, his expression turned into one of regret. Yeah, he looked as sorry as a model who'd gotten into the cookie jar. "Are you done?"

I wanted to knock something. Not him. I could never hurt him. "Yeah," I said. "*We're* done."

Before he could open his mouth, I flanked him and rushed out. I heard him call me to stop, but I didn't listen. Moving kept me sane. Moving away from him kept me from doing something I'd regret—like cry. Again.

"I'm not done talking to you," he said behind me.

I took the stairs to the lower level, where the TV had suddenly silenced, and started for the kitchen. I needed to keep my distance, and the counter between us would work just fine. I felt a plastic cup hit me in the back of my head and I turned around.

"Would you stop running for one minute!"

I shoved my fists under the opposite armpit just so I wouldn't start swinging. It was getting really hard to think happy thoughts right now. "Talk then. Say your fucking peace so you can get out."

"I'm sorry about my mother. I'm sorry I wasn't there when you woke up." He moved forward, and I moved back, cursing when I hit the countertop with my ass. Pinned down like a damn prey. "You want to know what I want? I want to be with *you*. I want to end my snowboarding career with one last ride. I want to get away from here and go to college. Is that good enough for *you*?"

No fucking way. Don't believe him. Keep that wall up or you are going to drown in all his bullshit.

We were standing toe to toe now. That damn mole he had on his cheek so damn endearing. It made me realize he wasn't a perfectly enhanced bot the way I had seen him in Dr. Newman's office the first day we met. No. Wade Wilson had imperfections like all of us. "I didn't tell my mother about us because I wasn't sure it's what you'd want. The risk of us being paraded in the media is high, and I can't make that decision for you."

Shit. I hadn't thought about all that. I wasn't even sure what I wanted yet. And he had thought this through. Thought about *me*.

Yeah, that fucking wall was about to be disintegrated until someone opened the front door and walked inside. Adam stomped on the mat near the front door before lifting his eyes to the room, catching sight of me. I exhaled a relieved breath.

Saved.

The first thought that came to my mind was that Adam was saving me from whatever I was about to tell Wade.

Adam pulled back his hood and dark shaggy hair fell in curls around his face. The guy was beautiful. No denying that. I realized then that we had an audience. Trini, Nick, Theo, Taylor, and Piper were spread around the living room, watching us with fascination, as if we were a documentary.

"Wade," Adam greeted, his voice deeper than I remembered.

"Adam," Wade said back.

Okay, so they knew each other. Why did that make me feel a helluva lot uncomfortable?

I didn't know what prompted the visit, but I suspected it had something to do with the sheriff verifying Trini's story and that I hadn't actually broken into his cabin.

Adam was only three years older than me. I considered that when I allowed myself to check him out, earning a curious glare from Wade, who hadn't moved from my personal space. I finally squeezed past Wade, feeling his eyes like daggers behind my head as I approached Adam.

Adam gave me a warm smile that highlighted his whole face. I wasn't sure what I intended to do when I got close to him. Fist bump, handshake, but Adam took control and drew me into a hug that lasted longer than I thought necessary. He cupped the back of my neck as if relieved. "Get me out of here," I whispered into his ear. A desperate plea that sounded pathetic even to me.

Thankfully, Adam didn't need coaxing. "You ready to head out?"

I ignored Wade's almost growl and sought out Trini. I hadn't talked to her since my meltdown on the snow. I hoped she wouldn't say anything.

"I'm heading out," I said, as if that wasn't so obvious.

Trini cocked her head in a way that spoke volumes on how she was not happy at my cowardice. I didn't care. I knew where I fit in, and it wasn't here. Not with them or Wade. She crossed her arms and glowered. "I thought you were staying the week."

"Change of plans. I'm uh …" I made the mistake of sliding my eyes to Wade, whose eyes had turned darker, though his features revealed nothing. Or at least not some emotion I could pick out.

"He'll be with me," Adam said. "Make sure you lock up when you leave," he told Trini. Then to me, "I'll wait for you in the car."

Right. My bag.

I sprinted back upstairs, plucked it where I left it on the bed, and turned back to the door to almost slam into Wade.

Those damn light blue eyes of his practically colorless felt like shards of glass digging into my skin. The best arsenal I had against people was indifference. I would play the part I'd been playing since I woke up from the hospital, since I learned my family was dead and they left me behind. I shoved all that pain to the back of my heart and acted as if I didn't give a shit that I was slowly dying inch by inch. A piece of my insides tearing from my soul. I needed to take control.

"You're just going to leave? With *him?*"

An ache in my chest clued me into how much I needed to run far away from Wade and never look back. It felt as if we were breaking up, and we were never in a relationship to begin with.

"I don't belong here," I said because I was an idiot. "This is your world, not mine." I started to flank him, but he grabbed my arm, and I stopped just inches from him. He leaned into my ear.

"Don't go."

My heart thudded against my chest. "Why should I stay? You said you want to be with me, but what does that even mean?" I wanted Wade to define us because I sure as hell couldn't find the term that fit us right now. He pulled back. A ghost of sadness flashed through his expression. It tore at my already edgy nerves. Wade deserved someone who could be what he needed. Anyone that wasn't me.

"I don't know," he said dryly.

With my bag in hand, I sprinted down the steps. I shoved myself into my puffer coat and slipped outside. Already dark with the world spread out in fresh snow, I ignored my heightened sense of mortality and dumped my bag into the trunk before settling beside Adam.

The guy had turned two shades paler while waiting for me. "Just drive slow and careful. If we have to wait out the storm in a hotel, then we'll do that, okay?" Adam told Bubbles.

"Of course. We'll be fine."

The SUV started to move, and Adam clutched my hand while I knuckle-gripped the door handle. "I hate this place," Adam breathed out.

I hated the snow, too, but my hero complex settled into providing Adam comfort. The focus of it allowed me to ignore the powder and the ice that could have us careening over the side of the mountain to our death on our descent. I decided to try my luck at deflecting with conversation. "Let me guess, you got a call from the County Sheriff's office today."

The dark interior of the car didn't allow me to see his expression, but I could sense his rising temper. It almost felt as if he really wanted to protect me. I'd never had anyone protecting me before. I didn't know what to do with that thought.

"I wasn't too far when he called to verify your stay at the cabin," he snorted. "The shit we do for people we care about, huh?"

My chest tightened at those words. Something inside me seemed to melt then harden when I strengthened the walls I'd erected to keep me safe from feelings a long time ago. I wasn't going to try to chip away at his wall. Hell, I needed mine to survive.

Weren't we a pair?

"What did the good sheriff tell you?"

"Wanted to verify that I let you stay at the cabin and you didn't break in. I didn't know it was against Mrs. Wilson." He said her name with clear distaste. "You should tread carefully with the Wilson family, Xander. Please don't tell me it's Wade you're crushing on."

I suddenly felt the need to jump out of the moving car. "I'm not crushing on anyone," I lied. By the look he framed my way, I knew he knew I was lying. "I got it handled."

"Victoria Wilson is a bitch of epic proportions, and Wade is her toy. She'll make your life a living hell. You just experienced a fraction of what she could do to you. Lies to get her way. Who the hell do you think the cops will believe?"

"I get it."

"Do you?" Adam snapped.

"Yeah," I shouted. "I get it."

He sighed and turned to look out the window. "People like us don't get an easy out just because we fall in love.

We've seen too much shit, experienced too much shit. And that stain stays with you, Xander. Always." I hated not being able to see his face, but I knew exactly what he was talking about. "You deserve better," he added as an afterthought. A lingering silence stretched between us, and I wanted to ask him what he meant but knew I wasn't ready to hear whatever he had to say. "You're still young. You have your whole life ahead of you. Don't mess it up."

And that was what I didn't want to hear him say. I didn't feel young. I'd been through too much to ever be young again.

We drove in silence in our own personal hell the rest of the way down the mountain.

CHAPTER 32

"Come on. We don't want to be late for the *pasteles*."

Puerto Rican *pasteles,* a must-have during Christmas in our household. Beatrice had almost been disowned the day she said she didn't like the dish. She had the nerve to saturate it in ketchup to eat it. I still had nightmares. And Katie was too young to appreciate it.

Carmen had convinced me to spend Christmas with the family. Since I had ejected myself from Wade's friendship pool, I wasn't feeling it. It didn't matter though. I couldn't say no to Carmen.

"I just want you to try, Xander, okay?" she admitted in the car.

I've been avoiding the *try* since I came to live with her. I hadn't tried during the *quince*. Instead, I had remained in the shadows, avoiding everyone. That would be difficult to do in a small house. So I pushed out all the bad thoughts I had of spending one dinner a year with the family who abandoned us in Chicago.

"I have to make a pit stop," Carmen said as she slid into the local grocery mart and found a vacant spot. I followed her inside, taking advantage and shopping for anything easily edible I could cook during the week. Since Moe left,

Carmen had started working longer evening hours, leaving me to fend for myself when it came to food.

Can't go wrong with ramen.

I shoved a few of those in my cart. Then I got a couple of water-flavored powders because anything tasted better than tap water.

I started to head toward the registers to look for Carmen when a familiar voice drew me out of my slump. I pulled back and peeked around an aisle to see a young couple. The girl was short. Straight blonde hair spilled out of her beanie. She was laughing and tiptoed to catch the lips of the guy beside her. The one I'd been thinking about endlessly since I left Boys Home and left him behind. Carmen had told me that his parents had taken him out after he'd completed the program six weeks later. I could never forget the thin scrawny kid with the wide green eyes and equally bright smile that had been my roommate for eight months. Jace had been at Boys Home three months before me and had taken me under his wing. Well, he showed me around and tutored me in school while I protected him from bullies. I was good with that. It satisfied my hero complex. But I couldn't protect him from what they did to him there. He hadn't been in like me, for committing a crime. He'd been there for being gay.

After only six months, this guy had grown a few inches and had packed a few pounds of muscle. I panicked, didn't want to interrupt him sucking faces with the girl, and turned to bolt. Except the world laughed at me. At that moment, a cart had peeked into the main aisle. I swung a sharp left to avoid it and rammed into the shelf of packaged spaghetti and the shit tumbled to the floor. *Shit. Shit. Shit.* I quickly started to scoop them up and shove them into the shelf when I heard a deep laugh behind me.

"Hey, buddy," Jace said. His voice too had deepened. I always knew he'd eventually pass puberty. I just hadn't known that he would fill to capacity. We had joked about it. But seeing him, being this near to him, I suddenly didn't know what to do. He helped me put the packages back, and we both got to our feet at the same time. I was still taller than him, but I hadn't changed much, evidenced by the shocked expression on his face when he finally looked at me. The last time I saw Jace he'd been lying on his side, his back to me, as I apologized for leaving him. He hadn't cried that night or anything, but I had managed to catch a look in his eyes, and they were blank. All the light had been stripped from them, leaving behind something dark and cold.

"Xander?" he whispered. His voice lower, softer, the voice I remembered.

The fact that he whispered my name as if I were a bad secret that came to haunt him made me stiffen. I didn't say his name back, unsure if I should at this point. Looking at him now broke my heart. I remembered the countless hours spent with him as he sobbed about how his parents expected him to be a mirror image of his dead older brother. The one who had been in law school, dating the most beautiful girl on the planet, making future plans to follow in his dad's footsteps before he died in a car accident. Jace was a musician, got mediocre grades, and liked boys, not girls. I knew he'd been broken in Boys Home after what they did to him. He'd been a wild spirit at one time. Had been adamant about keeping his soul intact. He'd been sweet and resilient for a sixteen-year-old kid who had been tossed away by the people that should've protected him. Should've accepted and loved him for being himself. Now, I saw a stranger whose smile did not reach his eyes, and I wanted to run away from him. To burn the image and the memories out of my retinas.

"Jace?" the girl said watching us, oblivious of the silent scream radiating from Jace just inches beside her.

Jace seemed to come to attention, as if he'd been electrically charged to respond. "Celeste, sorry, this is—" He let the lack of knowing my name hang, which hurt more than looking at his sad eyes.

"Xander," I said without reaching to shake her hand. I

didn't want to touch her.

"Right, Xander was a student at Morrison," he lied. The deadpan way he did it made me think he'd been practiced at lying. All of this shit made me uneasy.

"Oh." She smiled. "Are you here with your family?"

"Uh, no," I said before I thought of Carmen. I'd been used to being alone for so long that I forgot I had family now. I didn't correct myself though. I stupidly looked into my cart where I had stacked the ramen. It looked pathetic.

"Oh," she said as if that were a blasphemy of epic proportion. She seemed nice, but then they all were when they thought you were prey. "Why don't you join us?"

I looked quickly at Jace's dire expression. Sweat had broken out on his temple. A sure sign that the kid was raging inside. "Uh, no, that's okay. I have plans."

"With ramen?" she asked with a snort. And there it was. The underlying judgment of everything that was not her.

"Yeah, better company," I said.

She scowled and Jace jumped to attention again. "Well," he said. "It was so good seeing you again."

Then he did something I didn't expect. He hugged me. I felt a slight tremble course through his body for a moment, and my hero complex compelled me to kidnap him and run away with him. To protect him. But before I could even whisper some code word into his ear, he pulled away.

"I'll talk to you later," he said quickly and wrapped an arm around Celeste's shoulder, then led her away.

It wasn't until his back was to me that I realized he hadn't even asked for my phone number. I swallowed the wedge in my throat before tears rushed out of me, and headed straight to the register, where I found Carmen. She gave me a *what's wrong* look I shook away. I just wanted to get out of there.

"I'll meet you at the car," I mumbled and left her the cart before heading outside.

I couldn't get Jace out of my mind. I didn't want to be him. I didn't want to be fake and controlled. I didn't want to be alone, pushing the people in my life away because I was afraid to be happy. Undeserving of it.

My heart shattered into millions of pieces, and I heard Carmen's voice. *Just try.* For my own sanity, I had to do just that. *Try.*

The last time I'd seen my maternal grandmother before my family's funeral, I'd been three years old. And the story that became legend, and repeatedly told by my dad, was the story of how I clogged up Grandma's toilet. I'd apparently been on the cusp of toilet training and had ventured to clean my own butt. Except that I had used the entire toilet roll and clogged up the toilet. They had to get a plumber out to fix it. That wasn't the embarrassing part. No, the embarrassing part is how proud my three-year-old innocent self had been at that moment. I had declared to the whole family, *"¡Abuelita, me limpie el culito solito!"* I had proclaimed to clean my own ass.

I couldn't help but smile thinking about how Dad told the story over and over. It seemed to have been one of the proudest moments he had of me. Probably the only one.

Carmen squeezed my hand. "They love you, Xander. They're family."

I still didn't believe family had some sort of strict policy of loving each other. My dad ended up hating me. Hating all of us.

Nope. I heard Beatrice in my head again. *He only hated you. Maybe without you, he would've loved us, and we would've still been alive.*

I rubbed the pain in my chest. I no longer needed to think of the knives to feel the pain. Words hurt just as well.

The house we arrived at was small, but people were everywhere. Shorties had started a game of tag in the front. Some older kids were tossing a football. The women were in the kitchen setting the table while the men were watching the football game outside. Before anyone noticed us, I took in the sight. Mom's sister Joanna was corralling a group of toddlers who had pushed down the gate, locking them in a section of the house. She was flapping her hands and yelling as if the kids were a bunch of chicks. The oldest, Angela, was currently attempting to mix the arroz con gandules while dancing bachata and sipping her drink. That was multitasking in action.

Then there was the other middle child, Nelida, who sat at the edge of the sofa just observing everything in her path, as if trying to fold away and be forgotten. I totally knew how she felt. I wanted to sit right next to her.

The house smelled of adobo and sofrito, the way my house smelled all the time because Mom had cooked every day for us.

Once Carmen broke the trance and announced us, I was inundated with hugs and kisses. Grandma even started dancing with me right there in the dining room. I wondered if she was always this way or if she was on drugs. After about twenty minutes of having to politely answer questions like what grade I was in, where did I plan to go to college, do I have a girlfriend, and listen to how good I looked, I needed an escape.

Thankfully, my cousin Ray came to save me. He and I were both seventeen, but when I looked at him, I figured that's what most seventeen-year-old Latino males looked like. He wasn't as tall as me, but Mom's family wasn't tall. At five-ten, he stood average. Dark brown hair cut clean and short and brown eyes with just enough light in them to make him look like someone you'd like as a friend. I suspected he'd never been abused or never had to sleep on the streets and hope some serial killer wouldn't target him.

"Jesus, Mom," he said to Tía Angela, "You're embarrassing him and me by association."

"Don't be a *malcriado* and use Jesus's name in vain." She pointed a finger at him, the one not holding the drink.

Ray gave me a head's-up nod, and I followed him out the back porch and to the yard. "Thanks for coming, cuz," he said with a sly smile, pulling out a cooler and handing it to me. "Tio Cano owes me twenty bucks. He swore up and down you'd never make it. Thought you'd make a break for it." Ray pulled out one for himself, twisted the cap, and took a long chug.

I twisted mine and took a sip.

"Don't hurt yourself with that," he said and lifted the bottom of his bottle to mine to clink them together. "Haven't seen you in a while." He scanned the yard. More tables, more people. I suddenly felt guilty. Playing the blame game soured my stomach.

"Yeah, I've been fucked up for a while," I admitted.

That got him to look at me. His eyes were kind, and I kept thinking about my own interpretation of family. It had only been how my dad treated us. How Moe had treated me. That didn't mean everyone else were dicks.

"You telling me. I've heard stories."

I arched a brow.

He shrugged. "Tía Carmen talks to my mom, and Mom has picked up Tía crying more than once." He took another sip of his drink and I felt like shit. "Especially when you were at that place. You have no idea how we tried to get you out."

"Boys Home?" I hadn't realized I even said it out loud.

"Yeah, that fucked-up place. We were all doing our research and fucking up people's lives. You should've seen my dad on the phone with that piece of shit lawyer. That was scary. I thought the cops were going to come arrest him."

"I didn't know," I mumbled. I had felt so alone and only thought Carmen was the one fighting for me. "I didn't know it was a family effort. Carmen never told me."

"Of course not. If she finds out I'm telling you, she'll tell my mom, my mom will tell my dad, and he'll cuss me out. That's your business. We didn't want to get involved in your business, but we did anyway." He smirked as the bottle touched his lips. "That's family for you."

I didn't know what to say. I'd considered myself outcasted for so long. As if they hadn't cared about me.

"Dude, the coolers only four percent alcohol. You cry, I'll never let you live it down." He elbowed me softly. "Come on, let's go grab that football."

With that, we put our coolers down and had a game of flag football.

CHAPTER 33

"*Dime con quién andas, y te diré quién eres,*" my father said to me after I befriended Santos Espinoza, who was rumored to be selling drugs for the Disciples. We'd both been twelve at the time.

Choose your friends carefully for they shape who you are.

Friends were shunned in my household. Beatrice and I were too afraid of what they would think if we brought them home. It wasn't until I was on the receiving end of racism that I realized my dad was a racist prick. He'd tell us not to trust the white folks taking up residence in the new developments near our school. Or stay away from the black kids in the housing complex in the corner. And especially, do not talk to the Mexicans across the street.

But now I had friends. Like people in my study group. I'd even made plans to go watch the new Chainsaw Man episode over at Maury's crib with Ale, friends from my lunch weeb table. And then there was Wade, leaning against his fancy car with his arms crossed over his broad chest, wearing aviators that made everyone passing glance his way. Despite that I couldn't see his eyes behind the glasses, I knew he was looking straight at me.

I felt someone slam into my shoulder and saw Theo heading toward Wade. They greeted each other with whatever handshake they probably made up when they were bedwetters. Okay, my bad. Wade wasn't here for me. I secured my bag and started walking to the bus stop.

I almost made it when I felt a hand on my arm, and I was facing Wade. I would punch myself in the gut if it would lessen the effect this guy had on me. I both hated and liked it.

"Hey," he said a little breathless. He'd ran a bit to catch up to me.

"Hey," I said back.

Now he looked nervous. "Can we go somewhere?"

I would've gone to the ends of the world with Wade Wilson; all he had to do was ask. But I did have a heart to protect. "I really have to get home."

"I'll drive you."

"No, thanks, I'm good." Whenever a problem presented itself, I ran. It's what I was good at. No lie. So when I saw the bus closer, I ran. So color me surprised when I saw Wade's car in my driveway, with him leaning up against it, arms across his broad chest, wearing those damn sunglasses when I got home. His hair tousled just perfectly, a hint of sun on his cheeks, and a damn smirk that twisted all my insides. I forgot he knew where I lived.

"Hey, again," he said.

I ignored him and started for the house. Okay, so maybe that was juvenile, but I was still pissed off at him and his mother. More him though. I felt him close behind me. "I'm not going anywhere until we talk."

"Really?" I said. For some damn reason, I wanted to hear what he had to say. I wanted to talk to him. But him demanding, wanting to take control of the situation, had me fighting it. "Well, you can wait outside." I shoved him back, but not hard, and slammed the door on his face.

I couldn't do this.

Yes, you can, idiot, Beatrice said.

"You really need to make a decision if I'm worthless or worthy. This back and forth with you is driving me crazy."

Hey, who's the one talking to the ghost of a dead person?

Point taken.

I climbed the stairs two at a time and slipped into my room, changed out of my school clothes, and tried to do some homework. I didn't look out the window when I saw headlights flash through my bedroom window.

Wade gone.

He should've called. Texted. Something other than just shown up. No one just showed up nowadays.

I heard a knock on my door and figured Carmen was just checking in. "Come in."

The door swung open and a very pissed off Wade stood at my door. "Can we talk now, or should I ask your aunt to mediate?"

It was starting to be hard to be angry at him, but I was still stubborn as hell. "Are you sure I won't get *arrested* being seen with you?" Okay, maybe that was a low blow. I saw hurt flash in his expression for a second before he shook his head and started heading back downstairs without a word.

Okay, I panicked. I ran after him and caught him at the door. "Okay, fine. Talk."

"Everything okay, boys?" Carmen asked.

"We're just going to take a drive," I said and pushed Wade out the door before Carmen could get a clue.

He drove as I sat looking out the window. The tight space between us somehow constricting. It hadn't been the first time I'd been with him in the car, only now it felt too tight. "Are you going to talk?"

"Not while I'm driving."

Good plan, though I couldn't promise I wouldn't run once we got wherever we got to. I ran my palms down my jeans and started to bob my knee up and down. He finally pulled over into a narrow slip road that ended up opening into a clearing. It could've been beautiful if I wasn't so nervous. He seemed to notice because as soon as he put the car in park, he was already following me out of the car. I didn't run though. Just stood leaning against the side, my eyes shut, breathing in a deep lungful of night air.

Then I felt him close in front of me. He cupped my face and slowly ran his thumb along the ridge of my jaw. "I'm not going anywhere, Xander," Wade said, his voice deep and soothing.

The raw ache I'd carried in my chest since we parted seemed to burst open. "I'm not who you think I am, Wade. I don't deserve you."

The finger movements stopped, and I was afraid to open my eyes, only to see the same realization in his expression. That I was a piece of shit and would never amount to anything. Instead, I felt the heat of his body press against mine and his lips softly grazed my own. I gasped, not expecting the gentle touch. Our first kiss had been like a dream to me, our second one desperate with need, this one was exploratory. It was gentle and warm. Shit, I knew if I didn't stop this that I would be losing my heart to this guy.

He didn't press the kiss harder but kept the contact just a graze, and when he pulled back, I almost whimpered at the loss of his lips on mine. "We should talk," he said.

Right. We were there to talk.

He stepped away and to my left, leaning against the car beside me. We both just looked out into the night for a moment to clear our heads. "I'm sorry for not waking up next to you, but I'm not sorry for what happened. Are you?"

I licked my lips. "No. I'm not sorry either."

Another stretch of silence fell between us. I had no clue what I was doing. What I was saying, but I said it anyway. "I'm not into Adam, if that's what you think. I, uh, I like you. I've never felt like this, so I don't know what I'm doing." I looked down at the dirt under my shoes and kicked at it just to do something. "I'm not like your other *boyfriends.*" I bristled at the thought of him being with anyone else. Like something pinching at my nerve endings. "I'm not experienced. I'm not wealthy or have anything I

214

can give you. I'm an angry, controlling, possessive freak that will probably punch anyone that looks at you funny. I'm not what you need."

He didn't run away from me. I took that as a good sign. He did sigh, and I felt his shoulders brush mine as he ran his fingers through his hair. "Caleb was the only guy I've been with, and he was only a year and half older than me. Yeah, he hurt me, but I was a stupid kid who just needed attention, I guess. I didn't love him, and I don't want to be with him. I'm not looking for you to give me anything, Xander. Just you. And I know this is new for you, and I feel horrible for taking advantage of you that night."

"You didn't," I quickly protested.

"I did. You were asleep next to me, practically naked. Yeah, I took advantage, and I can't stop thinking that what I did was wrong."

I heard the guilt creep up into his voice, and I turned around so that now I had him pinned against the car and my body. "Don't do that. Don't make it wrong what happened between us. It was beautiful and perfect. The best thing that ever happened to me. Don't take that away from me." I caged him between my arms, loved that he was shorter than me, that he had to tilt up a little to look me in the eyes. "You have such beautiful eyes. You are beautiful." Then I narrowed the gap between us, and I didn't hesitate to kiss him properly. He opened up for me, submitted to me, and let me explore every inch of his mouth before we finally pulled away from each other. My chest felt tight, and I had to breathe hard just to take in oxygen. Him too. His hands on my waist felt so good.

"We're in public, Xander. This is risky."

I didn't care. But then I remembered Wade was famous. I remembered my past could come and slap me in the face, and that made me pull away from him. I felt empty when I did. We returned to our position next to each other. Just two dudes stargazing at an obvious make-out spot. Yeah, that was us being discreet.

"So what happens now?" I asked.

He licked his lips and pushed off the car. "Come this weekend to my mountain."

I arched a brow.

"I'll hook you up with a cabin. Just hanging out with friends." The smile on his face left no room for my heart to say no. I nodded and agreed to go to the one place I hated above all else.

Hell with snow.

CHAPTER 34

Don't do it, bro. Listen to Adam.

I didn't heed Adam's warning, but instead accepted the invitation to go up Wade's Mountain in ski gear.

He'd lifted the ban, apparently.

I stood in a vast mountain of snow hooked on skis as Piper talked about safety while Trini stood at the bottom of the slope with her arms outstretched waiting to catch me. They were friends again after Piper broke up with Chad. "You can do this," Piper said.

I shook my head. "No, I can't." I almost stuttered as I looked at the steep descent before me. A little person as tall as my knees shot past me down the hill. Okay, maybe it wasn't as steep as my imagination made it out to be.

I watched as the little dude shifted his body to the side, expertly stopping the descent before smashing into the building just twenty feet in front of him.

"Why don't they put bumpers?" I asked Piper, who was already laughing. "Like they do in bowling alleys."

"I believe in you!" Trini called from her spot far, far away.

I wondered how they ended up with the short end of the stick in training me. Or babysitting me. I was pretty sure

Wade had something to do with it since he was higher up the mountain with his entourage of spectators. I suspected he was doing damage control after being decimated by the news as having lost his touch; he'd have to save face. I hated the thought of him in danger. I could see him getting hurt with one mishap, which was why I couldn't watch. Thus, leading to my current predicament in the bunny slopes, which was misleading because I did not see bunnies.

Trini waited for me at the bottom of the hill. I just had to concentrate on getting to her. I pushed off with my poles and the skis did the rest. Heavier than the little critters who made this look so easy, I realized I was going faster and started to stop later than I should've. At least Trini broke my fall.

After we untangled ourselves, we decided to take a break from skiing, for forever, and headed to the coffee shop. It was packed like the last time Wade was here. The TV showed a live feed of the cameras on Wade as he maneuvered to the top of the incline. People were either encouraging him or wanting to see him faceplant. I wanted to hit someone until Trini led me to a table with Piper. Her eyes on the TV. I couldn't watch. My heart suddenly charged in my chest with that familiar aching fear. I should stop him. I should.

"Look," Piper said. "He's done this a million times. He's going to be fine."

"I don't want to look." I sipped my hot coffee, burning my top lip.

"Would you just look?" Trini admonished.

"No." I didn't want to jinx him. I didn't want to see.

Then a moment later, everyone started to cheer and clap. I looked in time to see Wade stop at the bottom of the incline, punching the air in triumph. I let out a breath I didn't know I was holding. My fears were ridiculous. Wade knew what he was doing. He was born for the snow. I hated the snow.

"See." Trini squeezed my hand. "This is him. This is

what he loves."

"I hate it." I couldn't believe I said that. She chuckled and shook her head, eyeballing me. "What?"

"Nothing. I just think it's cute."

I didn't think any of this was cute. Especially not me. "What's cute?"

"You, badass fighter. You're in love with him."

I snorted and sipped my coffee again, meeting Piper's eyes. I was totally being tag teamed here. "Right. Because everything about your kind has to be about love."

"I am not even going to come back with a comment for that sexist remark," Trini deadpanned.

I started laughing with Piper. Surprisingly they hadn't killed each other. Mission accomplished.

It must have been the successful jumps and the newfound positive attention in the media, but when Wade made his appearance at the coffee shop, he looked radiant.

Golden boy fit him to a tee.

At least that's what he projected on the outside. I had years of observing bullshitter tells and Wade had a few of them I caught as he clapped hands with folks and took selfies. His hands were shaking slightly. His eyes were unfocused, as if he couldn't land on one thing to ground him. Sure, it could've been the adrenaline, but the time it took for him to reach us from the top of that mountain the adrenaline should've worn off. No, this was something different. This was fear. His words back in the art room came slamming into me.

"I'm afraid of snowboarding. I'm afraid of getting hurt. I think about it all the time while doing tricks, and for me that's dangerous. One slip and I'm eating more than just snow."

Wade was unraveling in front of everyone, and no one saw him. Only me.

He finally made it to the table we were all sitting at and caught me staring at him. That smile he wore just for me sent all sorts of emotions rushing through me. He started to head my way, and I could already feel his lips on mine, but he seemed to realize what he was doing, stopped, and hugged Piper instead. Theo, Nick, and Taylor came in behind him. That hurt. A lot.

"Great jump!" Piper said as I sipped my cold drink. I was on my second already.

I avoided looking at him. His smile seemed to tune out the sun. Wow, I should be a fucking poet. He took the seat at the head of the table. The furthest away from me.

Okay, so we hadn't discussed how we were going to play out in public. Didn't mean he had to make shit so damn uncomfortable for me. He'd already came out, so what was the big deal? Unless, well, it wasn't him. It was me. Wade was fucking with me. Using me.

Told ya.

I didn't do well in uncomfortable situations. Made me itchy as hell. I got up, and Trini scowled at me. I didn't mention I needed a pee break, just headed to the bathroom. I had to squeeze through the crowd of people still praising His Highness. I was too big to be in the place. I finally managed to get to the bathroom and finish up just in time to catch the highlights on repeat on the big screen on the wall. Wade had been perfect. I caught him laughing and spilling out a verbal instruction on his moves, and it was all foreign to me. I couldn't stop wondering why me? Why the hell had he chosen me? And what the hell was I supposed to do about his fear, which led to my fear of him getting hurt?

I really had to stop thinking. My heart and my brain were not in sync right now.

Make a choice, asshole. You're either in or out. There's no in-between here. Make yourself an outcast or be free of your past. That voice in my head wasn't Bea. It was all me. I thought about Jace. I mourned my friend and feared becoming him. Becoming a fake version of myself.

Choose.

I headed for our table. Wade stumbled with his words a little as I sat down. Then he started chatting away again, returning to his casual persona. I took a moment to observe him the way I observed a possible threat. Watching for weaknesses I could exploit. Everyone had an agenda, and once I figured out what that was, I could determine the threat level against me. Wade was a smooth talker, something I caught when I met him at school. He thrived in the light. He leveled up around people, while I drained around them. Hell, it was draining me just watching him.

And when some asshole whispered something in his ear while handing him a napkin, I called it. Pushing away from the table, I got up and headed for the stools overlooking the tall windows. Nothing to see but snow. My heart told me to run outside. Be the same runner I've always been. But a part of me told me to stay. Don't rain on Wade's parade. Be something he needed too. Maybe we could find a happy medium.

"I don't care much for snow either." I recognized the voice and turned to Sage. He grinned at me with a "gotcha" expression. His blond hair was tousled and stuck to his skin. He wore a bright purple down jacket tied around his waist and ski pants. He leaned into me. "I hope you don't mind," he whispered. "Or should I act as if I don't know you?"

I shook my head, pressing my lips to keep from laughing. I hadn't realized how much I missed him. How much I missed the others too. "You're so crude."

He flinched back and cupped his chest. "Muah, no, really?" He patted the stool next to him and I sat.

"You look happy," I said dryly.

"As opposed to what? Unpleasant during those torturous sessions?"

"Touché."

He gave me a lazy once-over. "And you look very good."

I shifted in my seat, suddenly feeling unmasked. His dark blues met mine and that smirk deepened, revealing a dimple.

"What?" I even sounded defensive.

"Nothing. I've just never seen you without that dreadful school uniform. Didn't realize how"—he leaned into my ear—"handsome you are. If you need assistance with this new version of the gay you, I'd be happy to help." His breath tickled my neck, and I lifted my shoulder to keep him away. He laughed. It was a nice, new sound coming from him. "Who's your friend?" He shot a glance over his shoulder at Wade. "Is he famous or something?"

I laughed. Couldn't help it. A relieved laugh that I wasn't the only one who hadn't known who Wade was. "You made my day. He thinks he's famous."

Sage shifted in his seat. "Oh, oh, famous dude is coming this way." He leaned into my ear again and his breath made me shiver. "And he looks pissed."

"Hey," Wade said to me, then looked at Sage. "I don't believe we've met."

Asshole looked at ease. Good enough to keep in a dungeon somewhere away from all eyes on him. "This is Sage," I introduced. "Sage, this is Wade."

They shook hands. Sage even blushed. "Nice to meet you."

"How do you two know each other?"

I stiffened slightly, but Sage did not miss a beat. "Oh, we met a while back ago at the mall. This gentleman helped me with some bullying problems. You know, he's a terribly good fighter." Sage squeezed my bicep for emphasis, and I had to bite down on my lip to keep from laughing. He kept squeezing. "He's such a male hunk, don't you think?"

I could've sworn I heard Wade growl as he put a very possessive hand behind my neck, like some sort of collar, and squeezed. That was twice I'd managed to make Wade jealous, and I was enjoying it. Too much.

"Yes, that he is, and very much"—Wade leaned into Sage, and I sucked in a breath—"*mine*. You may want to remember that before you touch him again."

"Oh, darling," Sage said. "I think he's proved too much of a man for my heart. But you go ahead and tame the beast."

"Okay," I said, jumping to my feet. "Time to go."

I heard Sage's laughter as I slipped out the door.

CHAPTER 35

We made our way back to the cabin Wade rented for us. I refused to go to Wade's place, ever. Adam's warning about Mrs. Wilson had me a bit more guarded. Though the easy banter of the dorks behind me put me at ease. Trini and Piper reenacted Theo's failed attempt at a three-sixty, making them look like crazed ballerina dancers. Taylor had missed a hop and Nick pulled her into a hug and started apologizing, as if she were the beginning and end of his world. Which was cute in a nauseating sort of way.

I shook my head. "You guys are spoiled brats."

I didn't hear anything for a few steps, and when I turned around, a deluge of snowballs slammed into me, followed by laughter. One even caught me in my head. I stood there like a man and took it.

"Can I call you my ice bunny?" Wade laughed.

I lunged for him, and he spun too fast and started running down the narrow road leading back to the cabin. I followed. Snow boots and snow not conducive to running. I caught him just before he reached the house and tackled him to the soft snow. He rolled onto his back, a fistful of snow in his glove, and he slammed it against my face, still laughing.

Using my body, I pinned him flat on the snow and gripped his wrist tight over his head. "You are going to pay for that."

"Yeah, really, I'd like to see you try."

He tried to buck me off him, but I had at least twenty pounds on him, and I was taller. Before he could throw me off, I cupped some snow and shoved it down the front of his jacket. He squealed.

I loved the sound of his laugh, the peel of his squealing, and his inability to throw me off him because I was stronger. Then I leaned down and kissed him full on the mouth, biting his lower lip. I started to pull away, but he seemed already jolted and pulled me sharply toward him again, capturing my lips. We kissed for I don't know how long. By the time I came up for air, the others were already inside.

"I think my ass is frozen to the ground."

Shit. I got off of him and helped him to his feet, dusting him from the snow before we both went inside.

"Is this a thing now?" Piper asked.

Stripped of our coats, we all settled around the living room's fireplace and television. Wade plopped on the sofa, and I took a seat on the floor next to him.

"Define thing?" I asked.

Wade dug his fingers into my hair, and I leaned against the sofa. The gentle touch felt really good.

"Oh, you know," Theo said. "A thing we keep a secret, or a thing you're going to throw out to the world." Theo didn't sound as enthusiastic about this *thing* as Piper. And he aimed that question at Wade with a scowl.

"I don't think we have to label it," Wade said. "And it's no one's business." He threw Theo a pillow that he easily caught.

Which meant we'd keep it a secret. Wade was right. It was no one's business. But I needed to place it neatly in my headspace where it belonged, and I couldn't do that without a label. I wasn't going to push it though. Trini gave me a look of concern. I had totally cried like a dumped baby in front of her after Wade and I had sex and his mother had almost had me arrested. It had been my bit of weakness I wish I could erase. She didn't press it.

"Oh, hey, look!" Nick said and turned up the volume on the television, showing Wade's halfpipe descent into stardom.

"Wade Wilson, making a comeback?" the newscaster said. The room burst into applause and cheers and only caught the tail end of what she was saying. "We expect great things at the ESPN Exhibition games in February."

Theo threw Wade the pillow, and it hit him in the face. "Don't get cocky, Wilson," he said. "You've been pitiful lately. One round of greatness does not make you great."

"I'm awesome. Admit it."

There was a round of *boo*s, and I plucked myself off the floor to get something to drink in the kitchen. My nerves jacked. Trini followed me.

"Stop worrying so much," she said, plopping down on the stool as I rummaged the now-empty fridge.

I didn't tell her that I felt death graze the back of my neck. That everything about Wade being on that mountain sucked. Instead, I deflected. "So I see you and Piper are friends again."

Trini blushed. Her eyes moving away from mine. Even a small smirk appeared. "We're complicated," she said, tracing small circles on the countertop in front of her.

I wanted to ask her how complicated, but at that moment Wade approached me with a confident sway and a brilliant smile. My heart took notice. Although I hated him being on that snow, I knew he still loved the sport and I couldn't be the one to ruin that for him with my own fear.

"Hey, why the pout?" he asked me.

Was I pouting? "I'm not pouting. Don't ever say I—"

He slammed his lips against mine and everything else fell away, at least until I heard Trini clear her throat. Heat settled on my face as I pulled away from Wade, but he didn't let me go.

"I think I'm ready to take a nap, aren't you?" The words rushed out of his mouth, and even before I could respond, he was already pulling me up the stairs.

Trini started to giggle, and I knew it had something to do with the level of red on my face. I didn't complain, just went with it.

Just as we made it inside our room, he slammed me against the door, locking it behind me, his lips on mine again. We hadn't had sex since the first time, which had been chaotic and mostly without thinking. Now, was different. Now every emotion rushing through me felt magnified. Every touch he grazed me with burned right through me. And I didn't want to mess it up. I didn't want to give my past space in my head anymore.

Wade broke the kiss and leaned his forehead against mine. Our breaths intermingled in the narrow space between us.

"What's going on in that head of yours," he asked.

"I don't know what I'm doing," I blurted.

A smile teased his lips. "Do you want to stop?"

"No," I answered with a bit more desperation than I meant to show.

"You're safe, Xander. We won't do anything you're uncomfortable with. You have the power here. You say stop, we stop."

He was giving me the control I needed. A safe place to explore. And I wanted to explore it all with him. "I don't want to stop," I whispered. I didn't. "I just, I don't know what I'm doing."

Wade slid his fingers down my temple, grazing my cheek, and cupping my neck. "I'm with you, Xander. We have time. I'm not going anywhere."

He's not going to leave me.

I leaned in and caught Wade's mouth. I loved kissing him. I loved the way he made me feel safe and wanted.

I loved him.

Love. I didn't have a strong foundation of what loving

someone meant. I just knew that he made me want to be a better version of myself. Because he deserved better.

True to his word, Wade didn't leave me afterward. Lying in bed, I held him as he trailed his fingers along the scars on my body. The soothing rhythm of his heart pulsed against my side, making me hyperaware of every touchpoint.

"Why did you run away from your aunt when you were younger? Carmen seems nice," he asked.

"I caught Moe arguing with Carmen one day about me. He made her cry. I guess I just felt as if I didn't belong anywhere. It was easier to be angry than anything else."

Wade kept slowly tracing the scar, but I knew he had more to ask. I was okay with waiting, so I kept my mouth shut. "Did you ever tell anyone about what happened at the warehouse?"

"No. The cops wouldn't have believed me. I had a shitty lawyer, and they threw me into a residential treatment program for youth. Basically, a detention center. I met this guy, Jace. He was paired with me. At first, I thought he was there for the same reason as I was, you know. Maybe he got caught by the law for doing something, but he wasn't like me. He was sweet and had these large blue eyes that reminded me of a lost puppy. I should've known something was off about that place. Jace was gay. They'd take him out of the room at all hours and bring him back cold and starving. I'd give him my blanket, even socks. I'd save some food for him whenever he got back and do his schoolwork just so he could sleep. I always waited for someone to come get me like they would get him, but no one ever came for me. Then Carmen got me out."

"Conversion therapy," Wade said with venom in his voice. "I knew some guys who went through that."

"Yeah, I didn't know about any of that shit until I got out. That shit's not even legal." The thought of it made me sick. "I saw him, just before your party. He was with his girlfriend."

Wade lifted himself on his elbow to look at me. "That's

not your fault."

"Maybe I could've told someone. *Tried.* But I didn't because I didn't want to risk them sending me back to that place. I couldn't go back." Wade pressed his lips against mine, shutting me up. The anger and blame slowly dissipated as my focus shifted on this beautiful person with me. I trailed my fingers down his cheek, slipping his hair behind his ear as the kiss slowed. "Why me?" I whispered. My throat suddenly felt tight. I was giving Wade way too much control over my heart, and it scared me.

His light blue eyes perused every part of me, even inside my soul. "Because we fit. Because I think out of everything that's happened to us, this makes sense."

I wasn't sure if we made sense. I was still trying to find a reason why he'd want me, why I should deserve him. This. To be happy. The guilt of surviving still weighed me down, and I wasn't sure if I'd ever allow myself the chance to breathe. But Wade gave me the one thing I'd lost with my family.

He let me hope.

CHAPTER 36

The filling of college applications seemed like an unsurmountable task with no sense of reward at the end. I knew nothing about money, careers, or why any of these schools should add me into their student body. The millions I'd get after I graduated high school should last until I grew old and died, right?

I knew Wade was going somewhere in the East Coast with Theo, which made me a jealous asshole. Theo was begrudgingly a good friend to Wade. After the guy had protected Wade from Caleb, I couldn't really hate him. Hate was too strong a word. I could still dislike the asshole, and I had to learn to trust Wade. He'd chosen me. Not Theo.

Looking at the mess of brochures on my bed, I had no clue what I was going to be when I grew up. At one point I'd even considered joining the military and had gone so far as to talk to a recruiter and get an application, but I'd gotten a decent score on my SATs, so I considered applying to schools instead. And I didn't want to be far from Wade. Pathetically needy as that sounded.

I heard the doorbell ring, and a few seconds later, Wade strutted into my room with the same sunshine he'd had the first time he'd blessed me with his presence in my room.

The guy belonged anywhere. "Is that my competition?" He gestured to the brochures on the bed and sat on the chair near my desk.

"Any news on your end?" I asked a little hopeful.

"Not yet," he said without a care in the world, "but I'm pretty sure I'm getting into Harvard."

"Right, because you're so amazing." I rolled my eyes for effect. He cupped my hips and led me to his lap. "Dude, I'm bigger than you."

"I can handle you," he said.

I supported my weight by placing my hand at the back of the chair, not sitting on him … more hovering over him, then we kissed, and the applications that lay on the bed forgotten. We did some momentary grinding until I felt as if I was about to explode. Wade was too loud, risking us getting caught by Carmen, so I pulled away from him.

He groaned. "You're killing me, here, Xander," he complained. "I'll have you know I am a very sexually active male who wants my man whenever I'm horny, and I'm horny."

I laughed and led him to the bed. Moments like this with him were fleeting since he started training. "You have to be quiet," I said in a whisper.

He cupped my hips and dropped me on the bed, hovering over me as I scooted up so that we were stretched out with him on top of me. His blond hair was longer and fell around his face. I threaded my fingers into the soft strands as his blue eyes settled over me. The intensity of that look slipped into the crevices of the crumbling wall I'd built around my heart. "I thought I was supposed to be the controlling, possessive one in this relationship."

He tugged his lips in a quirky smile. "And I'm the teacher and I have a lot still to teach you." Slowly, with his eyes pinned to mine until my vision blurred, he lowered himself and grazed his lips against mine. A feather touch that already had me pliant under him. He grazed my jaw, the column of my throat, and back to my lips. "Why can't I get enough of you, Xander?" He asked that question with a slight crinkle between his brows as if trying to pry out an answer to his question.

"Because I'm handsome, a good kisser." I kissed him, hoping I wasn't lying. "And I'm the best thing that's ever happened to you." I kissed him again, feeling braver than my pounding heart allowed. "But—"

He let out a frustrated sound and lowered his forehead against mine.

"—not here." Not that I didn't want to do it, just not while Carmen was just downstairs. I wasn't that brave.

"Where? I'll rent the moon." He kissed me again. I was sure he would.

I pulled away again. "Surprise me," I managed to say.

The lustful look in his eyes forced me to shove him away before I consented to what he wanted to do to me right then and there. He rolled onto his back as I climbed out of bed and adjusted myself. Groaning, he pulled out an envelope that had lodged under his back and looked at it. I watched as the heated look turned into something feral. He shot up and swung his legs over the side of the bed, eyes still on the envelope. I racked my brain trying to figure out what I'd left on the bed to make him look so damn angry. I'd done nothing wrong. He got to his feet and shoved the envelope into my chest. "When were you going to tell me?"

He crossed his arms across his chest, his expression pinched in anger and hurt. I lowered my eyes to the Navy acceptance letter I'd received last week.

"You're going to the Navy? I mean, I have nothing against serving for your country, but ..." His voice trailed off.

My heart suddenly felt as if it'd wedged itself inside my throat. "But what?"

"Where does that leave *us*?" Before I could get anything in, he shook his head. "You know what, forget it. I shouldn't have said anything. Not my business, right? There's no future in this." He motioned between us. "It's just until we graduate and go our separate ways, right?"

Those words hurt. Stung in all the places I'd allowed him to penetrate. But he was right. We were still hiding whatever this was between us. We were in high school. Deciding the rest of our lives together made no damn sense. Telling him that I meant to follow him sounded creepy as hell, even to me. And why the hell would he still want me after high school?

"Say something," he spat out finally.

I couldn't say what I wanted to. I lied instead. "I just want to keep my options open."

He nodded, his jaw going tight, his eyes glistened as he swallowed and looked away. "Right. Options. Yeah, I, uh … I gotta go." He moved faster than I ever saw him move that wasn't on snow, and I let him leave. The coward that I was, I couldn't call him back. Tell him that I wanted to go where he went. That this wasn't just a thing for me. I just let him leave.

We never talked about it again.

It'd been a few weeks since I'd seen him last. He still had his advertisement gigs and traveled way too much. We kept conversations going via phone and FaceTime, but it wasn't the same. I missed him. Moping around the house didn't help, and even Carmen was relieved when he returned.

The media continued to report him as wishy-washy at best. Wade wasn't consistent in his maneuvers. Fell off track. His form was going to shit, and I couldn't help but think it was my fault. Even Theo was worried about him. Asked him to get his shit together or postpone the run. But Wade was a stubborn ass.

"I'm not postponing the run, dude."

We were all sitting around the television at the mountain cabin we rented instead of staying at Wade's place or leeching off Adam. I got up and walked to the kitchen just to get away from being so close to him and not being able to do anything, to say anything. After our discussion about college that had us already breaking up, Wade refused to talk to me about anything snowboarding, or whatever the hell was bothering him. Letting him go up to that mountain like this was killing me.

Trini followed me to the kitchen. She always did.

"He's going to be fine," she said with little conviction as if she sensed something too.

"What would you do if you had a sick feeling that something was wrong, Trini? Wrong with someone you cared about."

"Xander, you're overreacting. He's great."

I sighed. "I know." I did. I knew he was great. But I also knew the other side that had him terrified of competing. I knew he was risking himself being out there. I had to do *something*.

But the something got up and was already heading out. "I'm heading out," Wade said without looking at me. "I have an early day tomorrow."

Theo got up and mumbled something before starting up the stairs to pack his stuff while Wade headed for our room.

Our room.

Although I'd spent nights with him, we hadn't done anything but kiss and fall asleep in each other's arms. Wade was always so exhausted, and I always found myself sleeping, cuddled inside his arms or him in mine. I hadn't even had a nightmare with him. My sister's ghost had even gone silent.

I followed him into the room, and it took everything I had not to rip that bag from his hand and force him to stay. "Stay," I finally said. I wasn't *that* strong.

His body seemed to turn to jelly for a brief second. I saw the vulnerable Wade before he collected himself and turned rigid. "I can't," he barked out.

"Because you're awesome." My attempt at levity felt flat.

"You don't sound so convinced."

I hugged him, needing to be closer to him than ever

because I was losing him. I knew that in my bones. In my heart. Wade would decide our future now, and I had to make sure he had all the information he needed to make that decision. "I think you're awesome when you're not putting yourself in danger."

Wade leaned in and gave me a kiss just under my ear. "You like it when I'm dangerous. Admit it," he whispered over my ear, then suckled my earlobe. I moaned softly at his touch. Everything he did maxed out my senses. I wanted to keep him here with me and do things I'd never done before with him. Explore him and learn things about myself in the process. Like how I could hope for an us when we were so new. When I was so broken.

"I like it when you kiss me," I said, inviting his kiss. And he did not disappoint. The kiss scorched my body, pulled at all the strings tethering me to him. It made me hope, which was scarier than anything I'd ever experienced before.

I tried to pull away, but Wade held me and kept kissing me, so I just went with it until he finally decided to give me back my tongue. His smile was sweet and warm.

"I don't care about Wade the Olympic Gold Medalist. I care about Wade, the one who makes me feel everything," I whispered breathily. Those words were my own desperate attempt at letting him know that I didn't care about him being famous. I cared about him.

"Trust me, baby," he said. "I know what I'm doing."

"Please tell me you'll be careful out there. That you'll back off if it doesn't feel right."

For a moment I saw something in his expression that looked a lot like fear. Then he pulled away. "Where is this coming from?"

Shit. I knew where this would lead. But something in my gut warned me that he needed to hear this. I had let my family die. I had done nothing to stop my dad, despite the same gut-wrenching fear I had now with Wade. "You said it yourself that you're afraid of doing these tricks, so don't do them. Quit now."

He cupped his lips, hurt now flared in his light blue eyes. Then he ignored me and grabbed his duffel from the bed. "I gotta go."

He started to move past me, but I grabbed his arm and turned him to look at me. Panic filled me to the core. "Label us."

"What?"

"Label us. One word. What are we? Right now?"

"Xander, I don't understand."

"Just do it. How would you introduce me to your grandmother?" I held my breath. My heart pummeling inside my chest.

"I—Do you want to be my boyfriend?"

"Yes. I never wanted to join the military. I want to go to the East Coast with you. I might not get into Harvard, but I don't care. I'll go to a community school." I was rambling, and the look he gave me speared all my insides. That curtain wall I'd erected around my heart had just fallen. "We can make this work."

I love you.

The three words got stuck in my throat.

"Does that mean you're willing to go public with us?" Hope laced his words.

I cupped the back of his neck and kissed him again. This kiss was fueled with everything I had inside of me. Fear, guilt, anger, love. The kiss tore down my walls and opened up my heart to new memories. Good memories. To real emotions, and not just a tableau of a memory I held on to that would never happen again.

"Yes. If you want me."

He cupped my cheek. "Oh, sunshine. I want you." He kissed me again for a long time. At least until Theo knocked on our door.

"Are we leaving, or what?"

I didn't like Theo very much. We parted and I leaned my forehead against his. "Just please tell me that if you feel something off, you'll be safe. You have nothing to prove.

Please, Wade. I can't lose you too."

He cupped the back of my neck and kissed my forehead. "I'll be safe."

That night I woke up in a grip of a nightmare. This time it wasn't my family I had lost. This nightmare had me trying to claw my way out of a dark pit and no one came for me.

CHAPTER 37

Wade sent me a selfie as he stood at the top of the slope, getting ready for his descent. The clear blue skies at his back, his eyes gleaming with a beaming, toothy smile made for toothpaste commercials. *On top of the world,* he wrote as a headline.

Me: Waiting in hell for you.

Three minutes later my world had been ripped apart.

Theo: Wade was airlifted to the hospital. It's bad.

I hadn't been watching the run on the television like everyone else. I hadn't wanted to jinx him. I'd been too afraid to watch.

Now, it was all I could see.

The first few seconds of his run.

The jump.

The crash.

The blood.

I couldn't get it out of my head. Wade had been airlifted to a trauma center, and I couldn't get hold of anyone to give me information. I only knew he was alive because of what I read on social media from his PR people. They wanted to ease his fans while I was dying inside. Theo hadn't responded to my flood of calls and text messages. Trini,

Piper, and the others didn't know what was going on yet. They'd promised to tell me when they found out. It'd been thirty-six hours and I had gotten nothing. I would've flown to Colorado if I thought they'd let me see him, but I knew they wouldn't, so I found myself standing in front of Charlie's gym, needing to talk to someone who understood about pain. About *me*. It had been a matter of time before shit went wrong.

"People like us don't get an easy out just because we fall in love. We've seen too much shit, experienced too much shit. And that stain stays with you, Xander. Always."

Adam had been right. The darkness I'd fought against suddenly took center stage inside my body, and I felt like I was going to explode. I needed to still the chaos.

I needed a fight.

I rubbed my hands down my jeans, feeling a bit off the mark here. I stopped at the reception desk where Sal sat watching me.

"Welcome back!" he said with that smile. It didn't quite compete with Wade's, but it was close. "We're closed, buddy."

"I'm here to see Adam Brody."

"What do you want with Adam?"

"He told me to meet him here."

Adam came around the corner. "It's okay, Sal. Let him through."

Sal rolled his eyes. "You are going to get out of here on time, Brody. Right?"

"Yeah, stop being a little bitch and let him in."

"We have guests tonight, Brody."

"I don't think Xander is going to attack Lassiter Parker." I gulped at the mention of Lassiter's name and, yeah, had I not felt like shit, I probably would've lost my shit. Adam turned to me. "Right, Xander?"

"Right," I managed.

Sal rolled his eyes. "Fine."

Sal let me in. Adam watched me like a hawk as he

unwrapped his knuckles. He wore shorts and a T-shirt, sweat-drenched, his hair pulled in a bun, revealing his hearing aids he usually kept hidden. "Sorry about your boyfriend," he said.

I swallowed the wedge in my throat and shoved my hands in my pockets. "Thanks."

"How's he doing?"

I shrugged. "I don't know. No one will tell me anything."

Adam eyed me curiously, as if he knew exactly why I knew nothing about it. I'd been shut out. Wade didn't need me. He had Theo and his parents. I'd been given the awakening of a lifetime, and I didn't know how to bottle all this shit up.

Voices lifted from the boxing ring in the middle of the hall, and I caught sight of reporters with Lassiter Parker. I lowered my eyes and kicked at the dark rug at my feet.

"Cut the bullshit, Morales. Why are you here?" Adam sounded pissed. As if he had every right to be pissed because of how my life turned out. I clenched my fists in my pocket, and my teeth.

I hadn't expected that to hurt as much as it did. Finding people to call friends had always been hard for me. I just remembered why. It was better to have none than to have them treat you like shit when they finally tired of you.

"I wanted to talk."

He lifted both brows. "Yeah, I got as much. So talk."

I'd been running for so long. I already knew where that path would lead me. Back to the ruined remains of my past. Adam was right about one thing. People like us didn't get a free pass because we finally found something worth fighting for. People only saw what they wanted to see. The past. A broken piece of shit. A broken brown boy undeserving of anything good. Even when Wade got better, why would he want me? I felt as if I was losing my grip on it all, and I was holding on to something that wasn't real. Never would be real. Hope. And for the first time in such a long time, I was lost. Totally fucking lost. "Is there somewhere private?"

"No," he said sharply.

I felt the urge to crawl under something, anything, and curl myself into a ball and hide forever. Instead, I released the anger that had been building through me ever since I started this conversation. Because Adam Brody wasn't my friend. "You know what? Fuck you. I don't need this shit." I spun and started to head out.

"That's right, do what you do best. Run," Adam called out behind me.

Suddenly the whole place silenced. I spun back around, letting everything go. Fucker wanted a fight, he'd have one. "Fuck you, asshole. I'm not you. Don't toss your shit at me because you don't have your own shit together."

He curled his hands into fists, his chest rising and falling with every breath. His eyes darkened. The usual carefree demeanor he had used when we first met was gone. The optimism in the guy who approached me at Dr. Reyes's office was gone. Something feral had been left behind. I wasn't afraid of Adam. The fear I felt came from a different place.

Fear of abandonment. Shame. Guilt. Take your pick.

"You're right. I'm nothing like you," he hissed out. "Hiding and running like a coward. *You* let your family die."

Those words cut through all the walls I'd built to protect myself from the onslaught of a thousand cuts. I felt every one of the knives my sister hid inside my heart rip my flesh. Nothing would ever wipe that shit away.

But anger came close.

I lunged at him. He was ready, but I was fueled with more anger and pain to last more than one lifetime. I picked him up by the knees and slammed him down between two machines. A heard his breath rush out of his lungs as I took advantage and pounded on his ribs. Body shots. The torso had more surface area to hit. Pain rushed up my arm at each contact my knuckles made into his muscles.

"Fuck you!" I roared. Spittle flying from my lips, my eyes hazed out by the tears I couldn't hold back.

Chaos reigned around me. I heard people shouting. Movement around us. I didn't care. I didn't care.

"It wasn't my fault!" I cried out. "He killed them! He killed all of us!"

I felt someone pull me up sharply and fling me like a rag doll away from Adam. I didn't stop. I needed to bleed. Sal was larger than me, but I was nimble and taller. I kicked out into his knees, and he folded over. Then I aimed a kick to his balls, missed, and caught a good chunk of his thigh. He still fell over. I took that moment to leap toward Adam. My target. The person I wanted to hurt.

But Adam was faster than me and anticipated my move. He spun his body and came up behind me, grabbing me in a chokehold. I didn't care. I was done. Fucking done.

I stomped my foot, trying to use my body against him, but the guy was solid. The chokehold tightened. I heard the beating of my heart in my ears. A drumming sound pulsing in time with my heart.

"Calm down," he ordered.

"Fuck you!" I was on berserker mode.

"We have to hide the knives, X. He won't hurt us if we hide the knives." Beatrice's voice burst through my head.

The screams.

All of it my fault.

I kicked off a bench and sent us back, toppling over. My elbow dug into his ribs, and he released me. I inhaled sharply. My voice almost gone. I coughed but kept moving. I had to get away. I had to run.

Words left my mouth, but I couldn't hear them. I couldn't breathe. I got to my feet and ran toward the exit. I pulled on the handle, but the doors wouldn't open. I pounded and kicked for someone to let me out.

No one came.

No one came to save us. Not my mom's God. No one. My father had killed them, and I had kept that secret because I was afraid what that said about me.

Adam was right.

I let my family die.

"I didn't do anything to save them!" I cried out with my ruined voice as I punched the glass of my cage. "My father forced us into that coffin; I let him. It was my fault!" I pounded the glass again and again. My hands bled, leaving red marks behind. "He hated us. He hated her. Hated me! We hid the knives, and he killed them anyway!" I slammed my forehead against the glass and felt every trapped memory rush to the surface. My father's scent. The look of his hatred. My mother's voice as she pled with him to stop. "Why did we get in the van? Why?" I sobbed. No taking any of this shit back. No way to put it all back into my box.

"Xander."

I turned to Adam. I hated him. I really hated him. I wanted him to feel half the pain I was feeling. To know that we were nothing alike. I wanted to get this feeling out of me. I launched myself at him again, but something hard slammed into me before I reached him. I tumbled into the fighting cage and fell onto the floor. I jumped to my feet, rage giving me enough fuel to move, just in time to see an older man locking me inside the cage.

"Let me out!" I yelled, pulling on the chain link. "You can't keep me here. Let me out!" By that time, my voice was fried. The man moved back without saying a word as I kicked and clawed.

A tomb. They stuck me in a coffin.

Like the van. Like my dad.

The memory of it all rushed into my mind, forcing me to relive all of it, as my broken pieces finally tore me apart.

My mouth felt like sandpaper as I blinked away the tears and the memories of that night. Adam watched me with a horrified expression on his face. One that made me feel all the darkness I'd allowed inside my heart. I shook the cage, aiming all my anger at him. "You're right!" I croaked out. "I let my father kill them that night. *He* ran us off the road and killed them."

My legs finally gave out, and I fell on my knees, still

clutching the cage, as if I could melt it with my fingers. "My dad killed my mom, my sisters, and that truck driver. He meant to drive us off the road that night. Don't you see? Don't you get it? It wasn't an accident. I took that blood money because it wasn't an accident."

The adrenaline that had been coursing through my veins finally ejected out of my body, and I crumbled onto my side. I hugged my knees and closed my eyes. Except, I didn't find peace in the darkness. Everything I'd done finally burst free, and I heard my own voice, but I didn't fully understand the words I used to explain what happened that night. How Dad had woken us up to go to Canada. How he was still drunk. How my mom held my six-year-old sister tight. How Beatrice cried and pled for him to slow down. How I pled for him to slow down. How my mother's God abandoned us. Then the truck. And the screams. Their screams like knives inside my body I took with me everywhere.

Then I told him about running away. About Lawrence Whitman. How I fought and got arrested for it. How I was shoved into the Boys Home. I told them what I'd seen. What they did to Jace. How they made him docile. How they did things to him to condition the gay out of him. How I abandoned him in that place.

I spoke until I couldn't anymore, then I fell asleep locked in that cage.

That night, I had no nightmares.

CHAPTER 38

I woke up curled on my side on a bed in a bedroom I did not recognize. A large, spacious bedroom. Groggy, I sat up and ran my hand down my face, then winced. My hands were bandaged, and I felt as if I'd broken a few knuckles, ribs, and toes.

Then I remembered Adam.

Shit. I jumped to my feet and squealed—yeah, squealed—when I heard someone under the shadows in the corner. I recognized the man who had tossed me into the cage and locked me inside. He was built like a house. Thick muscles. A few inches shorter than me. Salt-and-pepper hair. A military guy.

"You're safe," he said, his voice gravelly, pissed. I took a step away from him.

"Where's …" My voice cracked, and it hurt to speak. "Adam?"

"He's in the other room still asleep. Rough night."

Yeah. I didn't say anything.

"Name's Charlie Cox. I don't believe we've met. I own this gym and a few others."

I remembered reporters. Lassiter Parker. And then I remembered everything I said last night. Everything I

247

admitted. I cleared my throat, unable to talk. The guy walked to a small fridge, pulled out a water bottle, and handed it to me. I took it, turned the cap, and swallowed half before I finally felt my throat a little bit better. "Why am I here?"

"You passed out in the cage. Adam carried you to the bed."

Adam. "Is he really okay?"

Charlie nodded. "Yeah, son, he's okay. Worried about you."

I wrapped my arms in front of me tight. "Are you going to have me arrested?"

"For what?"

I wiped my nose. "For, uh, fighting. Destruction of property."

The big guy snorted. "If I arrested every fucker who came busting through my door fighting, I'd be out of business."

I smiled. Duh. Boxing gym. I still felt off. This whole experience unreal. "But the reporters? Lassiter?"

"We managed to get them out the back way when the fight started. Lassiter did his job and kept the interest on him, so we're all good. But I do want to talk to you about some of the things you said last night. We did a little digging and found some things you might be interested in. You good now?"

I looked at my bandaged hands. "Not much use now anyway. I'm sure you could sit on me if I decided to go berserker again."

Charlie laughed. "Sal wants to kick your ass for going for his nuts."

I made a face. "Sorry."

Charlie laughed and clapped me on the shoulder. I winced. His heavy hand sent a burst of pain shooting through me. I had more than my hands messed up.

"Get cleaned up. I'll let Adam know you're awake."

I nodded and the guy walked out.

That was the strangest meeting in my history, and I

quickly scanned for an exit. A window. A duct I could crawl out of. I found nothing. After I used the bathroom, I followed the voices to a separate office. I was still in the gym, only the third floor had private bedrooms. I ended up in an office. Adam sat in front of Charlie's desk. Charlie looked up at me, leading Adam's gaze to mine.

Adam wasn't much better than me. He already had a bruise on his eye and his chin. He sat as if he, too, were sporting a couple of body bruises.

"Sit," Charlie ordered, motioning to a chair beside Adam.

As I walked in, I caught sight of three other guys in the room. Yeah, no fighting here. I sat down, keeping my eyes trained on Charlie. He slid a folder in front of Adam, who opened it.

"What you asked for. The accident scene and report, including forensic evidence."

I sat back, knowing what Adam was seeing. I closed my eyes.

"I'm sorry, son, but you need to hear this too. The Brody Corporation settled out of court for the death of your family because they didn't want it made known that Winston Murphy was driving that truck with five times the legal alcohol limit in his blood. He'd been spotted at a bar before he got in that truck. According to the skid marks on the snow that night, the truck *had* veered into your lane, Xander. Maybe, if your father was sober, he could've avoided the collision by taking evasive action. But most likely, he wouldn't have been able to anyway. Your accident had been caused by Mr. Murphy."

I let out a sigh as the aching tears ran down my face. I didn't bother wiping them away.

"So the settlement is valid," Adam said. "It's not blood money, Xander. It's for you to make a fresh start. Do something with your life."

I palmed my cheeks and wiped my nose.

Charlie leaned forward. His features hardened, and even

I felt threatened by that look. "And my people are going to track down Lawrence Whitman and deal with it."

I nodded, deciding not to ask what people, though I came close.

"Can you give us a moment?" I asked Charlie. "I'm not going to go berserk again. Too tired." I was tired and drained, both physically and emotionally.

Charlie nodded and took the other guys out with him, leaving Adam and me alone. I got to my feet with a wince because I was still mad at him. He'd attacked me first. Acted like a dick. I did remember that, and I didn't understand why.

"What the hell did I do to you?" I asked. "Why the hell are you so pissed off at me?" I'd never had the chance to ask my dad this question. Why he hated us so much, why he hated me. I needed to know with Adam.

Adam, too, got to his feet and turned his body to face me as he leaned against the desk. He shook his head and raked his hand through his hair. We didn't move from our position opposite each other.

"You think people like us get to choose to be happy or in love? Do you think we deserve any peace?"

I swallowed the lump in my throat. My heart banging in my chest. This was about Wade. I didn't need to hear this. I knew what lay behind my heart. I knew the darkness inside me. I didn't need it reflected back at me.

"Everything that we've been through, that we've seen, doesn't go away because we mask it in love, Xander. We may hide it better, deeper, but that rage, that guilt will always be there. And when that love is taken away, we risk releasing that darkness we hid to survive. Nothing good will ever come out of that." I hadn't realized that he moved closer to me until we were toe to toe. I could feel the heat radiating from his body. Coiled tight. "You can't love like that until you've let go of your past, man. It's going to eat you alive."

I knew he was right. I knew in my bones that he was right. My feelings for Wade were real. They gave me a glimpse of what I could have. If I lost it now, I don't know what I'd do. "What's the alternative?"

He flinched, as if not expecting that from me. "Make your peace with your past. It's the only way you can move forward. What happened last night should've opened your eyes to the worst that could happen. Imagine if you would've taken that anger to the streets, you'd be dead or would've killed someone."

I lowered my eyes. "Is that why you said what you did?"

"Yeah, man. I never believed you killed your family. I just needed you to fight it."

I wiped my nose. "I prefer Dr. Reyes's therapy. Yours suck."

He chuckled.

"What should I do?"

He let out an exhale. "Don't make my mistake. Make Wade tell you to piss off if that's what he wants. But you should hear it from him. Not his family or friends. You deserve to *know* either way how he feels."

"Why do you care?"

For a moment, I thought he was going to kiss me. But he cupped the back of my head and leaned into my ear. "Because I was you, and I'm still messed up. I want better for you." My body felt too damn hypersensitive to him. I couldn't move, and when he released me, I let out a relieved breath. His features were stone-like. His eyes rock solid. And I realized I didn't want to end up like Adam. He still needed his wall against the world. I had let Wade tear mine down, and I didn't want it raised anymore. "Are you sure it's him that you want to risk your heart with?" Adam asked.

"Yes," I said quickly.

Adam pulled back to lean on the desk. "Then you know what you need to do."

Someone knocked and Charlie peeked inside. "It's almost opening time. I need to know your answer."

"Answer to?"

Adam cupped his mouth, then turned to me. "Charlie's

gym helps kids like you," Adam said. I almost flinched when he called me a kid. "He can help you channel the shit inside of you. Teach you skills that will give you options and keep you out of jail."

Charlie gave Adam a look, as if something were wrong. Then he turned to me. "You have to want to work for it. Nothing in life is easy, and this won't be either. But it's a start in your healing."

"This isn't some therapy bullshit, is it?"

Charlie chuckled. "No."

I couldn't help but feel that maybe I found another family. "Okay, I'm in."

"Good." Charlie clapped me on the shoulder. "Now, go clean up the fucking mess you left downstairs. Both of you."

Adam ducked his head and walked out with me following behind him.

CHAPTER 39

It felt awkward to be back in Dr. Reyes's office without a court mandate. I almost wanted to apologize to him for asking him to see me again. He wore that same kindness on his features as I remembered, and it made me feel comfortable around him.

We sat. I talked. And he listened. I told Dr. Reyes about what happened with my family in that van. How I blamed myself. I told him about what happened before I got arrested. I honestly thought I had him floored with all the drama, but he just absorbed it as I let it out. I felt cleaner, lighter, sharing all this with him. Charlie had told me he'd deal with the guy who assaulted me and investigate further into Boys Home. I left that part out, a little afraid of how Charlie was going to deal with it. He didn't give out the impression of a man that would write a strongly worded letter to force change. More like something covert that required spyware.

I answered some of Dr. Reyes's questions and we made a follow-up appointment for next week. I left his office feeling emotionally drained. Trini was at my house when I got there. All evil sprites and glares. She had every right to be pissed at me after I hadn't returned her messages. Theo had gone silent after the initial news of Wade's injury. No one knew what was going on. But Trini had been the only one to reach out to me.

"Wade was transferred here this morning," she said. "Do you want to go, or what?"

I deserved the *or what*.

We arrived at the hospital shortly after noon and Trini looked ready to tear Theo's face off. "What do you mean family only? You're not his family."

"Just, how is he? Is he going to be okay?" I asked.

Theo ran his hand through his hair, which was already sticking up every which way. "He hit his head hard. They're thinking concussion and some facial reconstruction, but he's alive."

I felt all the blood drain from my body and dropped on the plastic seat behind me.

"Jesus," Trini said. "Can we see him?"

Theo shook his head. "No. Only family."

"Theo, come on. Wade would want to see Xander, don't you think?"

"No, he doesn't," Theo said sharply. "Look, he can't even talk right now. He's in bad shape. Just go home."

Wade blamed me. I knew it by the way Theo was looking at me. I told him to be careful. To pull out if he felt off. I jinxed him. Made it worse. I didn't stop it. I made it worse.

Theo deflated. "I'll call you later. His parents are with him."

"And you," Trini snapped out.

"Just go home," Theo said one last time and went back into the family waiting area.

Trini plopped next to me with a gruff.

I leaned into her, seeking her body for comfort. "It's my fault. I told him to be careful. I told him to quit. He told me he felt afraid of faceplanting. He hid it from everyone behind that smile of his. I should've convinced him not to do this. I should've done more. I let him go. I let him go." Trini wrapped her arms around me and let me cry. Just the way I cried for my family. Nothing I did was ever good enough. The tears tore out of me, as if being yanked from my soul.

"He's a stubborn ass, Xander," Trini said. "You warned him. It was his decision to make, and he made it."

We sat in silence for another hour before Trini finally called it. "Do you need a ride home?" she asked.

"No, I want to stay for a little while longer."

She planted a kiss on my head. "You are a good person, Xander," she whispered before she left.

Even with my eyes closed I saw Wade's accident, looping in my memories.

Get used to it, bro; everyone you care about dies.

I hated hospitals. The smell of antiseptic and the overbearing feeling of death trapped behind every door made my skin crawl. I hated being here, knowing that he was hurt and fighting for his life without me. I hated that Theo hadn't snuck me inside to at least see him. To talk to him. To let him know I was there for him.

When I opened my eyes, I saw Mrs. Wilson in the hallway talking to a nurse. She looked well-groomed as always, minus her dead mongoose. Then an older man walked out, bypassed the nurses' station, and headed my way, stopping at the vending machine in front of me. My eyes felt like dry sandpaper. The man was tall build, blond, and light blue eyes reminded me of Wade. This had to be his dad. Now or never.

I got to my feet and cleared my throat as I approached him. "Mr. Wilson," I said.

He turned around. Eyes bloodshot, disorganized. He almost dropped his cup of coffee, but I steadied the shaky cup as it fell into the notch to be filled. "You don't know me, uh, I'm—"

"I know who you are," he said gruffly, turning back to the machine. "Victoria told me about your altercation with her. Why are you here?"

"I just ... Wade and I ... we're together."

He picked up his cup and turned slowly to me with an angry look. Something hurtful. "No, you are not together. I know your kind, Mr. Morales. You will never be with my son. You should leave."

I rubbed my chest, hating the tears of weakness already hazing out my vision, and I cleared my throat, but I nodded anyway.

My days went by in a blur. I went to school and followed the motions that were expected of me. People whispered about Wade. They didn't know about me. No one did. We had been good at keeping the secret. Theo refused to talk about him during lunch when we all sat together. We all had slammed Theo with question after question, but he just got up and walked away. Trini had been my pillar through it all. Her love for me was unconditional, and apart from Carmen, I believed in it.

After school, I spent the evenings at the hospital. At first, I was ignored. Then I was scowled at by the nurses, and after day six, I was tolerated. I learned more from whispers in the hallway than I would've with Theo. I learned that he had facial trauma, had required extensive surgery, and a cosmetic surgeon had been called in. He had a broken wrist and a severe concussion, which should end his career. Whether that would keep him off the snow, who knew? He was too damn stubborn to let anything like near death keep him from snow.

I also got to see, if not meet, his younger brother. The resemblance between them uncanny. They both favored their father. I sat for hours doing what I always did. I drew. This time, I drew an image of Wade with his brother, both of them as anime characters. Before I left for the night, I did what I always did. I left it to Nurse Randall. She gave me a pitiful look but nodded. She'd promised to leave it in his room.

Theo showed up the following day. Without a word, he

sat next to me. We watched people come and go, as if we were two homeless dudes enjoying the cool air-conditioned waiting room. Kate, the afternoon nurse, kept a close eye on us, though she already knew me. I figured I might wear them down before I turned to mold.

"He's talking now," Theo said matter-of-factly.

I winced. "Why are you here?"

"I'm a big jerk," he started. He got no argument from me there. "I let Wade convince me that he doesn't need anybody. That he doesn't need you. He doesn't want you to see him messed up. He thinks you'll find him gross. He's a stubborn ass." Theo glared at me. "If you ever find him gross, I will end you."

I smirked. "You're a good friend."

He looked ready to fall off his chair with that bit of truth. "You're probably the best thing to happen to Wade since he won Gold."

I snorted. If I was the best thing, why would he ever believe I'd find him gross? Why hadn't he asked for me? Why had he forced Theo to cut me loose? I didn't say any of those things. I swallowed them back and dropped them somewhere behind my heart. I'd project my anger tonight at the boxing gym. Not here. Here I had to be ready for someone to finally give in and let me say my peace to Wade Wilson. I knew his parents had seen me waiting. His father's look had lingered, so maybe, just maybe, he'd let me inside.

"I have a plan," Theo whispered. "Just don't give up." With that little bomb, he got up and walked away.

It didn't happen until the tenth day. And it hadn't been his parents that let me in. I'd just brought the weekend nurse Patrick his coffee with one pump of expresso and four sugars.

"I still can't let you in," he said.

"I know. But he's still alive, right?"

He smirked as he sipped his coffee and made a sound like *uh-huh*. I took that as a yes.

"You know," I said, leaning over the counter. "I'm

thinking about majoring in nursing. Anyone I can talk to about that?"

He shook his head. "Yeah, sure, kid. Go wait in the family waiting room. I'll call our administrator for you."

I winked at him.

The closest I'd ever get to Wade was the upstairs family waiting room. After being thrown out twice, this was progress.

I was about to pull out my sketchbook when I heard a familiar snooty voice in the hall. I leaned over and peered around the glass wall to see pink hair on a thin tall guy wearing a matching pink button-down shirt and white slacks. Only Sage Morrison could get away with looking good in pink. He caught sight of me and hurried my way. Jack and David trailed behind him.

"What are you doing here?" I managed to get out.

"We saw the news. Knew you'd be here. Knew they wouldn't let you inside. Those bastards." Sage plopped down in the chair beside me, clutching his satchel for dear life and searching the room for informants, probably.

"Sorry about Wade. Sage told us how important he is to you," Jack said.

David just nodded.

I felt my cheeks get a little hot. "Thanks, but something tells me you're not all here to stare at the hallway with me. What's up?"

"Well," Sage said, stretching the one syllable word for ever. "We are friends, and friends with benefits—the PG kind of benefits—we have an in and a plan to get you in."

"I don't understand."

Just then, I heard a commotion in the hallway. A dark-haired woman cried out. "*¡Ayúdame! Por Dios, ¡ayúdame!*" She clutched a bleeding rag to her eye. The fact that she was in the fifth-floor pediatric intensive care unit did not register in my brain. A large, tatted-up man followed behind her.

"I'm sorry. I didn't mean to," the man said dryly.

Behind him, a soiree of fans practically bowling them

over.

Sage giggled. "That's my mom," he said with a hint of pride I'd never heard in his voice before.

I felt horrified. "Oh God, is she okay?"

Sage slapped my hand as if I were an idiot. "Of course. She's a telenovela actress and she's all about the love."

"My dad isn't an actor," David said, eyeballing the tatted-up man. "He actually sucks."

Jack shoved an ID card into my hands. "We got this from a friend of a friend. He says don't fuck it up."

Theo.

I looked up at the nurses' station. The *empty* nurses' station. Everyone paying attention to the two Emmy nominees and their fans, creating a hot mess as a distraction. All I had to do was sprint through, use the ID card to open the barred doors, and search for Wade's room.

"Go," Sage said. "Give that stud a kiss for us."

David snorted and Jack smiled.

"Thanks, guys," I said, my heart booming inside my chest.

Avoiding the telenovela chaos in the hallway, I sprinted past the desk, expecting fate to give me another kick in the balls. It didn't. And I slipped into the eerily quiet hallway leading to Wade's room.

He had a single occupancy room. The bed stood in the center surrounded by machines that took up too much space. I had expected his parents to be with him, but the room was empty except for him. I padded closer to him. My breath got caught somewhere behind my sternum as I took in his frail form under the covers. Stitches ran from his right cheek, across the bridge of his nose, to the other side. His face swollen as a result. His right hand was in a cast, so I walked to his left side and carefully, as gently as I could, slid my fingers between his, swallowing back the tears. I didn't come here to cry. I'd shed all the tears I could for him and for me. I had come here to tell him I loved him. To let him decide if he still wanted to take that chance and be together.

But guilt took center stage and threatened to shatter my resolve.

I sat on the available chair next to his bed, my throat tight. I kissed his fingers, and he blinked his eyes open. At first, I wasn't sure if he saw me, but then he tried to speak, and I shut him up with a careful kiss to his lips, then I sat back down. I stared at his hand in mine. His were much paler, smoother. Different.

"I never told you what happened when my family died," I said. Hospital sounds of drips and beeps the only other sound in the room. "My dad was a bad drunk who often hit my mom. We sometimes had to stay away from the house whenever he got into one of his binges, wait him out, and go back in when he'd fall asleep. It wasn't always bad though," I added, lifting my eyes to catch him watching me. "We had good family times too. Some of the happiest." I gave him a smile that didn't quite reach my heart. "That night he got it in his head to go to Canada in winter. I felt something off. I think my mom did, too, but I didn't do anything. We didn't do anything. We let him put us in that van and he started driving faster than was safe for conditions. It was snowing. There was ice on the ground, making everything slippery. We begged him to slow down, but he wouldn't. He seemed so angry. And then we crashed into a truck." I swallowed the lump in my throat.

You can do this, Xander. We're right here with you.

I closed my eyes and remembered Bea and Katie. They'd sometimes wait patiently for a drawing I was working on, wearing the same smile of anticipation. Katie liked Doc McStuffins. She wanted to be a doctor. So I drew her the Doc and all her animal characters while our parents argued in another room. Bea holding her tight, making her feel safe. Bea had made me feel safe too.

I wiped a tear before I realized I hadn't finished my story. "I always thought it had been my dad's fault that we crashed. That he had done it on purpose. That my dad wanted to kill us and I had let him. The reason I was always so angry all the time. But I found out that the driver of the truck had been drunk. The truck had veered into our lane. I don't think my dad meant to kill us." I lifted my eyes to his, still watching me silently. With all the swelling and the bandages on his face, I couldn't read his expression. If he had one at all. "I've been broken for so long, I don't know how to feel normal. Except when I'm with you. I don't know what you see in me. I … I don't deserve you."

I felt his fingers squeeze mine.

"But I want to try." I turned to look at him. I hated seeing the bandage and the pain. "This wasn't the way I wanted to tell you this, but I told you I'd be honest and tell you everything. I love you, Wade." The truth of those words no longer scared me. At risk of sounding like a damn cliché, the truth *had* set me free. I was in love with Wade Ashton Wilson. A boy who tore down every wall I had built around my heart. I knew it didn't mean that I was suddenly cured of all the shit still threatening to pull me back into the arms of the darkness inside of me, but it was a start.

Wade didn't speak.

I couldn't tell if it was the pain meds or what, but he didn't react at all. Not that I expected him to jump up and down or anything. Obviously. I really didn't know what I expected. My chest clenched in anticipation of the rejection. Maybe I had read everything wrong. Maybe he hated me for jinxing him, causing him to get hurt. Maybe he resented me for telling him to be careful. Maybe he didn't care about me the way I cared about him.

I remembered Adam's words. Find the truth. Make him tell you to fuck off so you'll know for sure. I had to know for sure.

"Look at me, Xander," Wade finally whispered gravelly.

I looked at those blue eyes that held me like a vice grip.

"No," he grumbled. "*Look* at me."

It took me a moment to register what he meant. He'd have scars. No longer the perfect bot I'd met in Dr. Newman's office. I wasn't sure and didn't care what he'd look like after all the swelling went down. I got up and leaned over him again. His light blue eyes a little darker, his lips full and pink. I kissed him softly again. I knew he didn't have much energy to kiss me back and that was okay. I pulled away and looked over his bandages. "I like it. It gives you character. Makes you a little less perfect. More human." I waited a heartbeat, wondering if I said the wrong thing, and then his lips turned up in a half-hearted attempt at a smile and he winced. "What? I'm just saying, my boyfriend is not the perfect avatar I thought him to be the first time we met."

He arched a brow. "You thought I was perfect when we met in Dr. Newman's office?"

"I did. Perfect like some droid. I like *this* version of you. I want to kiss every one of your scars and I'll let you kiss mine."

"I'm going to hold you to that," Wade whispered. "I have a very strong sex drive, and I'm a horny teenager."

I chuckled. "My, you do have a one-track mind. I like it."

His eyes trailed my face, and I suddenly felt the weight of it all. Almost losing him and having to live with the broken pieces of my life. I just hoped that somehow, I'd be able to fit him into the chaotic mess that followed me.

"I love you, too, Xander Gael Morales," he said.

I swallowed the lump in my throat and wiped a traitor tear from my cheek. "You better be sure, because I'm a stubborn ass who won't ever let you go."

His eyes lit up. "I'm going to hold you to that, too."

I leaned in to kiss him again when someone cleared their throat behind me. I jolted, as if burned. His father had just come out of the washroom. His eyes bloodshot from crying possibly. How long had he been there? How much had he heard? Oh God, I was going to jail.

But Mr. Wilson just gave me a look. Then he looked at Wade, then at our interlaced hands. "I'm sorry, Mr. Morales. I misjudged you unfairly."

I almost swallowed my tongue at those words.

"I'll make sure the nurses know to give you access so you don't have to break in next time."

I could only nod.

"And Mom?" Wade asked.

Mr. Wilson tapped Wade's knee. "I'll have a discussion with her," he said to Wade, then turned to me. "Can you stay with him? I could use a shower."

"Yeah, of course. Can you, um, make sure I don't get arrested?" I handed him the stolen ID card.

He arched a brow, smirked, shook his head, then walked out.

CHAPTER 40

Six Months Later...

"What do you think, X? Do you think you'll survive going over the falls in a barrel?" Beatrice asked me.

I looked out into the raging waters. "Maybe, but I'm not stupid enough to try it."

Beatrice shrugged and leaned over the cement barrier. "I don't know, X. Sometimes you just have to jump in order to land."

"Are you sure about this?"

Wade wrapped his arms around me. A movement that made me feel at home. "For the hundredth time, yes."

"And your mom—"

"Won't have anyone arrested. I promise."

I inhaled. Carmen and Victoria had planned this merging of family and friends at Mrs. Wilson's big mansion, and I couldn't help but to think that nothing of the expensive house would be left standing afterward. "This is a bad idea. You know Jack gets sick when he gets nervous, and David, well, he's just—" I made a motion of explosion with my fingers against my temples. Sound effect included. I kept going when I should've ended things there. "And let me not get started with Sage. He's going to go after the cheese dip. Mark my words. And then there's that rivalry between our friends Piper and Trini that has—"

Wade planted his mouth against mine and nothing else seemed to matter but us. Well, maybe except for our crazy families about to meet head-on like a tsunami against a cyclone. I felt Wade's smile on my lips as I tried to pull back away from the kiss.

"My grandma likes to dance. Like not in a really good way, but in a tear-your-eyeballs-out-of-your-head way. And we have shorties galore that are going to—"

Groaning, Wade kissed me again.

"—make a break—"

Another kiss.

"—for your pool without swim diapers."

That made Wade laugh, and I loved hearing his laugh.

After six months of surgeries and therapy, Wade was just as perfect as when I'd first laid eyes on him that day in Dr. Newman's office. Perfect, except for a thin scar just above the bridge of his nose that only I could see whenever I kissed him. And a few scars at his hairline. A reminder of everything that he meant to me, of the promises we made to each other to mend our broken pieces together.

"You need to stop worrying so much. My mother has been forewarned not to assume servitude, my father is keeping her on a tight leash, my brother will handle all the swim babies, and you"—he nuzzled his lips against mine— "are an adult. And I am an adult. And we are going to be heading out to college next week and start the next chapter of our lives *together*."

Together.

"And," he went on. "I am never letting you go. You still have a lot to learn." The edge of his lip tugged up in a half smirk.

I couldn't believe the asshole still made me blush with those words.

I couldn't believe that I had fallen madly in love with

him. A guy. A famous model, actor, and gold medal snowboarder.

I couldn't believe that my family accepted him, accepted me for who we were to each other, and who I was for me.

Told ya, silly. You're just easy to love.

I still heard my sister's voice inside my head sometimes, but I no longer felt the knives in my chest. My night terrors had been getting better.

I felt the prickles of tears on the edge of my eyes and swallowed them back. "I miss them," I said.

Wade's smile didn't fade. He didn't give me the pitying look I got from so many people when I told them how my family had died. When I told them how much I missed them. Instead, he gave me his most dazzling smile that hung above me like sunshine. "They're here with you, Xander. A part of you. Always."

And Wade was right. My family hadn't left me behind. They were here all around me. In Grandma, in Carmen, inside me.

"I love you," I said to the person who mended all the broken pieces of me.

"I love you, too," he said back. "Now, are you ready for this?"

I'd always felt as if I'd been falling with no place to land. No sense of belonging anywhere.

Until now.

Surrounded by friends and family who cared about me.

I squeezed Wade's hand, and he showered me with that smile he shared only for me, and I knew then that I had landed.

"Yeah, I think I'm ready for anything."

ABOUT THE AUTHOR

Elizabeth Arroyo is a Latinx young adult author.

Before she started writing, Elizabeth earned her undergraduate degree in Psychology with a minor in Criminal Justice. She then went on to work in foster care programs, mental health facilities, and youth organizations within the Latinx Community.

Elizabeth spends a ridiculous amount of time on twitter where you can find her ramblings at @EArroyo5. You can also find her musings on her blog at https://elizabetharroyo.wordpress.com/ and Instagram https://www.instagram.com/earroyo5/

She also enjoys binge watching anime and spending time with her family.

Elizabeth currently resides in Chicago.